don't you forget about me
a gossip girl
novel

Gossip Girl novels created by Cecily von Ziegesar:

Gossip Girl
You Know You Love Me
All I Want Is Everything
Because I'm Worth It
I Like It Like That
You're the One That I Want
Nobody Does It Better
Nothing Can Keep Us Together
Only In Your Dreams
Would I Lie To You
Don't You Forget About Me

If you like gossip girl, you may also enjoy:

Bass Ackwards and Belly Up by Elizabeth Craft and Sarah Fain

Secrets of My Hollywood Life by Jen Calonita

Haters by Alisa Valdes-Rodriguez

And keep your eye out for **Betwixt** by Tara Bray Smith,
Coming October 2007

don't you forget about me
a gossip girl novel

Created by

Cecily von Ziegesar

LITTLE, BROWN AND COMPANY

New York ❧ Boston

Little, Brown and Company
Hachette Book Group USA
1271 Avenue of the Americas, New York, NY 10020
Visit our Web site at www.lb-teens.com

First Edition: May 2007

ALLOYENTERTAINMENT   Produced by Alloy Entertainment
151 West 26th Street, New York, NY 10001

On the cover:
Dresses by ABS Evening
Earrings by H&M
Crystal necklace by Yvette Fry Inc.

ISBN-10: 0-316-01184-3
ISBN-13: 978-0-316-01184-6

10 9 8 7 6 5 4 3 2 1
CWO
Printed in the United States of America

There is only one thing in the world worse than being talked about, and that is not being talked about.

—Oscar Wilde

gossipgirl.net

hey people!

It's finally August, and you know what that means: New York City is officially *hot, hot, hot*. Not that I would actually know. My friends and I have spent the last month hiding out in our quaint beach houses in the dunes of Montauk and in little country cottages on Gin Lane in Southampton—and by *little* I mean eight bedrooms and five baths, of course—soaking up the summer sun and working on our Bain de Soleil tans.

So who are we? If you really have to ask, then the question is, Darling, where have you *been*? We're the girls in batik-print Marni sundresses, nursing our hangovers with Veuve Clicquot mimosas under wide-brimmed straw Philip Treacy hats while we watch the show-jumping at the Hampton Classic. We're the crowd skinny-dipping on Main Beach at daybreak, waking up at 2 p.m. and going to bed at 6 a.m.—who has time to sleep when there are so many poolside soirees to attend? We're the ones you love to look at—not to mention talk about—and we're at our summer best.

But summer's almost over, and change is in the air. The Hamptons are emptying out, the jet-setters are jetting back from Europe (by private jet, of course), and our families' decorators are already out there collecting samples for us to choose from for our dorm room décor. Yup, the countdown has officially begun: in just ten days the most recent graduates of Manhattan's most exclusive private schools are headed to college. Pretty soon you'll find us settling into our dorm rooms on Ivy League campuses across New England, the first fallen leaves crunching beneath our new, camel-colored Coach riding boots as we stride purposefully to classes with names like Explorations in the Romantics and Chaos Theory. No more back-to-school coffees on the steps of the Met, no more sneaking out of AP French class for a cigarette, and no more itchy poly-blend uniforms . . . unless you're planning on driving all the frat boys wild by dressing up as a pigtailed schoolgirl for Halloween.

College is the time to reinvent yourself (read: your chance to pretend you weren't a colossal loser in high school), so with only a little over a week left before we leave for those institutions of higher learning, it's time to figure out who you're going to be next. What color is your parachute, my dears? The options are endless, but let me help you eliminate one: the role of observant, fabulously chic Web-logging gossip is already taken.

And while we're all busy reinventing ourselves, there will be a whole new set of gorgeous girls in our school uniforms and TSE cashmere cardigans trying on oversize tortoiseshell sunglasses at Barneys after school. It's hard to believe, but we'll soon be—*sigh*—replaced by the guys and girls who have been carefully studying us from afar. So consider this our last hurrah: it's our chance to take the silver Range Rover LR3s we got for graduation for a ride at daybreak around Manhattan's silent streets. Our last chance to wake up the investment banker next door with rooftop parties at our Fifth Avenue townhouses. To spend a fortune on Chloé bags and Marchesa gowns at Bergdorf's on daddy's black AmEx card. Ah, heaven. Speaking of which . . .

trouble in paradise . . .

Everyone who's anyone saw or has heard about the spectacle of **B** and **N** at **S**'s birthday party up at her country house in Ridgefield, Connecticut, last month. But was I the only one who saw **S** standing out by her pool that night, dipping her toes in the water and wiping her face with the back of her hand after **B** and **N** disappeared upstairs? Were those real tears? Seems mighty close to a certain perfume ad if you ask me. . . . And what did she think of their early a.m. departure on her birthday morning? **B** and **N** may have sailed off into the sunset— literally: their sailboat was last seen due south of Hyannis—but how long can they really stay at sea? Something tells me there's more drama on the sun-splashed horizon.

. . . and trouble on the home front

No one's ever accused **D** of being happy, but I'll be the first one to call him out on being pretty darn . . . gay. And not just the metrosexual, let's-go-shopping at Thomas Pink kind—although his wardrobe could do with a little spruce-up—but the kissing-other-boys-kind. Is he ready to come out? Or will he succumb to **V**'s prickly-headed charms and go hetero once again? If not, I can always hire him to redecorate my bedroom . . . or not.

your e-mail

Dear GG,

 I was at **S**'s legendary pre-birthday bash in Ridgefield last month, and I could've sworn I saw her sneak out to **N**'s Aston Martin at, like, 6 a.m. and shove something in the glove compartment. Okay, so I'd had *way* too many Tanqueray gimlets, but it looked awfully suspicious. Whatever she had in her hand looked a lot like an envelope—but full of what, I wonder. Whatever it was was probably totally illegal, but I passed out before I could find out. Any ideas?
—Confused and Still Hammered

A:

Dear CSH,

Confused is right. Our sweet **S** may have dated a rock star, but she does not party like one—at least not lately. I'll bet anything what you saw in **S's** hand was a simple letter. So the real question is, What did it say? I'm one curious cat, and believe me, my kittens, when I find out, we'll all be purring with contentment.
—GG

Q:

Dear GG,

My dad is a producer here in Beverly Hills, and last night he screened a rough cut of *Breakfast at Fred's* in our screening room, and all I can say is . . . wow! I always thought that **S** was just another ditzy, genetically blessed socialite, but that girl can really act!
—Beverly Hills Brat

A:

Dear BHB,

Tell me something I don't know. The buzz over *Breakfast at Fred's* has reached the East Coast, too—I overheard two studio execs at an Amagansett cocktail party (and, no, I'm not divulging which one) agree that *BAF* is going to be the breakout hit of the fall season—can you say pull-out *Vanity Fair* cover? Buzzzzzzzzz. . . .
—GG

sightings

S wandering all over New York City in a pair of enormous, quilt-patterned black Chanel sunglasses, feeding the ducks in **Central Park** and going to old movies at the **Angelika** by herself, looking rather lonely. I'm sure there are more than a few boys out there who'd be happy to keep her company. . . . A thirty-foot boat that looks a mighty lot like the *Charlotte* approaching the wharf at **Battery Park,** one brunette girl and one sandy-blond boy aboard. S might have company sooner than she thinks. . . . **V** at **Barnes & Noble** on Eighty-third and Broadway, standing nervously in the checkout line, a book entitled *Love Me, I'm Gay* tucked under one arm. A little light summer reading? Our old friend **J** at the airport in Prague waving goodbye as a wild-haired woman in a turquoise caftan boarded a New York-bound plane. Isn't **J** the one who's supposed to be heading back? Maybe it's an exchange program. . . . **K** and **I** in **the Conran Shop** on 60th and 1st, selecting dorm room furniture to be shipped to Rollins next week. Umm, word to the wise, girlies: you might not have room for that cherry-red Eames sofa in your ten-by-ten double unless you're both planning on sleeping on it. . . . With those two, you never know.

Okay, my darlings, I'm off to the SoHo House rooftop pool with my favorite gossip rags in hand to enjoy the last days of this hot and sultry summer. Want to join me? Oops, too bad, it's members only. Maybe you can sneak up the back stairway. After all, it's almost time for that pre-college, back-to-school shopping spree at Barneys, and I want to look my tanned and freckled best for my dressing room debut. I've had my eye on a little ivory wool Stella McCartney jumper for months. And, as always, you know I have my eye on *you*.

You know you love me.

gossip girl

a new york state of mind

"Hello, Manhattan!" Blair Waldorf cheered, hopping off the *Charlotte* and onto the Battery Park wharf. A huddle of unnaturally tan bikini-clad girls stood next to their private yacht, the *Miami Mama*, glaring at Blair while their hot, polo-shirted crew unloaded their bulging Coach duffels onto the weathered gray wood of the dock. The high-rises of Battery Park City stood in the distance, the bright August sun reflecting off thousands of windows. Across town, the South Street Seaport boardwalk bustled with tourists wearing unflattering horizontal-striped polo shirts with overstuffed fluorescent fanny packs, and aggressive rollerbladers weaving their way through the crowd.

Blair licked her red and completely bare lips—who needed lip gloss when you'd been kissed that much?—and glanced back at the *Charlotte*. Nate Archibald's lanky frame appeared on deck, tanned, bare-chested, and grinning, his wavy brown hair streaked with gold, his eyes perfectly matching the green Billabong board shorts hanging low on his hips.

Yummy.

Blair resisted the urge to get right back on the boat and drag him down to the *Charlotte*'s ridiculously tiny bedroom. Even though they'd been together 24/7 for the last month, drinking frosty-cold mango margaritas all day and getting hot and sweaty all night, she still couldn't get enough of him.

Apart from enjoying each other's company, there had also been the requisite visits to charming New England seaside towns like Rockport and Camden for cups of clam chowder—she'd actually learned to enjoy it, despite the fact that chowder was just hot, heavily salted cream with little pieces of chewed, gumlike clams in it—and adventurous forays up rivers and inlets so Nate could feel like the sailor he was.

Blair closed her eyes and inhaled the scent of Guerlain sunblock still coating her skin, taking in the feel of the fine grains of sand still stuck between her toes, and the cool ocean breeze that tickled her cheeks. She sighed happily as she remembered last night, stretched out beside Nate, who was wearing light blue linen pajama bottoms, on the *Charlotte*'s miniscule bed, falling asleep with the sound of his heartbeat in her ears. She ran her hands through her seaspray-tangled hair and watched as Nate tied the last knot on the bowline and jumped onto the dock.

"Well, don't you look happy?" He wrapped his arms around her tiny waist, burying his face in her dark, windblown hair. "You even smell nice, for once."

Blair squealed as he began to tickle her, squirming away. "Thanks a lot!"

Nate just grinned as he slid his feet into the black worn Teva flip-flops he'd worn every day at sea.

"I wish I could say the same for you!" She punched him lightly on the arm, fantasizing about the L'Occitane honey-and-almond body wash and Frédéric Fekkai shampoo awaiting her at home. The shower on the *Charlotte* was so fucking small she almost smacked herself in the face with the glass shower door every time she turned around. Though she'd been happy to make space for one more when Nate wanted to join.

Scrub-a-dub-dub!

Despite the memory of the dollhouse-size bathroom, Blair felt a tinge of sadness as Nate threw her apple green Hervé Chapelier tote over one shoulder and grabbed his own dirty monogrammed canvas L.L. Bean tote. This had been the most blissful month of her life. After a few days at sea, she'd almost forgotten why she'd been in such a hurry to get aboard—and stay aboard—the *Charlotte* in the first place: the love letter to Nate that her *supposed* best friend Serena had slipped into the glove compartment of his father's Aston Martin before they left. Blair had found it while Nate was at a rest-stop bathroom, read it, and promptly shredded the thing to bits. Not that it mattered now. She could totally find it in her heart to forgive poor, lonely Serena—after all, who could *not* fall in love with Nate? Besides, and most of all, Serena had no chance of coming between them ever again.

She and Nate were more in love than ever and heading to Yale together in just ten days. Sure, Serena was going to be there too, but she and Nate would barely even see her once they ditched their separate and totally-unsuitable-for-living-happily-ever-after dorm rooms and found a shabbily elegant New Haven town house to move into. Once they were settled, they could reenact their cozy time on the *Charlotte*. She'd laugh at Nate for not knowing how to cook anything—not that she could make much more than caviar on toast points—and he'd have gin gimlets waiting for her when she got back late from one of her pre-law lectures. It was going to be *perfect*.

"Your house or mine?" she asked with a sultry smile. Nate's emerald green eyes glittered in the sun, and Blair affected a little pout, which she knew he couldn't resist. She turned around to face the water and closed her eyes, basking in the sun like a contented cat.

Meow.

Nate dropped the totes he'd been carrying and put his hands on Blair's smooth, tanned shoulders. She leaned back into him and he nuzzled her neck, looking out at the shimmering blue water. He thought about the last few weeks. He'd been so happy out on the waves, with nothing in front of them but the clear blue sky and the roaring ocean.

A ringing noise erupted from his pants and Nate jumped back. *Shit.* His cell. They hadn't had a connection out at sea, and he hadn't heard the damn thing ring in weeks. Nate pulled the Motorola Pebl from his rumpled khaki cutoffs and looked at the screen: HOME. *Double shit.* He pressed IGNORE and resisted the urge to throw the thing into the water behind him. Then he grabbed Blair's soft shoulders, a little tighter this time, already worried about the unavoidable confrontation with his dad over his future, which was kind of a mess now due to some recent mishaps.

The message Coach Michaels had left him before he climbed aboard the *Charlotte* repeated itself on a loop in his head. He wouldn't be getting his diploma from St. Jude's; Yale was out of the question. Of course, Coach had probably broken the news to Nate's strict former Navy captain father by now, which meant he'd be getting a serious reaming as soon as he walked in the door. Knowing his dad, he'd probably been calling to rip him a new one every day for the last month, and this was the first time the signal had come through. Obviously he should have dealt with the situation, like, weeks ago, but surrounded by all that ocean and Blair's bikini-clad body, who could think straight?

Nate pushed his parental worries aside and refocused on Blair. He hadn't told her about the diploma—or lack thereof—yet, and he wasn't looking forward to it. He wondered if he could just head to New Haven with her and Serena and sneak into the occasional class on Western films or nude portraiture and tell everyone he had a lot of AP credits so he was taking an easy load this semester.

A load, indeed.

Nate sighed. The truth had waited this long—what was one more day? He bit down on his chapped bottom lip and tried to concentrate on how tan and smooth Blair's shoulders were under his fingers. All he wanted was to crawl back down into the *Charlotte*'s tiny bedroom, get under the covers with her, and never come out, except maybe to smoke a joint.

It's good to see that he has his priorities in order.

"Let's go to your house," he suggested, releasing her. "Myrtle makes the best quesadillas, and I'm freaking starving."

She turned around and grinned at him. "Okay, then, let's get the hell out of here, sailor."

Nate headed back to the boat to grab the rest of their bags, whistling as he jumped on board. He'd avoided his moment of truth with the Captain—and Blair—for so long, maybe he could keep on avoiding it a little while longer.

Blair slid her enormous tinted Prada aviators over her eyes and starting walking down the gray wooden dock. Things couldn't have worked out better—Blair and Nate, the couple always most likely to end up together, heading off to Yale in ten short days. It was almost too good to be true.

Yes, quite.

the devil wears dolce

Serena van der Woodsen sat in the Waldorf Rose living room, flanked on either side by Blair's mother, Eleanor Waldorf Rose, and Davita Fjorde—party planner to those residing on Manhattan's Golden Mile. Serena had no idea why she'd been invited to Blair's house, but when Eleanor called she couldn't very well say no to her so-called best friend's mother, whose wedding she had been a bridesmaid in less than a year ago.

"Now, I want it to be surprising and wonderful and luxurious, of course, but I don't want anything too over-the-top. Nothing *vulgar*." Eleanor wrinkled her ski jump of a nose and straightened the hem of her skintight bronze silk Valentino skirt. After giving birth to baby Yale that spring, she was on a strict Pilates-and-no-carbs diet, and it was clearly working. "Although Cyrus just *loved* the belly dancers in Corfu."

"Eleanor, my dear, stop worrying. This party will be *fabulicious*," Davita drawled, scribbling notes in her hot pink, leather-bound notebook with a gold Montblanc pen, her signature pencil-straight ass-length platinum blond hair draping almost to her knobby fishnetted knees. Davita fumbled, dropping the pen, and then pulled an exact replica from her enormous apricot-colored Marc Jacobs tote without missing a beat.

Serena ran her fingers over the miniskirt she'd made herself out of her faded Seven cutoffs. Ever since Blair and Nate had sailed off into the sunrise on her birthday morning, she had been struggling to be her usual cheerful self. Sitting in Blair's living room wasn't helping any. As she looked around at the gleaming oak floor, the heavy crimson silk drapes, the overstuffed toffee-colored, silk-jacquard sofa, all Serena could think about was how she'd spent most of her childhood running around this apartment. She and Blair used to make forts out of all the silk pillows, throwing them off the couch and piling them in the center of the room, pretending the rest of the rug was the ocean while they were stranded on an island. They hid beneath their soft, dark weight for hours, whispering secrets and giggling the day away. Things were so much easier back then—before Nate had come between them. Not that it was his fault.

Why is it never the boy's fault?

Serena sighed and tried to concentrate as Eleanor's nervously loud voice chattered away in her ear, the ice cubes in her Bloody Mary clinking against the glass as she waved her arms about.

"Because, you know, when the Reynoldses had their party last year, they chose that hideous bisque color scheme, which completely washed out Mitzi's complexion," Eleanor was saying, her brow wrinkled in worry. "I was envisioning shell pink or ivory, because those are Blair's absolute favorites, but I just can't stop thinking about Mitzi looking as though she was about to be *sick* all over her very own soiree."

Davita leaned in conspiratorially. "My dear, that event was planned by *Samantha Powers* and her troop of under-lings. *Amateurs*. You have to relax and realize you're dealing with a *professional* here!" She threw her overbleached plat-inum locks over one shoulder and turned toward Serena, her tanned face nearly as leathery as the distressed calfskin bag on the sofa beside her. "Eleanor tells me that you're Blair's best friend," she said with a stewardess smile, scribbling more notes on the pink pad.

Or worst enemy.

Serena nodded. "We've been friends—"

"Forever!" Eleanor finished enthusiastically.

"Mmmm," Davita murmured as she picked up a thin cucumber sandwich—crusts cut off, of course—from a ham-mered silver tray. She sniffed it delicately, then returned it to the tray.

"Now, Serena," Eleanor began, smoothing her sleek, Fekkai-blond shoulder-length bob, "I hope you don't mind me calling you over, but Blair has been positively *unreachable*, and I thought that since you two have known each other since you were toddlers, you'd be the perfect per-son to help plan this event I have scheduled at the Met. We have more than a few milestones to celebrate—Blair and Aaron going off to college, for one. And then there's also—"

Just then Davita's gold Motorola Slvr cell phone began to ring frantically, beeping and burping in the most annoying way possible. Davita jumped up, holding her bony, manicured index finger out in the air, and walked quickly out of the living room, her pewter Jimmy Choo slingbacks sparkling like firecrackers in the light that streamed through the south-facing windows. Serena returned to picking at the frayed threads on her cutoff skirt again. She could barely concentrate anyway. As of today, Blair and Nate had spent exactly one month together, alone on a boat with no one around for miles. They were probably, right at this very minute, eating steamed lobsters with clarified butter and gazing dreamily into each other's eyes. Serena blinked back hot tears as she pictured it.

"So," Eleanor said brightly, inching closer to her on the couch and resting one tanned hand on Serena's forearm. "How has your summer been? With Blair gone I've hardly seen you at all, and it's only a matter of days before you kids are off to New Haven!"

"It's been okay." Serena forced a smile as she squirmed on the couch. She'd spent the last four weeks wandering around the city under the pretense of getting her fill of New York in before leaving it behind. In truth, she was just trying to distract herself. Unfortunately, everywhere she went—to the Central Park pond, to feed the mallards; to the mod boutiques on Little West Twelfth Street, to shop; to the steps of the Met, to drink coffee; even her one venture into Brooklyn to see a warehouse art show—reminded her of her friends. They'd grown up together and experienced the city together, and, supposedly, they were leaving it behind together. But here she was, completely alone. "Just the usual. Nothing special," Serena finished, noticing how lean and tanned Eleanor's legs were. Maybe she should take a Pilates class too.

"Nothing special!" Eleanor exclaimed in the way that

only mothers can. "May I remind you that your first feature film is going to be released very soon, *and* you're starting Yale in a week and a half!" She squeezed Serena's knee so hard it hurt.

Serena knew that she had a lot to be excited about, but she just couldn't seem to match Eleanor's enthusiasm. Maybe it was because the thought of heading to Yale in ten days with Nate and Blair and watching them be blissfully in love for four torturous years loomed over everything. "Has Blair . . . mentioned me at all when you've talked to her?"

Eleanor grabbed a white silk handkerchief from the antique coffee table and began to frantically pat her brow with the soft cloth, then sprayed herself thoroughly with an Evian facial mister and dabbed at her face again. "I'm sorry, dear, but is it hot in here? I'm telling you, never turn forty-seven. The hot flashes are unbearable!" She sighed dramatically, throwing the now-damp hanky behind her. "Now, sweetheart, what were you saying?"

Serena shrugged her shoulders, not at all fazed by Eleanor's outrageous behavior. At least there was one thing around here that wasn't going to change. She just wished she had Blair or Nate to giggle with her about it.

Davita flounced back into the room, snapping her cell phone shut with a decisive click. "Okay, ladies," she said, breaking into an enormous smile, her obvious veneers as wide and white as Scrabble tiles. "Where were we?"

"Well . . ." Eleanor motioned to Serena, her gold Cartier Love bracelets clinking loudly against one another. "I was just telling Serena we have a lot to celebrate right now. In addition to everyone leaving for college, there's—"

"We're hooooooooome!" A taunting, singsongy girl's voice called out from the foyer, a voice Serena would know anywhere. Her heart fluttered. The sound of bags being thrown onto the marble floor was followed by the unmistakable patter of Blair's light, quick steps. Serena swallowed hard, watching as Nate and Blair appeared in the doorway of the Waldorf Roses' massive, antique-strewn living room, hands clasped, looking sun-kissed, glowing, and more gorgeous than ever.

As if that were even possible.

Nate's green eyes lit up when he spotted Serena sitting on the couch, and she smiled weakly, her stomach folding like pancake batter. Just the sight of him in his stained and wrinkled cutoff khakis and ratty gray T-shirt made her feel lightheaded. The last time she'd seen him, standing at the top of the staircase at her family's house in Ridgefield while she hovered at the bottom, the whole world had gone quiet as she overheard him telling Blair he loved her. *Loved.* With those words ringing in her ears, something in Serena had finally clicked. She'd watched him lead Blair upstairs and right then she knew as surely as she'd ever known anything that *she* loved Nate. And now that he was standing right in front of her with her on-again-off-again best friend, she knew it was really true. She loved Nate with her entire heart. It was something she'd always known, deep down. Why hadn't she done anything about it until it was too late?

She shook her long blond locks, trying to remember to act like a normal friend and not a love-struck freak. She jumped to her feet and ran across the room, her fuchsia flowered Calypso flip-flops thwacking all the way, and threw her arms around Blair, squeezing tightly. All at once Serena felt suffocated by the scent of Nate's Right Guard deodorant clinging to her best friend's skin. She pulled back, looking hopefully at Blair, who was still latched onto Nate's hand. "I missed you."

But Blair wasn't smiling back. In fact, she looked less than pleased to see Serena—she looked downright pissed. Serena began to gnaw on her Sephora Supernova-polished thumbnail. Blair could be so scary sometimes. Had *she* found the letter? Oh God. Why hadn't she thought of that before?

As she wrapped her arms again around Blair's rigid, sunbaked body, she couldn't help looking over Blair's shoulder at Nate. His golden-brown hair was wavier than usual from the salt water. It fell across his tanned forehead and he pushed it away, smiling widely as they made eye contact. His lips looked chapped and swollen, like he'd been making out with Blair all night long—which he probably had been. The thought nearly made her choke.

"Looking good, Natie," Serena sighed wistfully, unable to keep the words from escaping her lips. She pulled gently away from Blair, tendrils of golden hairs escaping her ponytail. Nate dropped Blair's hand abruptly and moved toward Serena, opening his arms. Serena rushed in to hug him, wrapping her arms around his taut waist and holding on tight. He squeezed her back with a fierceness that Blair's hug had lacked. Had he found her letter after all?

"What are you guys doing here?!" Serena's voice was breathless as she buried her face in Nate's warm, soft neck. Blair stared at them, her blue eyes narrowing.

Shouldn't they be asking *her* that question?

a yabba-dabba-doo time, we'll have a gay ol' time!

Vanessa Abrams staggered out of the Humphreys' living room, her pale arms weighed down with piles of old coffee-stained newspapers. Her army green Triple 5 Soul cargo pants were rolled up to the knees, and her fitted black Old Navy wifebeater was soaked in sweat. *"God."* She exhaled heavily as she dumped a pile of decades-old New Yorkers in a large blue recycling bin, exposing the dusty parquet floor beneath. "It's amazing these piles of crap haven't toppled over in the night, killing us in our sleep."

Dan Humphrey grunted in assent as he walked down the hall to the kitchen and washed out his coffee-grit-encrusted blue plastic Evergreen mug for the third time that day. He wouldn't mind being dead right about now. They'd been cleaning out the Humphreys' ramshackle, grime-coated Upper West Side apartment for a grueling two hours, but it felt more like two days. Dan just wasn't cut out for hard labor, and he could feel the heart palpitations coming on. At least if he died now, he'd die young, like his idol, the poet John Keats, which he always thought was sort of romantic.

They could bury him beneath the Strand, a copy of Baudelaire's *Fleurs du Mal* over his ashen face. Maybe Vanessa would weep dramatically as she said her final good-byes. Or wait, maybe Greg would. This was one of the many problems with recently discovering you might be gay—it was totally unclear whether your future widower would be your longtime ex-girlfriend or your newish-maybe-boyfriend.

After he and Dan had shared a semi-conscious drunken kiss at their literary salon earlier in the summer, Greg seemed to have decided two things: that Dan was gay, and that they were a couple. Dan wasn't sure how he felt about either of those conclusions, but he hadn't had very long to think about it, because Greg's grandmother had passed away a few days later, and Greg had left for Phoenix for the funeral and to spend time with his extended family. He'd been gone nearly a month, and in that time Greg had sent Dan dozens of beautifully crafted e-mails, all with the same theme: absence makes the heart grow fonder. But every time Dan wrote back, he wasn't sure if he was growing any fonder of Greg . . . or just more confused.

Dan tried to shake his uncertainty away. "I'm going to keep cleaning," he announced with a sudden surge of determination, and marched into the living room with the purposeful steps of a military general.

Dan in the army? Don't ask, don't tell!

"Be my guest," Vanessa retorted as she threw another huge stack of newspapers into the recycling bin. "As far as I'm concerned, it's a lost cause."

Earlier that summer, her older sister Ruby had returned from Europe with her new Czech boyfriend, Piotr, in tow and had proceeded to kick Vanessa out of the cozy Williamsburg apartment they'd shared for the last three years. Thanks, sis! Since then, Vanessa had been living in Dan's sister Jenny's room while Jenny was at art school in Prague for the summer. Since Dan was heading to Evergreen College in Washington State in less than two weeks and Jenny would be off to boarding school in upstate New York, it looked like Vanessa would be keeping her room in the Humphreys' apartment when she started NYU—after all, somebody had to keep Rufus, Dan and Jenny's lesser-known Beat poet editor father, company. So she'd decided to spend the weekend redecorating the totally dismal pad. And really, what better way to try out Dan's new *Queer Eye* decorating skills? If he even had any. He was so fresh out of the closet it was hard for her to believe it was really true. But maybe that's because she didn't *want* it to be true.

Didn't she?

Dan closed his eyes, remembering the feel of Greg's lips on his, his scratchy blond chin stubble scraping against Dan's jaw. The more he went over it in his mind, Dan wasn't even sure how he felt about the kiss anymore—or about Greg—except that he was pretty sure he didn't really have any desire to do it again anytime soon. He'd promised himself he was going to get to the bottom of this before he hopped into the 1977 Buick Skylark his dad had given him for graduation and drove to Evergreen in ten days. If he were going to reinvent himself in college, which was basically the whole point of going to college in the first place, figuring out his sexuality would be a good place to start. He'd even picked up a book at the Strand, where he'd worked all summer, called *Unlocking the Closet*. It explained that feelings of confusion and despair were natural while you were transitioning from one sexual identity to another, and said that one should be totally willing to ask oneself the really "tough" questions. Which he really was trying to do. Like, if he wasn't truly gay, then why had he kissed Greg in the first place? Then again, why was Vanessa suddenly looking so hot with newsprint smudges across her pale cheek?

Good question.

Dan moved over to the sad gray curtains shading the floor-to-ceiling windows in the musty living room and attempted to tie one limp side back with a twist tie he'd found with the garbage bags under the kitchen sink. The yellow twist tie fell to the ground and he bent down to pick it up.

Vanessa sighed as she watched him. He was really going to have to get in touch with his inner diva if he was going to make a go of it as a New York City–bred gay man.

"There, how's that?" Dan secured the garbage tie and stood back to admire his handiwork, looking more optimistic than he had all day. He placed both hands on his hips. "*So* much better, right?"

The fabric hung to the side, exposing the dirty hand-printed and dust-streaked window. Vanessa looked from the window to her ex-boyfriend—who now apparently had boyfriends of his own. "Uh . . . yeah," she intoned, fluffing a lumpy brown leather sofa pillow that resembled a giant potato. "That's just great. I'm sure we'll be featured in *Town & Country* next month."

The truth was, Vanessa kind of missed him. After returning from a hellish stint as a nanny and then some sort of fashion muse out in the Hamptons, and since Greg had left for Phoenix, she and Dan had spent the last month hanging out in the city, but it had been . . . different. They had fallen into a comfortable, friendly sort of small-talk-making rapport—with none of the sexual tension or heated argument you'd expect from two exes living in such close quarters.

With so little time before Dan left for college, Vanessa couldn't believe that this was the way they were going to leave things. Not even one last lingering kiss or one last roll in the hay? Every time Dan brushed past her when he was making his umpteenth cup of Folgers crystals, or on the way to the bathroom, when she caught a whiff of stale Camels and coffee grounds, she had to stop herself from throwing him down on the dust-bunny-littered floor and ripping off his brown, frayed-at-the-bottom, zillion-year-old cords. In fact, now that Dan was gay—and completely unattainable—the thought was more appealing than ever.

A key jiggled in the front door and it swung open with a bang as Rufus Humphrey's bulk filled the doorway. He wore a pair of denim overalls splattered in white paint with a faded brown ANTEATERS HAVE FEELINGS TOO T-shirt underneath, and scuffed, red bowling shoes on his feet. A white straw Panama hat was perched jauntily atop his wiry, shoulder-length gray hair, and his bushy salt-and-pepper beard was partially braided, with a hot pink elastic at the end.

"Hey Dad," Dan called from his station at the window. "Check out—"

"Close your eyes, Dan!" Rufus boomed, holding up one

hand, palm out in a stop-in-the-name-of-love pose, as if he were auditioning to be the next Supreme. Dan was too surprised to do anything but comply. He closed his eyes, his mind racing with the possibilities. Chinese food for lunch? He was starving. An iPod to take to college with him? A first edition of his favorite novel of all time, *The Sorrows of Young Werther* by Goethe?

"Danny, darrrrrrrling!" A preening, soprano-pitched voice sang out behind Rufus. Dan's eyes snapped open. Whatever he was expecting, it definitely wasn't this.

"Mom?!"

Jeanette Humphrey flew into the room like an exotic bird just released from captivity, dressed in a turquoise floor-length sundress and carrying two large brown shopping bags. She threw her long, gray-streaked mousy brown hair over one shoulder, elbowed Rufus aside with an exasperated sigh, and flung her skinny arms around Dan in a cloud of poisonously strong floral perfume. Dan just stood there in a state of shock, his arms like chow fun noodles as he tried to wrap his mind around the fact that this was actually happening. What the fuck? Was this really his mother, after, what, *ten* years? Or was this an acid flashback, like a real-life Howl poem? Oh wait, he had never done acid. What was she *doing* here?

Vanessa watched with a fascination that bordered on horror as the mythical Mrs. Humphrey proceeded to kiss Dan all over his face, leaving violent tracks of bright pink lipstick smeared across his sunken cheeks.

"How *are* you, my pet?" Jeanette chirped as she squeezed her son so tightly it looked like he might suffer internal organ damage. "It's been absolutely *ages!*" She cupped Dan's pained, mortified face and led him, zombielike, to the couch. Vanessa had never seen him get whisked around before and with so little complaint. Rufus winked merrily at Vanessa from beneath his white hat, and sauntered through the chipped, oak-trimmed doorway into the kitchen. Vanessa followed him, not quite sure where to go. Rufus pulled out a clear Tupperware container full of weird brown goo that had been shoved in the back of the fridge, peeling back the lid and sniffing happily.

"Redecorating?" His voice boomed as he opened the utensil drawer and rummaged through it. "The curtains look phenomenal! That your golden touch, Dan?" Rufus yelled toward the living room. "This place could use *something*, that's for sure." He pulled out a lime green spatula and began using it as a spoon.

"It could use something—like a wrecking ball!" Jeanette's voice rang out from the other room. "Or a can of gasoline and a lit match!" She came striding into the kitchen, the blue folds of her sundress flying to and fro, while Dan trailed behind, carrying her bags. Gliding up to Vanessa, she smiled broadly and extended one hand laden with turquoise rings for Vanessa to shake . . . or kiss . . . or high-five? It was hard to tell, the way she was holding it, and finally Vanessa just bumped fists with her like they were old homies.

What up, dawg?

It was so strange meeting Dan's mom after all this time— it was like looking at a slightly more feminine version of Dan—complete with long brown hair and too much hippie jewelry. "You must be Vanessa," Jeanette exclaimed, her hazel-blue eyes sparkling manically. "I've heard *so* much about you."

"You too," Vanessa lied, because in truth, she really hadn't. As far as she knew, Dan's mom had disappeared with Count Dracula or Count Chocula or something and was never heard from again.

Dan's palms were slick with sweat and his wrists trembled under the weight of the bags. His mother. Really, she was the last thing he needed. On top of trying to figure out once and for all whether or not he was gay, he was going to have to play catch-up with this person who had basically abandoned him when he was only eight. Or was he ten? She's been gone so long he really couldn't remember. He'd certainly stopped missing her years ago, but now here she was in all her perfumed, turquoise jewelry-wearing glory, acting like her presence was really no big deal. Jesus. Jenny had seen their mom in Prague. Why hadn't she *warned* him?

Dan brought in his mother's packages and placed them gently on the kitchen floor. Vanessa tried to make eye contact with him but his eyes were glued downward, and he was seemingly deep in thought. Or in a trance. Maybe his mother had hypnotized him? Maybe she was a New Age gypsy?

"Now, Dan," Jeanette began, as she rooted through the cavernous bags, pulling out assorted packages and placing them on top of the piles of newspapers covering the kitchen table, "Jenny told me all about your special announcement, and I'm here to help you celebrate!"

Vanessa stifled a nervous laugh as Dan's face turned sheet white.

Rufus held the spatula, piled with what Vanessa was now

convinced was dog food, even though they didn't have a dog. "What announcement?"

"Coffee!" Jeanette chirped excitedly opening a large pink box and shoving the contents under Dan's nose. "Will go perfectly with *these*."

Dan craned his neck and peered inside. Cradled in white wax paper was a chocolate éclair. Two plump cream puffs nestled on either side of the long, frosted pastry. His face flushed red with embarrassment. Maybe he was just being paranoid or perverted, but that looked a whole lot like a—

"It's a penis!" his mother trilled, as if reading her son's thoughts. "It's to celebrate Dan being gay!" Jeanette practically screamed. "The cream in the center is the sweetest part." She winked.

Um, ew?

"Gay?" Rufus brought the spatula to his lips and chewed thoughtfully. "When did this happen?"

All eyes turned to Dan. "Like . . . I don't know exactly," he stammered, wishing the parquet floor would just open up and swallow him whole. His mother had traveled three thousand miles just to give him a penis pastry? She was back because he'd come out of the closet? He was going to *kill* Jenny for opening her little mouth. Besides, what did penises have to do with anything? There was nothing sexual about his conundrum.

Wasn't there?

Rufus shrugged and took another bite of mustard-brown slop. "And here I thought Jeanie just missed me—ha!" Dan's hand flew to his chest in an unconscious and totally effeminate gesture. Rufus continued, an insane-looking grin now plastered to his bearded face. "Well, you'll remember what you're missing now, won't you Jean-Jean? And *then* you'll be sick of living like royalty in Europe." He shook the lime green apparatus at her and turned back to Dan. "Does this mean I need to learn to cook quiche?" he asked.

"Anyway," Jeanette sang out, ignoring her estranged husband as she began pulling what looked like yards of magenta silk out of a large white box. "I brought you some gifts to mark this very important transition into your new lifestyle. Look!" She held up what appeared to be a fuchsia pink jumpsuit with sparkling gold laces up the front. As she excitedly held it up to Dan's body, it became immediately apparent that it was about ten sizes too small—which was only fitting, since the last present she'd sent had been size-four lederhosen from Düsseldorf when he was ten. Dan closed his eyes again and silently wished that he and Vanessa hadn't removed the ancient stacks of newspapers today—maybe then the piles of clutter could have fallen down and killed him, if not in his sleep, then in this, perhaps the worst waking moment of his life.

"I knew this would be perfect on you! Can you imagine what kind of *splash* you'll make at the Chelsea nightclubs?"

We can imagine—and it's already giving us nightmares.

"I have another gift," she continued conspiratorially, taking Dan's elbow and leaning in close, her singsong voice dropping to a low whisper. "But this one is for your eyes only." Jeanette reached into the hip-length macramé tote still hanging from her shoulder and drew out a large, black-bound book, which she handed to Dan.

He ran his fingers over the gilt label: HOMOESENSUAL: THE

GREATEST GAY LOVE POEMS OF ALL TIME. The book must have weighed over fifteen pounds. Dan stared down at the cover, not sure what to say. It actually was a really thoughtful gift. After all, he *was* a poet, and he was pretty sure he might be gay. It would do him good to read some gay poetry.

Still, couldn't she have just given him a card?

"I figured you might want something more *artistic* to celebrate your awakening, and I knew you'd appreciate this new European compilation. I picked it up at this delightful little 'alternative' bookstore in Paris—they have gay movies, too! I'll be sure to pick one up for you next time I'm there."

Dan frowned down at the book. Had his mother just offered to send him gay porn? She seemed really excited by the idea of having a gay son, and he hadn't seen her in at least ten years—why not humor her? He shrugged, picked up the penis éclair, and took a giant bite. It tasted like a Bavarian cream donut.

"Delicious," he declared, smacking his lips and really camping it up. His mother nodded, beaming with pleasure. Vanessa giggled and dipped her finger into the box to taste some of the cream. *"Truly divine,"* he added, for their benefit.

The family that's gay together stays together!

s takes the wind out of b's sail

Blair's pretty blue eyes narrowed, catlike, as she looked at Serena in her cutoff Sevens skirt and white Imitation of Christ tank. The light poured in through the enormous living room windows and bounced off Serena's angelic blond wisps of hair. She looked predictably, infuriatingly stunning. Even though it was obvious that Serena hadn't put any effort into her outfit, she was as gorgeous as fucking ever. It wouldn't matter if she were wearing saggy-butt shorts and a stained wifebeater—she'd probably still get stopped on the street by Patrick Demarchelier on her way home and get put on the cover of September's *Vogue*. It wasn't fucking fair.

Yes, but look who has the boy, honey.

Blair willed herself to smile and maintain her composure as Serena slithered her lithe arms around Nate's neck. Wasn't it bad enough that Serena had planted that stupid, three-page love letter in Nate's car when she could *obviously* see that Blair and Nate were totally back together? Did she have to show up in Blair's living room the second they got back to the city, like some scary stalker?

Or like your best friend?

Blair seethed, watching as Serena leaned in even closer to Nate's body, and Nate gripped her tightly, closing his eyes like he was really *enjoying* it. Serena nestled in Nate's arms like she belonged there, like she had *always* belonged there. Any more of this and Blair was going to scream. She shifted from one foot to another, angrily twirling her ruby ring around her finger and silently shouting at them to let go of one another and notice her standing there.

"Blair, honey!" Blair whipped around as her mother practically pounced on her, while a skinny, bored-looking bleached-blond woman stood behind her scribbling in a fuchsia leather organizer. Eleanor wrapped her arms around Blair, enveloping her in a cloud of Chanel No. 5. Blair squeezed her eyes shut tight and dug her short buffed fingernails into the palms of her hands, tolerating the embrace. "Welcome home!" Eleanor finally stepped back and gestured to the blond woman, who had now taken a seat on the couch. "Ooh, and I'm so glad you get to meet my new friend, Davita Fjorde!"

Blair offered the orange-lipstick-wearing blond woman a limp hand, all the while looking over her shoulder as Nate laughed at one of Serena's annoying little jokes.

"Charmed, Blair," Davita drawled, tapping one pewter-colored Jimmy Choo slingback against the caramel-and-burgundy Bokhara rug. She didn't seem to have any patience for family reunions. Well, good. Neither did Blair.

"Now, Blair," Eleanor began, speaking rapidly—the way she always did when she was worried about something, sweat breaking out in small, jewel-like beads on her brow. She practically pushed Blair onto the sofa. "Davita is here because . . . because . . . well, I'm glad you're sitting down, because I have big, big, big news!"

Blair *really* didn't like the sound of that—what could be bigger than Serena manhandling Nate right in front of her? They had finally stopped hugging, but were now paired off in the corner of the room, whispering. Serena's delicate, bell-like laugh grated in Blair's ears like the whine of a chainsaw.

"I've invited Davita and Serena to help plan a going-away party for you and Aaron at the Met the night before you leave for college!" Eleanor grabbed Blair's arm, squeezing tight with excitement, her eyes glassy and bright. "That's just nine days away!"

Davita grabbed a clipboard from off the coffee table. "Let's see . . . so far we've got fabulous gift bags full of Kiehls and Frédéric Fekkai products, and of course flower arrangements by Robert Isabell—I was thinking stargazer and Casablanca lilies, but that may be too bridey for your taste . . . truffles from La Maison du Chocolat, a tower of cupcakes from Magnolia Bakery. And I thought it might be really cute to run a red carpet outside and down those fabulous Met steps. . . . Blair? What do *you* think?" Davita frowned, her leathery skin crinkling. Her face looked like it was about to peel off in layers, like a withered onion.

Blair couldn't concentrate. She continued to stare at Serena and Nate, willing Nate to turn around and notice her. *Hello! Remember me? Your girlfriend? The girl you just spent a month alone with on a boat in the middle of the Atlantic? The girl you said you loved about eighty thousand times?* What the fucking fuck was going on?

". . . and it's all for you, sweetie! Well, you and Aaron and . . . the rest of the family too! Because . . . we're moving to Los Angeles!"

Blair's head whipped around to face her mother. *"What?"* She suddenly felt like she was choking. "What are you *talking* about?" Eleanor's smile wavered for a moment and she reached up, patting her sleek, golden bob to compose herself, her six-carat Harry Winston diamond wedding ring sending glittering reflections across the room.

"Cyrus's real estate company just landed a huge contract in L.A.—they're building a luxury resort in Malibu! Isn't that fabulous?" Eleanor waved her hands excitedly in front of Blair's stunned face. "And with you and Aaron off to college, it'll be a fresh start for baby Yale . . . who really should be raised *properly*—with a real backyard she can play in." Eleanor grabbed a stack of blueprints from the coffee table and shoved them on Blair's lap. "Look at these plans for the new house! Your bedroom will be here, with its own terrace, and Yale's is going to have a sleeping loft for the nanny and—"

"Jesus Christ, Mom!" Blair yelled, swatting away the blueprints. "Los Angeles? Where people die from earthquakes like every day? You raised *me* in Manhattan—*without* a backyard! What's wrong with Central Park? This is our *home!*"

Davita stiffened at Blair's little outburst and stalked out of the room, clutching her jewel-encrusted cell phone. She was paid to plan parties, not navigate family drama. Serena and Nate were still chattering away obliviously in the corner, staring deep into each other's eyes. The greatest catastrophe of Blair's life, and they didn't even *notice?*

"Yes, dear, I'm well aware we raised you in Manhattan, but we were innocent new parents," Eleanor answered, distractedly surveying the plans for the new house. "We just didn't *know* any better!" She tried to make her voice a bit more soothing. "Please be happy for your family. I promise you're going to love it. If you'll just look at these blueprints, you'll see we're going to have a swimming pool and everything. And oh!" She jumped up and grabbed a photo from the coffee table. "I forgot the other surprise—even your father is coming over from France to celebrate!" she exclaimed, shoving a photo under Blair's nose. "With these *darling* Cambodian twins he's adopted with that sweet Giles."

Blair looked down and tried to focus on the photograph. Her tan, handsome father sat smiling happily, a pink bandana tied around his neck, two decidedly Asian-looking babies cradled in his overly worked-out arms. Blair stared down at the photograph uncomprehendingly, feeling nauseous. *Babies?* Her father had adopted *babies* from Cambodia? What, was one beautiful, Yale-bound daughter not enough? Was she not enough for *anyone*? "Really, Blair," Eleanor continued, "I think Giles is just about the best boyfriend your father's ever had!"

Blair jumped to her feet. For the first time in her life she couldn't think of a single thing to say. Los Angeles? Cambodian *twins*? She couldn't fucking *believe* her family would do this to her. This was supposed to be the happiest time in her life! It was supposed to be all about her and Nate, heading off to Yale with no more distractions, just smooth sailing all the way from now until they climbed into her brand new bisque-colored BMW and drove away, leaving her crazy family behind.

In the corner, Serena laughed again, and Nate ran his hands through his wavy, salty hair. Clearly they were in their own little world, with no clue what the hell was happening to her. Blair clutched her stomach. Projectile vomiting was a distinct possibility. Her family was seriously moving? What would it be like on Thanksgiving or Christmas break? She'd be in L.A. with her stupid family, hiding out in their bomb shelter or wherever the fuck people went during earthquakes and Nate would be . . . here. With Serena.

She heard her mother calling after her as she clutched her stomach and ran down the hall to her old bedroom. Baby Yale was lying in her white wooden crib, her head topped with a Mohawk of strawberry blond peach fuzz. She smiled delightedly at her big sister as if to say, "What's all the fuss about?" Blair went over and picked her up, glad to see her chubby little friend after almost a month away. Then she noticed that Yale was wearing a tie-dyed onesie with the words CALIFORNIA DREAMIN' stenciled on the front of it.

Without a moment's hesitation, Blair whisked her tiny sister over to the changing table, yanked off the offending article, and replaced it with the adorable pink DKNY onesie she had bought for her at the DKNY flagship store on Madison Avenue. Yale giggled as Blair tickled her in all her favorite spots.

"There." She dropped the tie-dyed onesie into the airtight Diaper Genie, where it would be lost forever. "Much better!" Yale clung to Blair's shoulder as Blair carried her over to the celery-colored cashmere throw rug to play with blocks.

At least someone was happy to see her.

s and n's mission impossible

"So, what have you been doing here all by yourself?" Nate asked. He shook the sand-colored hair from his eyes. Across the elegant burgundy-and-ivory living room, Blair was arguing with her mother, as usual.

"Nothing much." Serena hoped she didn't look as nervous as she felt. "Nothing" was the truth—she'd spent the past month doing a whole lot of nothing, bumming around on her couch, wandering the streets of New York aimlessly, iced latte in hand, going to movie theaters alone. Just trying to distract herself from the gnawing, anxious feeling inside her. "You know, hanging out—the usual." She couldn't tell Nate what she'd been up to—it was too pathetic. She took a deep breath and wiped her sweaty palms on her cutoff skirt. Why was she so nervous? This was *Nate,* the guy she'd chased around this very living room when she was six because she wanted to wear his new Superman Underoos.

Has anything really changed?

"What about you guys—you're the ones who went on this big adventure!" Serena looked into Nate's eyes and edged her fingers closer to his on the settee where they were huddled together. She smiled shyly, her blond hair curling slightly around her temples. She wasn't trying to flirt, but when it came to Nate, she couldn't seem to help herself. "Captain Archibald," she said with a sly smile.

"Don't *ever* call me that!" he laughed. "Seriously, though, being out on the water all that time was amazing. Sun every day, and the stars at night—you just can't imagine how great—"

"That's awesome, Natie." Serena cut him off distractedly. She turned to stare as Blair got up from her seat and stormed out of the living room, holding her stomach with one hand and wiping her face with the other. Throwing a tantrum five minutes after coming home wasn't exactly unusual for Blair, but Serena wondered if she should she go and check on her friend. *Wait, shouldn't that be Nate's job now?* she wondered. Wasn't checking on your girlfriend kind of a boyfriend thing to do? Serena turned to look at him. He was gazing straight at her, completely oblivious to the fact that Blair—the supposed love of his life—had just run of the living room in tears. What the hell did that mean?

Umm . . . maybe that he's stoned? Again?

"So," Serena started again, focusing her gaze on the gray Abercrombie T-shirt Nate had had for as long as she could remember—anything to avoid looking up into his glittering green eyes. She shuffled her flip-flops against the floor and steeled herself for the question she knew she had to ask, no matter how much the answer hurt. "Did you find—?"

"We found so much cool shit." He grinned widely. "Little sandbar islands, these caves up in Maine—we even saw fucking *puffins*!"

Serena looked up into his beach-glass green eyes, her heart thumping crazily in her chest. She kept replaying Blair's sudden exit over in her mind. What was she so upset about? Had Nate found the letter and said something to her about it? Or what if Blair had found it and told *him*? Or, worse yet, what if Blair found it and *didn't* tell him? What if Nate loved her too and that was why he wasn't running after Blair? Or what if the letter was still nestled in the glove compartment of Nate's father's Aston Martin, unread, all her questions unanswered?

"It was really amazing," he said, speaking slowly, the way Nate always did when he was happy or relaxed or stoned, which was basically all the time. "I didn't want to come back."

Just looking at his angelic face, she couldn't stand not knowing what had happened to her letter—not knowing whether or not he knew. She had to say *something*.

Serena smiled weakly. "Nate, did you ever find—?"

"Just a minute, you two!" Eleanor appeared before them and sat down, wedging her skinny butt between them on the way-too-small-for-three settee. Serena and Nate both inched over—not that they had a choice. It was either move or have Eleanor sit on their laps. She linked one arm through Serena's and the other through Nate's, a mischievous look on her face. The overpowering scent of Eleanor's Chanel No. 5 made Serena feel like she was in a department store.

"I'm so glad to get the two of you alone," Eleanor whispered conspiratorially, as if they were all planning some kind of top-secret mission. "I'm working on a surprise for Blair for the party. It's a slide show of Blair's life—kind of like a-greatest-moments-so-far thing." She smiled brightly, turning her head back and forth to look at Serena and Nate as she spoke, like she was watching a tennis match. "But the problem is that I don't really have the time to go through the *thousands* of snapshots of Blair I've amassed over the years—and that's where you two come in!" She squeezed each of their knees with her hands. "I need you to go through this *immense* stack of albums and choose some appropriate photographs. But I'm afraid we're on a bit of a deadline—I need them by next Friday at the latest." Serena tried to glance at Nate over Eleanor's head, but when she leaned back on the couch, Eleanor leaned back too, fanning herself with her hand. "But remember—this has to be a top-secret mission, you two, so no telling Blair!" Eleanor's loud whisper reverberated off the living room's paneled walls, and she held her finger up to her mouth.

Hush-hush!

Serena tried not to giggle. Eleanor was terrible at keeping secrets—she always managed to tell her children what they were getting for Christmas *before* she'd even bought their presents. Most likely she'd tell Blair by tomorrow—*if* Blair hadn't already heard their entire conversation. Nate just nodded mutely. He never said much in Eleanor's presence: she was far too overwhelming.

"We'd be happy to do it," Serena answered for the both of them. "And we promise to keep it a secret from Blair."

Yeah. They're good at that.

a very short engagement

"I am just too pooped to pop!" Dan's mom stretched her arms overhead and wiggled her butt back and forth on the lumpy brown leather sofa in the living room, her mouth open in a yawn. It was only eight o'clock, and Rufus was at one of his anarchist poet jamborees in the West Village. She looked around, blinking like a sleepy Siamese cat. Her mousy brown hair was sticking out in every direction, and her watery blue eyes were now red and bloodshot. "Jet lag really gets you at my age. And cocktails on the plane are only a temporary fix!"

She looked at Dan and then turned in the direction of the kitchen doorway, where Vanessa was standing, obviously expecting them to say something. Dan sat stonily in the tattered armchair across from his mom, still not sure what to make of her.

"But you kids really shouldn't be drinking!" She wagged a finger back and forth, apparently unaware that she was chastising them for something *she'd* done. "Although if you want to taste some—just a taste—you just let me know, okay? Because that would be fine. So, where am I sleeping?" she added to her rambling.

Dan attempted to exchange a what-the-hell? glance with Vanessa, but she just stood there, lazily licking the remains of the penis cream puff from her fingers. The contrast of her snowy, white skin against her close-cropped dark hair, the curve of her red lips, her slightly mocking brown eyes—she really was beautiful.

"See?" His mother leaned forward and prodded his knee with her turquoise-embellished fingers. "*She* likes the cream filling."

Dan quickly snapped out of his reverie and stood up. "Um, well, we're sort of filling up around here. I guess if you want to take my room I could take the couch?"

His mother stood up, holding onto her neck with one hand and rubbing furiously. "The *couch*? Don't be silly. I mean, now that you're . . . well, you know—" Jeanette broke off, waving her turquoise-laden hands in the air. "I mean," she began again, "sharing Vanessa's room shouldn't be a problem, right? You girls can pillow talk all night!"

"Sure, um—yeah—that's fine," Dan stammered, glancing over at Vanessa. She looked a little surprised or horrified—or maybe she was just trying to hold in her laughter after hearing Dan called a girl by his own mother.

Jeanette stood on her tiptoes and kissed Dan on the top of his head, mussing his hair. "Dan, dear, do you mind if I use your computer before I go to bed? I just want to send off a few e-mails. Don't worry, I won't download any granny porn!" Without waiting for an answer, she flitted toward

Dan's room, whistling Gloria Gaynor's "I Will Survive" completely off-key.

Sure, *she'll* survive. But will Dan?

"Good night, ladies!" they heard her trill as she closed the door to Dan's room.

Dan swallowed hard, trying to hide his embarrassment. He never would have imagined it possible that four little words—specifically, the ones on his postcard to his sister that read, "Dear Jenny, I'm gay"—could cause so much trouble. He went into the kitchen to find Vanessa, who was now smearing pastry cream on the Formica tabletop, swirling it in intricate designs. If he was really gay, then how come he still thought about running his palms over the prickly hairs of Vanessa's shaved head, or seeing if the flesh on her stomach was still as soft and warm as bread dough.

"So, *roomie*. Wanna go to bed?" Vanessa raised one eyebrow mischievously, her lips curved into a smirk. Before Dan could answer, Vanessa stepped away from the countertop and walked into Jenny's old room, her combat boots slapping against the floor.

Dan could hear the snapping of sheets as Vanessa made the bed—something she rarely did. Making the bed. Did that mean she wanted him to come to bed? But it was barely dark out. Maybe she was just tired of the apartment being such a total mess? Dan's head hurt. It had been a long, long day. He sighed and walked into the room behind her.

"Hey, roomie," he parroted back to her, grabbing one corner of the sheet and pulling it tight around the mattress. Vanessa let go of her end of the sheet and threw a pillow at his head. Was she *flirting* with him? A fine sheen of sweat coated her face, and her cheeks were flushed, giving her a radiant glow. Dan resisted the urge to crawl across the bed and lightly kiss each apple red cheek.

Right. Sharing a room will be *just like* a girly sleepover.

Dan waited to see what Vanessa would do next, but then a shrill buzzing sound came from her pocket, startling them both. He still wasn't used to Vanessa having a cell phone—she'd gotten one shortly after moving in with the Humphreys so she could pay her own bill. Probably a good thing, since Rufus was not known for his skill at relaying messages. Usually he left sticky notes on the fridge that read, A GUY CALLED, and then the time of the call, to the minute—like that was helpful.

Vanessa dug for her phone, not all that thrilled with the interruption. Flirting with Dan was so fun now that he was supposedly gay. She flipped open her phone. "Hello?"

"Lil' sis!"

"Ruby?!" Vanessa hadn't spoken to her sister since she returned from Prague and kicked her out. Fun times. So why was she calling now?

"What's up, girl!?" Ruby yelled, sounding uncharacteristically manic. "God, it's great to hear your voice!"

"Um, you too. What's going on?" Vanessa tried to keep her voice neutral, but she was still mad as hell at her sister and wasn't about to forgive her without first receiving some serious ass-kissing. She crossed her arms over her chest, waiting for Ruby's apology. Maybe she and Piotr had broken up and she wanted Vanessa to move back to Williamsburg and into her old room. She could almost smell the sweet, burnt scent of the sugar factory directly across the street from their apartment. Soon she'd be having breakfast at Eat and late-night coffee at Diner surrounded by pale, skinny boys with hair that looked like it had been cut with a butter knife, her days of decoding Dan's flip-flopping sexuality finally over. . . .

"Listen, V, I'm sorry I've been out of touch for so long, but I've just been really busy. . . ."

Vanessa gripped the receiver with one hand and stuffed a pillow back into its case with the other. Right. She'd probably been busy holding Piotr's *brush*. Ick. Vanessa shivered at her own perverted thought and threw the pillow onto the almost-made bed. Dan sat on the end of the bed, eavesdropping and examining his fingernails in a typically gay way.

"Piotr's working on a new series of paintings and he's been using me as a model—I can't wait for you to see them."

Scowling at the receiver, Vanessa stomped out of the room. Okay, so Piotr was still in the picture. And presumably he was still using Vanessa's room as his studio. But maybe Ruby wanted her to move back in anyway: she could get a cot or something. She walked down the long crumbly hallway to the kitchen and began to spoon granules of Folgers into a lumpy yellow ceramic mug Dan's mom had sent over from Europe ages ago.

"Um, sure, I'll check the paintings out at some point. . . ." The last she'd heard about Piotr's "art," he'd been doing a series of paintings of "monolithic nudes and their canines." She pictured a huge canvas of Ruby naked, astride a slobbering German shepherd. Not exactly her idea of "art."

This from the girl who prefers photographs of dead pigeons and spat-out gum?

"Anyway," Ruby went on, her voice as breathless as if she'd been running the 10K, "That's not the really *big* news. Are you sitting down?"

"Yeah," Vanessa lied, distractedly placing her ceramic cup in the microwave and setting the timer.

"We're getting married!!!!!"

"What!?" Vanessa sank to the floor in front of the microwave, Folgers crystals scattering all over the linoleum they'd just mopped this morning. *Married?* To *Piotr?* They'd just met a few months ago! He made paintings of naked women and *dogs!* And now he was going to be *family?* There was something seriously wrong with the world.

Just then Dan's mom glided into the kitchen, wearing a diaphanous, floor-length pink dressing gown embroidered with hundreds of exotic birds. A pasty, fragrant white cream that smelled like pound cake covered every inch of her face. Her fuzzy pink slippers shuffled against the linoleum floor. "Pardon me, I forgot to take my vitamin drink!" Jeanette whispered, opening the refrigerator and pouring a noxious-looking brown liquid into a Scooby-Doo glass. "Vitamins are nature's gift to us all!" she trilled. Vanessa just shook her head as Jeanette smacked her lips and started to walk back to Dan's room, drinking the disgusting-looking concoction and humming as she went.

"Vanessa? Can you hear me?" Ruby's voice broke the silence.

"Um, yeah. Whatever. I mean, congratulations," Vanessa murmured into the phone. She looked up to see Dan standing in the doorway. He shot her a quizzical look and mouthed, "Are you okay?" Vanessa just nodded and brought the phone closer to her ear. Ruby was still chattering away happily, totally oblivious to her less-than-peppy response.

". . . maid of honor," Vanessa heard her sister's voice say over the low hum of the microwave.

She sat up straighter. "Maid of *what*?" she asked incredulously. "Who are you? Where's my sister?"

Ruby cackled. "Come on, you know you're dying to wear a big Laura Ashley dress." Vanessa got to her feet just as the microwave beeped noisily. No fucking way.

"So, will you do it?" Her sister's voice rang in her ears. Slowly, she removed the mug from the microwave, handling it carefully so that the water wouldn't spill over and burn her. Although maybe a third-degree burn would get her out of any wedding-related duties.

Tempting.

Vanessa sighed. She knew she couldn't say no to her sister, even if Piotr did have horrible teeth and bestiality issues.

"Yeah, fine. Whatever. I'll do it." She took a sip of scalding coffee and promptly spat it out all over her cargo pants. "But only if I can wear my own clothes—there's no way in hell I'm putting on one of those totally gay pastel bridesmaid dresses."

She glanced over at Dan, who had pulled the hot pink silk jumpsuit out of one of his mom's bags and was holding it in front of his skinny body as if picturing what it would look like on. She mouthed, "Sorry," smiling weakly. "I mean, so totally *lame*," she said into the phone, wiping her thighs with a ratty brown kitchen towel.

Ruby laughed, and Vanessa could hear her mumbling to

Piotr in the background in some insane language she couldn't understand. Probably Martian.

"Don't worry about that. The ceremony is a week from Saturday, a picnic kind of thing at Prospect Park—so it's totally casual. Everyone's bringing some food and wearing their own clothes anyway." Vanessa could hear the click of her sister's lighter and then the sound of her exhaling as she blew out the first drag. Ruby never smoked before she met Piotr. Was "Eurotrash" a contagious disease?

And is there a vaccine?

"Thank God." Vanessa held the coffee up to her lips, letting the steam float over her skin. "You really had me worried there for a second."

"Listen, the bachelorette party is on Thursday. You're kind of supposed to plan it. I've got some ideas though, so don't worry too much."

Bachelorette party? *Plan it?* "Yeah," Vanessa managed to mumble while taking another sip of her coffee, which tasted like ass. "I guess." Was there some unwritten rule that all coffee in the Humphreys' apartment had to be terrible?

"Of course you're going to film the whole wedding, too. And before I forget, listen—can you ask Dan if he'll write a poem to read at the reception? You know, something about love, that kind of thing. Piotr's friends are planning some performance art, but we'd like someone to read something and don't know any other poets. It would mean a lot to us."

Vanessa snorted into the phone. Straight love poems weren't exactly Dan's thing.

"Anyway, listen, I have to run—I have a dress fitting at Kleinfeld first thing in the morning and I gotta get some sleep. Oh, and my last gig as a single woman is on Monday at the Galapagos Art Space—if you're free, come check it out!"

There was a click, and then the dial tone began buzzing rudely in Vanessa's ear. Waking up early for a *dress* fitting? Ruby really *had* been abducted by aliens.

"My sister's getting married," Vanessa intoned flatly, staring at a postcard of some really old building in Prague that Jenny had sent. The building was so completely covered in pigeon shit it looked like it was made of wax.

"Are you *serious*?" Ruby was the last person Dan ever thought would get married—except for maybe Vanessa. Vanessa had told him once that she thought marriage was all about money and status and that it always had been, all throughout history—in the Middle Ages it was practically a form of slavery. Still, Dan had always believed that someday he would get to watch Vanessa walk moodily down the aisle in a long black dress, carrying a bunch of brilliant white daisies. He'd even written a poem about it. But now he was gay, and gay marriage wasn't even *legal* in New York.

". . . anyway, she wants you to write a poem and read it at the ceremony." Vanessa's voice broke into Dan's thoughts.

"Who? Me?" Dan tied the sleeves of the fuchsia jumpsuit around his shoulders like a cape—that was the only way it was ever going to fit.

"Yeah." Vanessa downed the rest of her coffee in one gulp. "You. The one in the cape."

Supergay? Captain Gaypants?

Dan scratched his head. Ever since his recent "revelation," he hadn't felt much like writing. In fact, he hadn't written a single word since he'd kissed Greg. It was as if all his confused feelings were trapped inside, circulating furiously, and he couldn't get any of them out and onto the page. "But, what's it supposed to be about?" he wondered aloud, rubbing his unshaven cheek against the magenta silk. The only thing he could possibly write about right now was penis-shaped cream puffs, and he didn't think that was going to go over too well at a wedding. Even a European one.

"I don't know." Vanessa pulled out a chair from the table and sat down beside Dan, her now-empty coffee cup in front of her. "Love, I guess." She shivered, suddenly cold.

"Okay," Dan responded. It occurred to him that the only person he'd ever really loved was sitting right next to him. Certainly he could write a poem for Vanessa's sister, who he actually happened to like. "I can do that."

"I just hope their friends don't like, boo you off the altar or whatever," Vanessa joked. "And that they understand a little English."

Suddenly the weight of what Dan had agreed to sank into him. Get totally mushy and, well, completely . . . *gay* in front of a whole bunch of Williamsburg hipsters?

That's one way to come out.

can n weather this storm?

Creeeeeeeeeeeeeak.

Nate Archibald opened the glass-and-wrought-iron front door of his Park Avenue town house, cringing at the moan of the hinges. With any luck, the Captain would be long asleep, and Nate could just stumble off to bed—avoiding his father completely. He had waited until almost midnight to come home for just that purpose. After he'd left Blair's, he'd headed for the boat pond in Central Park, smoking joint after joint and watching the clouds of smoke drift over the calm surface of the water. It reminded him of sailing, of how peaceful it had been out there on the ocean, surrounded by nothing but water and more water.

As Nate stood looking out at the boat pond, his brain all fuzzy from the pot, he couldn't help remembering the way he and Blair and Serena had spent afternoons at the park when they were kids sailing miniature boats. Their nannies would sit talking quietly on glossy, dark green benches, and the three of them would throw rocks in the water and lick their Popsicles—which both girls would eventually grow tired of, and Nate would promptly eat. And now here he was, sneaking around his own home at age eighteen, and not much had changed. He was still a troublemaker. He still loved sailboats and popsicles. And most of all, he still loved Blair and Serena.

Nate sighed, walking down the carpeted hall as noiselessly as possible. Somehow, things seemed so much simpler back then. He didn't need to be reminded that lately, things were far from simple. After getting caught stealing Coach Michaels's Viagra, Nate hadn't received his diploma at graduation. He was supposed to work for Coach all summer, helping to fix up his house out on Long Island and earn his diploma that way. But after Mrs. Michaels started coming onto him, Nate took off without a word of explanation to anyone. He'd stolen his dad's car, kidnapped Blair, and *then* stolen the *Charlotte*. Jesus, what hadn't he done? And because of all his screwups, his future was totally up in the air. As he tiptoed past his father's study, it was impossible to miss the sliver of yellow light that peeked out from the half-open door. Nate's heart sank in his chest. *Fuck*. He ran his hands through his hair and tried his best to straighten up. He wasn't really *that* stoned, was he?

Is that a serious question?

"Who's there?" His father's voice boomed out into the hall, echoing off the polished wood floors. "Nate? You home?" Nate sighed, ran his fingers through his hair one last time, and slowly pushed open the door.

The study was paneled in rich, dark wood, and it reminded Nate of the sea caves he'd once explored while sailing off the Amalfi coast in Greece. Captain Archibald was sitting in a rust-colored leather chair. His feet, clad in gray cashmere Ralph Lauren socks, were propped up on a matching leather ottoman. A crystal tumbler of Glenlivet rested on the armrest, the amber liquid sparkling in the light. His father's hair was gray, with a touch of yellow—a reminder of his younger days as a hot-young-Yale-lacrosse-player-turned naval-captain. His eyes were bottle-green, like Nate's, without the sparkle. As usual, he was wearing a gray cashmere suit tailored in England expressly for him, his navy blue silk tie slightly askew.

Nate braced himself for the shitstorm that was surely about to rain down on him. All he wanted right now was to take a long nap—maybe sleep until this whole stupid thing blew over. But then, shockingly, the Captain's face broke into a wide grin. Was he *seeing* things? Nate blinked his eyes rapidly, trying to clear them.

After three hours of smoking, he was kind of past the point of Visine.

"Nate, my boy! Home at last!" The captain threw down the *Wall Street Journal* and jumped to his feet, throwing his arms around his son and squeezing tightly, clapping him roughly on both shoulders as he pulled away. Nate felt dazed, as if he'd just woken up from a long sleep. What the hell was going on?

His father sat back down and motioned to the matching leather chair across from him. "Sit, my boy. We've got a lot to catch up on."

Nate sank down in the chair and started fiddling with the gold lighter in his pocket. Blair had given him that lighter two summers ago, and the smooth weight of it under his fingers calmed him down a little.

"So, you've been on quite the sailing adventure, haven't you?" Captain Archibald noted, peering contemplatively at his son. It was more of a statement than a question.

"Uh, yeah. With Blair. It was great." Nate shifted uncomfortably in his seat. It wasn't like his father to make small talk.

"Tell me, son, are you looking forward to Yale?" The Captain reached up and loosened his tie even more as he spoke, finally pulling it from around his neck and dropping it on the desk, where it lay like a puddle of blue silk. So that was it. The Captain had no clue that Coach hadn't granted Nate his diploma and that there was no way Yale would take him.

"Yeah," Nate answered, letting out some of the breath he'd been holding. "Um, I think so." His father didn't know. But how long could he keep it from him?

As if reading Nate's mind, the Captain sat forward in his chair, a fierce look in his green eyes. "You *think* so?"

Uh-oh.

His father sat back in his chair and waved one hand in the air. "Let's stop all the pussyfooting around—we've got some important things to discuss."

Nate's heart sank in his chest. He dragged a scuffed Stan Smith tennis sneaker back and forth across the Oriental rug, knowing what *that* meant. He squirmed in his chair, wishing that he was just about anyplace else—but most of all that he was out on the water, with the waves lapping against the sides of the boat. He braced himself, waiting nervously for his father to speak.

"I've heard from Coach Michaels, and I know exactly

what's going on." Captain Archibald's voice was neutral but firm, and Nate began shifting nervously again in his chair. Whenever his dad adopted this tone of voice, it meant that he'd decided something with complete finality—usually something that Nate didn't want to do. "And this time, I'm not bailing you out. You'll repeat senior year at St. Jude's. End of story."

Nate stared at him, openmouthed. He'd never really considered that not getting his diploma would mean he'd actually have to *repeat* senior year. Maybe take a year off, do some "community service" building outhouses on a beach in Costa Rica or something, but another year of high school? Taking the same boring classes, doing the same boring things, while his friends were all off at college, having fun without him?

Next stop: total humiliation.

His father took a slow, deliberate sip of scotch, and Nate could hear the frosty sound of ice cubes rattling against the crystal. He fingered the stubbed-out joint that remained in his pocket, wishing he could pull it out and light up right there. He'd promised Blair that he wasn't going to smoke so much anymore—she didn't think it was mature, or collegiate, or whatever—but this was an emergency. He had to calm down. Then maybe he could think.

Or *not* think.

His father swallowed and set his tumbler down on the armrest of his chair. "And there's something else."

Something else? What other torture could his father possibly inflict on him? What could be worse than not graduating with the rest of his friends? Military school? Reform school? *Prison?*

Nope, repeating senior year would be far more humiliating and way less exciting.

The Captain's face was so somber that Nate had to lower his eyes to his father's nautical-striped dress shirt in order to keep from completely panicking. Once a year his mother ordered a complete custom-made wardrobe from one of the exclusive men's boutiques on Jermyn Street in London—new suits, ties, and dress shirts—all fitted to the Captain's proportions.

"I want you to meet my friend, Captain Chips White," his father continued. "I obviously haven't gotten through to you, but if anyone can, it's my old navy mentor."

Nate slunk down further in his chair. Not only did he have to get chewed out by his father, but this scary Captain Chips guy his dad was always going on about would be in on his demise too? Chips would probably use some archaic navy torture technique to teach him a lesson—hold him underwater until he nearly drowned, or take him sailing, cut off his nuts, and then throw him overboard to swim back to Manhattan through the polluted Hudson. Nate would probably grow an extra arm or a tumor on his back, and he'd go from being happy-go-lucky, easygoing Archibald to a hunchbacked, three-armed, no-balled freak. Blair would be all over him then.

Captain Archibald raised his glass with a smug smirk, and Nate felt his chin begin to quiver as he gripped the roach in his pocket.

Prison's not looking so bad now, is it?

gossipgirl.net

Disclaimer: All the real names of places, people, and events have been altered or abbreviated to protect the innocent. Namely, me.

hey people!

The days until we leave for college are tick, tick, ticking away, and our mailboxes are piling up with college orientation packets. You might be tempted to actually read those flashy booklets sent by your school in their collegiate colors, but really—get-to-know-you camping trips? Meet-and-greet on-campus sessions? Let me tell you, there's no better way to be labeled a dork than to fall for that one. Do you really want to get introduced to that lax hottie down the hall with leaves in your hair and bear poo smeared all over your never-before-worn-and-never-to-be-worn-again North Face hiking boots? Honestly. Trust falls are for losers without trust funds. You've just got to trust me on this one!

So here's my question, people: why can't the deans figure out a way to make college orientation not a repeat of fifth-grade summer camp? As usual, it's up to me to show those stuffy academic types the way.

suggestions for making college orientation fun instead of unbearably loserish

(1) Bonding activities. Ban all camping trips, sightseeing tours, or campus scavenger hunts. *Nobody* wants to be dragged around a muddy forest, sit in a stale-smelling tour bus all day, or check retardedly obscure objects off a list as part of a "bonding experience." If there's one thing we know how to do, it's bond. Just lead us to an open bar and leave us to our own devices.

(2) Age limits. Any freshmen welcome event that involves adults—read: deans, RAs, and other people who will soon be responsible for getting us in trouble—is a total killjoy. IDs should be checked at the door, and anyone *over* the age of twenty-one should not be welcome!

(3) No more nametags. They ruin every well-planned outfit and practically *invite* skeezy losers to stare at your chest. If you're cute, I'll tell you my name before you even ask.

While the college deans may not know how to throw a welcome party, Manhattan girls sure know how to throw *goodbye* parties. I'm so tired from last night's festivities that if I don't eat my morning H&H bagel (toasted, please, with extra butter) soon, I may just pass out on my keyboard. Too many vodka gimlets, too many floral-patterned silk wrap dresses from Biba and Diane von Furstenberg, and too many cute boys wearing yummy, sherbet-colored polo shirts. If there really can be too many. But the soiree all over the gossip airwaves is a goodbye blowout planned at the Met next week. What better place to say *bon voyage* than at one of Manhattan's most timeless and exclusive venues? One thing's for sure: when that night finally rolls around, we'll all be looking like works of art.

your e-mail

Dear GG,
I was walking past the boat pond in Central Park on Friday night when I saw **N** sitting on a bench smoking a doobie, *alone*, looking all worried about something. Does this mean that he and **B** could be over?
—Giddily Hopeful

A: Dear GH,

The yumminess of **N** is totally undeniable, but unfortunately for all of us, I don't see him breaking free from **B**'s siren song anytime soon. Look on the bright side—the city is positively crawling with sweaty, practically half-naked boys in need of a nice cool soak down. Remember, friends don't let friends shower alone, especially during a heat wave. Conserve water—it's all about the environment, people. So break out the Bliss lemon-and-sage body wash and lather up.

—GG

Q: Dear GG,

My boyfriend is leaving for college soon, and I'm heartbroken. I'm only a junior, so I have another year to hang around, waiting to graduate, and I'm worried that he'll be tempted by all those college girls. Do long-distance relationships really work?

—Left Behind

A: Dear LB,

In my experience, long-distance relationships are dicey—even if you only live across the park from one another. If that's got you down, here's my Rx: go to your kitchen and find some Godiva cocoa powder (you may have to dig around in back for the good stuff—the cook always tries to hide it), and whip yourself up an iced hot chocolate. Sip it while sitting at your iBook. Look—you're multitasking! Don't you feel better already? Now go to eLUXURY.com and buy yourself something fabulous. When that's done, cruise all the cute guys on Facebook and MySpace and send the ones you like best some cleverly flirtatious e-mails. By the time the weekend comes, you'll have a bunch of hot dates at your beck and call—and an even hotter outfit to wear! Trust me, by Sunday you'll barely remember College Boy's name.

—GG

Q: Dear Mme. Gossip Girl,

My darling son has recently had a sexual awakening and is coming to terms with his long-latent homosexuality. After not seeing my dear boy for some years, I want to be there for him in this most exciting time, but I'm not quite sure how to go about it. I've already given him some gifts relating to his new identity, but I want to do *more*. Hallmark doesn't seem to make an "I love my gay son" card. Please help!

Sincerely,

Loving Mother of a Gay Son

A: Dear LMGS,

I'm going to give you the same advice I give to anyone looking to celebrate something exciting and new: have a party! And invite *everyone*. There's no better way to say "I love you." Plus it'll give your son the chance to get all dolled—er, dressed—up. Here's to partying the gay (I mean day) away!

—GG

sightings

B in the **La Perla** store on Fifth Avenue buying a sky blue bra-and-thong set. Can the flames of desire between **B** and **N** be waning already? We hope not—although I'd be happy to help him out if he's bored with monogamy. . . . **N** sitting outside his town house looking contemplative—or maybe he was just under the influence as usual. . . . **V** at the **NYU bookstore** on Washington Place, asking if they had any school logo T-shirts in black instead of their trademark purple. Not exactly the school spirit, **V**! . . . **K** and **I** shopping for their back-to-school wardrobes at **TSE,** buying armloads of cashmere sweaters—even though they're going to school in Florida? Well, cashmere *is* nice over a bikini. . . . **C** at the **Shake Shack** in Madison Square Park, chomping down on a cheeseburger and feeding that spoiled little white monkey of his French fries with extra ketchup. I wonder if they get cited for health code violations. If so, we'll know why.

It's time to watch some *Laguna Beach* reruns—gotta love to hate those ridiculous nouveau riche kids—before I skip out for my mani/pedi appointment at Elizabeth Arden Red Door Spa. Nothing like buffing up and staying silky smooth for the dog days of summer—not to mention the devilishly handsome French waiters at Pastis. . . . Down, boys!

Vouz m'adorez, ne dites pas le contraire,

gossip girl

TO: <u>undisclosed-recipients</u>
FROM: <u>jeanieinabottle119@yahoo.com</u>
Subject: Dan's gay—hooray!

Dear recent graduates of Riverside Prep:
I hope you don't mind my abusing your
school yearbook's contact list, but I'm
sure you'll be happy when you find out
why: I'm writing to invite you all to a
momentous occasion, the coming-out party
for your dear classmate and my dear son,
Daniel Jonah Humphrey. After four years of
going to school with Dan, I'm sure you've
all been waiting for this big day!

Please be our guests in apartment #9D,
815 West End Ave., this Saturday (tomorrow!)
at 2 p.m. Food and drink will be served,
and it's sure to be a merry time. But
hush-hush—it's a *surprise*! Whatever you
do, don't tell Daniel!

Hope to see you all on Saturday! Please
dress your colorful best for the occasion.

Love and rainbows,
Jeanette (Daniel's mom)

TO: svanderwoodsen@constancebillard.edu
FROM: kenthemogul@gmail.com
Subject: Get ready for your close-up . . .

. . . because it's showtime!

Due to the fact that even the fuckhead
critics love my film, the release date for
BAF has been moved up to September.
Sweetheart, you are about to be a *star*,
thanks to me.

That freakworm Bailey Winter is probably
peeing himself trying to sew you a choice
of couture gowns for the NYC premier next
month, lucky girl. You'll have to wear
your own clothes to the press conference,
though. You and that queen Thad are
scheduled to do press this Tuesday at
5 p.m. in one of those tacky penthouses at
SoHo House. Don't worry, I'll handle all
the questions—I just want you two to sit
there look and pretty. Think you can
handle it?

See you Tuesday.
KM

honesty is totally overrated

"So, *why* can't you come over?" Blair couldn't keep the irritation out of her voice. She was annoyed. Actually, she was more than just annoyed—she was totally fucking pissed. At Nate, and at pretty much everyone else—*especially* her stupid, traitorous, moving-to-L.A., dysfunctional *mess* of a family.

No, please, tell us how you really feel.

She sprawled out on her stepbrother Aaron's old bed, rubbing her legs against the all-natural, organic, puke green hemp comforter cover he'd bought at some hippie supply store last winter. Even though Aaron had moved out of the room ages ago—he'd been on a road trip all summer doing God knows what, leaving his bedroom to Blair, since hers had been turned into Yale's nursery—it still smelled of boy sweat and Mookie, Aaron's disgusting boxer dog. Then, to make matters worse, Blair's cat, Kitty Minky, had decided to move in and mark her territory—spraying everything until the whole room reeked of cat pee, wet dog, and the herbal cigarettes Aaron was always smoking. Blair loved her baby sister, but really, did she have to get displaced from her own beautiful bedroom and into this shithole?

"There's um, some *stuff* I have to get done. It, like, can't really wait," Nate mumbled. Blair could always tell when he was lying—he sounded even more incomprehensible than usual. She picked at the rough cloth of the comforter with her French-manicured fingernails. Blair loved surprises, but somehow she didn't think Nate was hiding anything fun.

"Well, I'll just come over there then." She rolled over onto her back and held a strand of shining chestnut-colored hair in front of her face, mentally reminding herself to book an appointment at Warren Tricomi—she desperately needed a trim. The tips were bleached and parched from all the sun and salt water from when she was at sea.

Poor thing.

"No," Nate answered quickly, "I mean, uh, you can't come over here."

Excusez-moi? They just spent a month together on a boat, totally in love, and now they'd been home for twenty-four hours and he didn't want to see her? She sat up and impatiently switched the phone from one ear to another. She was probably going to get brain cancer from talking on her cell so much. Then Nate would be sorry.

He's probably sorry *now.*

"I mean," he stammered, "my bedroom's being repainted and the fumes are killer."

Blair narrowed her eyes and remained silent. That was about the lamest excuse she'd ever heard.

"I didn't even know it was scheduled to be done until I got home last night," Nate offered weakly. "Really."

"Let's go to the Plaza, then," Blair suggested, doing her best to shrug off the nagging sensation that things were just not right between them. She knew Nate was lying, but *why?*

"Blair, I can't." He was starting to get annoyed with her—she could hear it in his voice. "I *told* you, I have some stuff to do right now. Maybe later?"

"Fine. Whatever." She closed her cell phone with a hard snap and threw it across the room, where it landed with a thump on a pile of needing-to-be-hand-washed Wolford stockings. Why was Nate being so secretive all of a sudden?

Blair heard the low murmuring of voices in the hallway and her bedroom door flew open to reveal her mother, dressed in a gray silk Oscar de la Renta blouse, black Cynthia Rowley pencil skirt, and gray suede Manolo slingbacks. A woman in her early forties stood behind her carrying a red crocodile Hermès Birkin bag, her whip-thin body encased in a red-and-brown tropical-print Diane von Furstenberg wrap dress. Her definitely-not-natural-red hair was pulled back in a neat chignon, and black, rectangular-framed Alain Mikli glasses perched on her nose. She sniffed the air delicately.

"Blair, this is Diana Riggs from Sotheby's. She's the real estate agent in charge of selling our apartment!"

The real estate broker's eyes swept the room. "Another great bedroom, Eleanor." She attempted to wrinkle her Botoxed forehead and counted on her fingers, "One, two . . ." she muttered distractedly, "four beds total?" She grabbed Eleanor's arm for emphasis as she spoke. "I know the *perfect* family for this apartment—they have the most gorgeous triplets!"

Blair stared at her mother in horror as she cooed appreciatively at Diana. *Triplets?* She was being forced out of the only home she'd ever known so a bunch of test-tube infertility treatment triplet fuckfaces could slobber and vomit all over it?

"The Carlyles—do you know them?" Diana asked. "Edie Carlyle? I believe she grew up in the city as well."

"Oh my goodness, of course!" Eleanor squealed. "I attended Constance with Edie. Where has she *been*? I haven't see her since, well . . . it must have been seventeen years ago!"

Blair jumped off her bed and pushed past her mother and the broker standing in the doorway. Who cared if Nate was busy? Fuck busy. Wasn't he supposed to be there for her in her time of need? She was his girlfriend, and he was going to pay attention to her—whether he liked it or not.

She fumed all the way down in the elevator and into the bright Saturday afternoon, replaying the scene over and over in her mind as she marched determinedly toward Nate's house. Triplets. Living in *her* house—some annoyingly perfect family taking over her space? She stomped along in her new D&G coral ballet flats as cabs rushed by in the street. As she turned away from the park, she remembered how when she and Nate first got together, they'd meet in Sheep Meadow after school and make out for hours, lying in the grass. Maybe she'd yank him away from whatever the hell he was doing and they could go over to Sheep Meadow and repeat history.

Then, just as Blair began crossing the street to Nate's town house, a *very* familiar-looking blond in worn True

Religion jeans and a black Tory Burch logo tank rounded the corner. With her huge black Chanel sunglasses covering half her face, Serena looked like she was dressed for a stealth mission. And as she pushed open the heavy door to Nate's town house, Blair swore Serena looked just the tiniest bit guilty.

Blair stopped in the middle of the street, not even caring if a taxi rammed into her. She felt like she'd been punched in the chest. All the air rushed out of her lungs. What was Serena doing at *Nate's*? And why was Nate lying to her? Why wouldn't he rather see his own girlfriend than that two-faced fake, Serena?

Good question.

Queasiness overcame her. In fact, she thought she might be sick right there on the pavement. She took a few steps back until she found a fire hydrant to steady herself on. She'd kill them both, except then they'd be together in the afterlife and that would kill *her*.

A bus drove by, burping clouds of stinky black exhaust in her face. Blair began coughing furiously, and through the hot tears in her eyes, she saw Serena's gorgeous, airbrushed face in front of her, larger than life, staring out from the side of the bus, the words BREAKFAST AT FRED'S in pink rolling script above her gleaming blond head, and below, in hot-pink letters TRUE LOVE NEVER LIES.

Apparently, that depends on your definition of true love.

smile! things can only get worse

"Surprise!"

Dan walked into the Humphreys' apartment after a long day of stacking musty books at the Strand and blinked in shock as the lights snapped on. Multicolored balloons hung from the ceiling, and rainbow crepe-paper ribbons twirled from one end of the room to the other. Rainbow flags hung from the doorway, waving in the early evening breeze that wafted through the open windows. What the hell was going on? He smiled as he looked around the room, crowded with so many familiar faces—his parents, Vanessa, his dad's Beat-poet friends, even the crazy old lady from apartment 5F who liked to take her mangy cat for walks around their crumbling apartment building's hallways. And wait, weren't those dorky guys in the corner from his calc class at Riverside?

"Are you surprised!?" His mother sang, pulling Dan into the room. She was wearing a candy pink shirt that said PFLAG over a fuchsia-and-white batik-print floor length skirt. Her electric blue toenails peeked out from the straps of her battered Birkenstocks.

"What's PFLAG?" Dan demanded, staring at the front of her shirt. "And what's all this . . . for?" There were so many rainbows it made him nervous.

"PFLAG, my darling, stands for 'Parents and Friends of Lesbians and Gays'—" Jeanette began.

"And it's a party—to celebrate your coming out." Vanessa appeared at Jeanette's side, holding a ballpark frank festively slathered in mustard in one hand and a small digital video camera in the other. She was wearing a black tank top with the words HE'S MY GAY BOYFRIEND printed on it in hot pink lettering. "Happy Gay Day!" she called out from behind the camera.

For a second, Dan couldn't help feeling a little touched at how supportive she was being. Maybe they could be like Harper Lee and Truman Capote—he'd be the gay, brilliant star of the New York literary scene, and she could be his grounding, stabilizing force and literary muse, all rolled up into one cute, bald-headed package. Then he remembered where he was—apparently at his own *surprise* coming-out party. He tried to focus.

"I thought I'd video your journey into gaydom," Vanessa told him with a smirk. "Your mom thought it was an *excellent* idea."

"Come with me, Daniel." Jeanette pulled him toward the kitchen. She handed him a glass of bright pink liquid. "I know I've missed a lot of things in the last couple years. I wanted to do something special for you right now."

Couple? Try *ten* . . .

Dan stopped walking and stared at his mother's not-entirely-familiar face. The truth was, he'd gotten used to her being away a long time ago, but he'd always felt especially bad for Jenny, growing up without a mom and all.

"But really, teenagers all just hate their parents anyway, so I'm sure it wasn't much of a problem." Jeanette sniffed dramatically. "And this summer, I was really able to reconnect with Jennifer when she was in Prague," she went on, her voice warbling as though she were about to cry. "And then when this opportunity to support you came up—well, it just seemed like the right time for a visit."

Dan nodded, not sure what to say. It made him happy that things were right between Jenny and their mother, but did that really mean she had to fly to New York and ruin his life? "Well, um, thanks," he finally stammered.

"Now!" Jeanette blinked her eyes rapidly and grabbed his hand. "Your darling boyfriend was just teaching me how to make Cosmopolitans!"

Dan frowned. Boyfriend? He looked across the room and was shocked to see Greg at the kitchen counter wearing a pair of brown American Apparel cargo pants rolled just past the knees, rainbow suspenders, and a crisp white T-shirt, vigorously shaking a chrome cocktail shaker, his glasses sliding down the bridge of his nose. Dan lifted a hand in a tentative wave, trying to look cheerful, and walked over with his mother at his heels.

"Hey!" Greg grinned widely as he approached, putting down the martini shaker. He opened his arms to give Dan a hug, his shaggy blond hair falling into his eyes. "Sorry I didn't tell you I was coming back—I wanted it to be a surprise, and I wouldn't have missed this for the world," he whispered, his breath tickling Dan's neck. "My parents didn't do anything *half* this nice when I came out to them last year." He gave Dan an extra squeeze before releasing him.

"Thanks," Dan said, stepping back from Greg's arms. "It was, uh, sweet of you to come back for this. How did my mom, um, find you?" He took a nervous sip of his way-too-sweet drink. As a rule, he liked bitter drinks—truly lousy black coffee and vodka straight from the bottle. This punch was way too . . . fruity.

Better learn to love it!

"Oh, I just went through your e-mails," Jeanette piped in. "Your gmail was open when I borrowed your computer. What a writer this Greg is!" She patted him affectionately on the head, and Dan noticed that Vanessa had followed them into the kitchen and was now zooming in on Dan's red face.

"I've been showing Greg here the most *adorable* pictures of you, Daniel!" Jeanette linked her arm through Greg's and grabbed a worn manila envelope off of the kitchen counter with her other hand. Dan watched in horror as his mother released Greg and proceeded to spread out a bunch of creased old photos of Dan as a kid on the kitchen countertop. "I was just telling Greg how funny you were as a little boy—whenever you played dress-up, you always raided my closet. Dresses and jewelry, the sparklier the better!" Dan stared down uncomprehendingly at a photograph of himself at five years old, dressed in a frilly purple cocktail dress, his hips cocked defiantly.

"And you see!" Jeanette continued, tapping a sloppily painted rainbow nail against the photograph. "He was always stealing my lipstick, too!" Greg and Jeanette chuckled together, lightly touching each other's arms.

"I did the exact same thing when I was a kid!" Greg giggled. "And yet my parents were somehow surprised when I came out—can you *even*?"

"Oh, we always suspected things might turn out this way." Jeanette smiled admiringly, reaching over to smooth down Dan's messy brown hair.

Dan looked up to see if Vanessa was still filming, but she seemed to have headed back into the living room, probably to do some interviews on who had known he was gay when. He sighed. Dan knew his mom's heart was in the right place, but he couldn't help but feel squeamish seeing himself as a girl-boy and having it implied that his gayness had been practically predetermined. Had everyone known all along? Looking at the photographs of him wearing dresses and tap shoes, hugging plush stuffed animals, his mother's lipstick ringing his mouth, the evidence seemed irrefutable.

Suddenly Chuck Bass appeared from the direction of the bathroom. What was *he* doing here? Chuck was dressed in a white tank top that showed off his ridiculously tan and buff summer body, and a pair of aqua-and-pink flowered Hawaiian shorts. A rainbow-colored lei hung around his neck, the petals bright against his dark skin. His ever-present white snow monkey, Sweetie, was perched on his shoulder, pulling at strands of Chuck's over-produced hair. Sweetie was dressed in a tiny black T-shirt with the words SILENCE=DEATH printed in white lettering. The monkey screeched loudly, waving its furry white arms in the air.

"Congratulations!" Chuck raised his Cosmo. "It's about

time!" The small crowd murmured their agreement, holding up their glasses and clinking their cups against Dan's untouched drink. Great—even a complete moron like Chuck Bass had known Dan was gay before he did. Was it, like, stamped on his fucking forehead or something? As if it wasn't weird enough that he was here, Chuck suddenly pulled him by the elbow into the corner so that they were out of earshot of the rest of the group.

"Chuck, what are you *doing* here?" Dan blurted out before Chuck could say anything.

Chuck flapped a hand, as if waving off the silly question. "I got the e-mail from your mom—everybody did. Subject line: 'Dan's gay—hooray!' Anyway, is that your boyfriend?" Chuck asked, pointing across the room at Greg. Greg was now standing next to Vanessa, who was laughing loudly with her head thrown back.

Dan's gay—hooray? Dan resisted the urge to climb out on the fire escape and throw himself onto the street below. He gave Chuck a weak smile. "Um, Greg and I . . . we're—"

"You know, Dan," Chuck interrupted, one hand resting on his shoulder, "I never really had anything against you." He looked meaningfully into Dan's eyes. "I think we were both just feeling some unresolved . . . *tension*, if you know what I mean." Chuck smiled and casually let his fingers trail from Dan's shoulder down his bare arm. Just then the monkey reached down and stuck its tiny brown hand in Chuck's drink, spattering the pink liquid everywhere with a high-pitched screech.

"Bad Sweetie!" Chuck exclaimed, dabbing at his Cosmo-stained tank top with his fingers. "Excuse me for a moment?" Chuck flashed him an apologetic smile. "I have to go spank my monkey." He laughed at his own perverse joke and moved toward the kitchen sink, chattering to Sweetie under his breath. Maybe Dan was losing his mind completely, but it sounded like Sweetie was actually answering Chuck in some kind of crazed monkey-speak.

Dan shook his head and wove through the crowded kitchen to the living room. His dad stood in the center of the room, holding court before an enraptured audience of middle-aged guys with straggly, bushy beards. Rufus was dressed in a light-pink '70s leisure suit with a PFLAG pin on one insanely wide lapel.

"Dan!" Rufus bellowed. "There you are!" He put his arm around his son's shoulders and turned to the group of bearded Rufus clones surrounding them. "Dan, these are the members of my gastronomic society—they brought the wild boar pâté." The group of men raised their glasses in greeting, and Rufus pointed to a plate of suspiciously lumpy brown pâté over on the battered wooden coffee table. "Try some— it's fantastic."

Silence = death.

"And Dan." Rufus leaned in to speak more privately, "I was thinking about this whole transition you're going through." He stopped and scratched his mess of a beard. "Well, maybe its not so much a *transition* as it is a realization," Rufus mused, stuffing a mushy glob of pâté into his mouth. "But I think," he continued, the boar pâté sputtering out of his mouth in chunks, "that in the long run it will probably make you a better writer, like Oscar Wilde or W.H. Auden." Rufus took a gallant swig from the Cosmo in his hand, washing down his meaty mouthful. "Just think of all you'll have to say now!" he exclaimed. "I imagine that your marginalized position will be very productive for your writing."

Marginalized position? Dan didn't feel very marginalized— more like completely overwhelmed. And curious. What else had his mother e-mailed? And to whom? He noticed out of the corner of his eye that Greg had taken a seat on the sofa next to Chuck and his idiotic pink-Cosmo-stained monkey. They seemed to be giggling over the rims of their martini glasses. Just then Greg looked up, caught Dan's eye, and waved, smiling happily. "C'mere," he mouthed, gesturing with one hand.

"I'll be right back," Dan told his father, who was chewing another massive slice of pita bread with some of the scary pâté smeared on it.

Greg untangled himself from Chuck and met Dan halfway across the living room. Some of the rainbow crepe paper was falling down, and it brushed Dan's shoulders as he moved.

"Listen." Greg ran a hand through his shaggy blond hair. "Not now, but sometime soon, I'd really like to talk to you about some stuff." He looked meaningfully into Dan's eyes, and Dan took a sip of his Cosmo—fruit punch flavor be damned—and swallowed hard. What with Greg's grandmother dying, Dan knew he had to be supportive—be there for him in his time of need and all that. But what if what Greg wanted was to make things between them more . . . *official*—just like everyone else?

Dan's head was still spinning with the discovery that he

was gay—and that he'd probably *always* been gay. But if he was going to be gay, shouldn't he at least find a boyfriend who made him feel something besides awkward and nervous? His eyes scanned the room, finally landing on Vanessa, who was talking to his mother and nodding like she actually had some clue as to what Jeanette was talking about. She caught his eye and winked, and Dan instantly felt a little bit better.

"Sure," he replied weakly. "That'd be good."

A look of relief swept over Greg's face. "Thanks. You're the best." He gave Dan's hand a little squeeze before returning to sit next to Chuck, who was feeding his monkey wild boar pâté, its fingers covered with the soft brown goo. Dan watched in horror as the monkey screeched, throwing its furry head back and smearing the pâté all over the freshly washed white wall.

So much for redecorating.

things worth having are worth cheating for

"Oh my God, you *have* to burn this one!" Serena held out a picture of her first-grade self in a fuzzy alligator costume and dug her feet into the butter-soft forest green Pratesi sheets covering Nate's bed. His bed was always unmade, despite the fact that his family had a maid who bulldozed through his room every day, washing everything in sight. Serena and Nate lay side by side on their stomachs, a worn leather photo album between them.

"I don't even remember *wearing* that," she mused, tossing the aging photo onto the already messy floor. Even though he'd only been home for one day, his room was a total disaster. Piles of clothes were strewn everywhere, and his huge wooden desk was completely covered with notebooks, magazines, and PlayStation games. A broken Brine lacrosse stick leaned dejectedly in one corner.

"*I* do." Nate laughed, retrieving the photo. "It was Halloween. We'd just gone to the Bronx Zoo on some field trip, and you became obsessed with alligators." He smiled lazily at her. "You ran around telling everybody you were going to live with the alligators."

Serena's bare foot was right next to Nate's, and she moved it a fraction of an inch closer, feeling the heat from his body as he turned the pages of the photo album. She bit her lip. She needed to focus on the job they'd come there to do—to choose the pictures for the slide show at Blair's graduation party. Blair. Nate's girlfriend. The love of his life. She looked down at the tan leather photo album again and took a deep breath, letting it out slowly. There was Blair's tanned, happy face, her arms entwined around Nate's neck as she pulled his face closer to hers, grinning into the camera. They'd probably kissed moments after they took that picture. Because they were *in love*. Her heart sank with the thought.

"This is so weird," Nate said, turning the page.

"What is?" Serena asked, hoping Nate hadn't suddenly developed the ability to read minds. She twirled a lock of blond hair around one finger, waiting for him to finish his thought.

"Oh, no *way!*" she exclaimed, pointing at the photo album as he turned to the next page. There was Nate, blissfully passed out between a smiling Serena and Blair, the words BUCK NAKED scrawled in red marker across his bare, hairless chest. "I didn't even know we had this! I'll let you keep the alligator one if you promise *never* to burn this one. . . ." She looked up and gave him a mischievous smile.

"Deal." Nate stuck his hand out, and she shook it, slowly drawing her hand away.

Looking down at eighth-grade Nate, so peaceful and

sleepy, Serena couldn't help remembering how warm his skin always was, and how, on the night they'd lost their virginity to each other, she hadn't needed a blanket at all—sleeping with Nate was like sleeping with your own personal furnace.

And just as dangerous . . .

"What were you saying though before—what's weird?" Serena looked down at the ends of her hair again, afraid of his answer.

"I don't know." Nate flipped the page and pointed to a picture of Blair on the steps of the Met with Serena, their arms wrapped around each other, tongues sticking out at the camera. "Things seemed so much easier back then. No college. No worries. No responsibilities."

"Like taking the *Charlotte* for a month without asking?" she said, grinning. "It must've been awesome." She cleared her throat and rolled over onto her back, her hands on her belly. Her stomach dipped and rolled in anticipation and nervousness. She wasn't sure she really wanted to know the answer to that question, but at the same time, she couldn't seem to stop herself from asking.

"It was." Nate closed the photo album and looked at her. "Being out there with no parents, nothing to worry about, just me and Blair . . . it was probably the best month of my life," he said, although he was really thinking about how kissable Serena's lips always looked—the way they were always a little parted, with just a trace of a smile.

Serena's heart plummeted in her chest. She wanted so badly to have been the one out there with him, totally alone, nothing around but the endless expanse of blue water and their half-naked bodies. She wondered for the millionth time if he had found her letter and read it. Somehow, she doubted he had. If he'd found the letter, he would've said something, right? But there was probably no point in asking anyway. He loved Blair. There was no question. She felt dizzy at the thought. How could she go up to Yale with them in a week and watch as Nate and Blair stared into each other's eyes for four long years? She didn't think she'd be able to stand it.

Nate's phone rang, breaking the peaceful silence. He grabbed it from the floor and as he reached out, his T-shirt rode up a little, exposing the smooth, tanned skin of his back. Serena swallowed and tried to look away. Nate pushed the speakerphone button and a gravelly, decidedly grumbly voice was released into the air.

"Nate? Is that you?"

Nate looked over at Serena in confusion, wrinkling his forehead.

"Uh, yeah," he said cautiously. "This is Nate."

"Well, this is Chips," the voice growled menacingly. "Meet me at the New York Yacht Club in half an hour." There was a click, then the sound of a dial tone.

"Fuck," Nate mumbled under his breath. After a moment he jumped to his feet and slid them into a beat-up pair of black and white Marc Jacobs Vans.

"I'm sorry," he said, putting his cell phone into his pocket. "But I've gotta go."

"Sounds like you've got a hot date." She winked and waited for his sly comeback, but he only gave her a half-hearted smile. Serena searched his eyes, trying to figure out what was going on. Nate turned and started digging through one of his desk drawers, pulling out some rolling papers, a stick of deodorant, and some random unicorn stickers Blair had probably given him in, like, seventh grade or something. "But before you go, I just wanted to tell you that they're pushing up the release date for *Breakfast at Fred's*. . . ."

"Seriously?" He turned to look at her again, producing his iPod from the drawer and throwing it into his navy blue Jack Spade canvas backpack along with his keys. "I guess you'll be a real movie star soon." He grinned, closing his backpack. "Sure you'll still have time for us little people?"

"I'll always have time for you, Natie." Her voice was small but serious. As she held his green-eyed gaze, Nate leaned over and kissed her softly on the forehead, his lips lingering for a moment on her skin. He stroked the top of her head briefly with one hand and then walked quickly to the door. Before the door swung shut, he looked back at her —a kind of wordless question swimming in his green eyes. And then he was gone.

Serena sat there in a daze, one hand tracing the path of his lips on her face. Her forehead felt strange and electric— like her skin had just been branded by the soft pressure of Nate's mouth. She could still feel the silky warmth of his lips, and all she wanted was to chase him out the door and kiss him back.

But not on the forehead this time.

b stakes out her best frenemies

"Hot dogs! Get your hot dogs here!"

Blair perched on a fire hydrant directly across from the Archibald's town house on Eighty-second Street. A Sabrett hot dog cart was parked on the sidewalk a few feet from her, and the salty aroma of hot dogs, sauerkraut, and hot, golden pretzels was making her feel slightly insane, and very hungry. Her stomach growled and she rolled her eyes in annoyance. Even though she was totally starving, she wasn't going anywhere or eating anything—especially not a greasy, disease-filled hot dog—until Serena came out and explained to her what the hell was going on and why she was hanging out at Nate's house. Rumbling stomach or not, right now the only kind of dog Blair was interested in was her lying, cheating boyfriend.

Woof!

She crossed her arms over her chest, her forest green canvas Kate Spade tote resting in her lap. She pushed her tinted blue Prada aviators up on her forehead and watched as the heavy wooden door to the town house swung open. Nate came tumbling out, shoving his white iPod headphones in his ears and practically running down the street. Where was he off to in such a hurry? Maybe the "paint fumes" had gone to his head. Moments later, Serena appeared, looking right, then left, her black leather tote swinging from her shoulder, blond hair gleaming in the sunlight. Aha!

Blair watched as Serena proceeded to practically *tiptoe* down the street toward the park. As she reached the corner, she stopped suddenly, pulling her cell from her bag. Who was she calling now? Did she need to call Nate only seconds after parting to plan their next rendezvous? Blair leaned forward on the bench, trying to make out Serena's expression as she held the phone to her head.

Beeeeeeeeeeeeeeeeeeep.

Blair jumped as her cell began to vibrate and ring from the confines of her tote. She grabbed it and looked at the caller-ID screen. Well, of course.

"Hello?" she answered shrilly, unable to keep the iciness from her voice.

"Hey." Serena's voice was bright and casual. "What are you doing?"

"Hey. Nothing. Contemplating killing my family." *And you?* Blair added silently.

Serena laughed. "What'd they do this time?"

"I'll tell you later." Blair sighed. She watched as Serena stopped walking and held onto a streetlight, kicking one foot against the metal base.

Oh-kaaay . . .

"So, where are you right now?" Serena asked, her voice questioning. Blair watched as she leaned against the pole, crossing her legs at the ankles.

"You know, just out and about." Blair kept her voice neutral.

An ambulance rushed down the street, siren wailing, and the sound echoed through both phones. "That's so weird—it sounds like you're right next to me." Serena sounded confused . . . and maybe the slightest bit nervous?

"It's funny you should say that." Blair's tone was icy as a January frost. "Because I'm looking right *at* you."

She watched as Serena whirled around, checking the crowd frantically. "Oh!" she exclaimed, spotting her. "I'll be right over."

Now this should be a fun reunion!

Ten minutes later, they sat side by side on the cool stone steps of the Met, smoking cigarettes, iced vanilla lattes sweating in their hands. The sun beat down on their heads and shoulders like a reprimand, and brightly colored banners hung from the entrance to the museum, advertising the latest Picasso and Van Gogh touring collections.

"So," Blair's voice was cool and measured, "what were you doing over at Nate's?" She glanced at Serena's low-cut black cotton Tory Burch tank top. "Because it certainly doesn't look like there was any *painting* going on."

"Painting? What are you talking about?" Serena knew it must be weird for Blair to have caught her and Nate hanging out without her, but the iciness in Blair's voice felt totally wrong, especially *here*. The two of them had met on these steps countless times. They'd drunk hundreds of coffees and smoked probably thousands of cigarettes here. Usually they would gossip wildly until the sky grew dark and it was time to head home, linking their arms and walking down Fifth

Avenue. But now it didn't feel calming or familiar to have Blair sitting next to her—it felt *tense*. Serena shifted on the hard stone, trying unsuccessfully to get comfortable.

"Nate told me earlier he couldn't hang out because they were painting his room and the fumes were too much to bear. But clearly *you* were able to handle them," Blair accused, looking straight ahead.

"Listen, I think you've got things all wrong. Please don't freak out before I tell you what's really going on." Serena snuck a glance at Blair, whose eyes were hidden behind enormous blue aviators. She *seemed* mad, but Serena couldn't really be sure, since cranky was kind of Blair's natural state. She hadn't wanted to ruin the surprise of the slide show, but she knew Blair would never trust her again if she didn't explain what she and Nate had been doing.

Um, maybe she should've thought about that *before* writing her best friend's boyfriend a three-page love letter?

"So you know the party at the Met?" Serena took a gulp of iced latte and looked out at the street below. A tired-looking mother was attempting to strap her writhing toddler into a stroller while her husband looked on helplessly. "Well, your mom asked me and Nate to go through all these photos to make a slide show for the party: a 'This Is Your Life, Blair Waldorf' kind of thing. That's why we were hanging out today." Serena reached into her tote and rummaged around at the bottom. "She asked us to keep it a secret, but clearly you're too much of a sleuth for us," she joked, hoping to lighten the mood.

"Seriously?" Blair perked up. She hadn't even considered the possibility that Serena and Nate might be getting together to do something nice for her. And she loved surprises, as long as she knew about them.

That makes sense.

"Uh-huh," Serena replied excitedly. "Look at *these.*" She pulled some old photos from her bag and handed them to Blair.

Blair stared down at the picture of Nate sleeping, the words BUCK NAKED scrawled across his adolescent, scrawny chest in black magic marker. She'd written the "BUCK" part, and Serena's wavy script had filled in the "NAKED"—they hadn't even talked about it, they'd just had the exact same thought at the exact same time. Blair laughed, running her fingers over the slick surface of the photograph. "I can't believe you found this! What were we, like, thirteen? We were so freaking immature!"

They looked so innocent, lying there with Nate between them. Blair smiled, suddenly feeling nostalgic. The Three Musketeers—that's what their parents had called them since grade school, a cluster of adults shaking their heads and smiling as Serena and Blair tackled Nate in their various living rooms, sitting on top of him until he screamed.

Sounds like a dream come true.

"Oh my God." Blair turned to face Serena and pushed her sunglasses up on top of her head. Some girl's art portfolio nearly slapped Blair as the girl hurried up the stone steps. "Remember in seventh grade when we all drank a bottle of champagne, and Nate had to go out to dinner with his dad afterwards, totally tipsy?"

Serena laughed as she stuffed the photos back into her bag. "How could I forget? And remember how we went back to your house and tried to make brownies? Except we were both so uncoordinated we spilled the batter all over the floor, and then Kitty Minky ate it and threw up in your mom's closet—all over her new pair of Fendi boots? I've never seen your mom that mad before."

Blair laughed, moving slightly closer to Serena on the steps. Her anger was slowly dissolving. If Serena would just confess about that fucking love letter, Blair could just forgive her and they could move on. With her family turning on her, she really needed her best friend.

"Can I bum a smoke?" Blair eyed Serena's slouchy black leather Gucci bag. Serena nodded and pulled out her pack of Gauloises, handing one to her. Even though she'd brought her own Merit Ultra Lights, Blair decided that with Yale coming up so soon, she'd better start smoking a more serious brand of cigarettes.

Doesn't she mean more pretentious?

A horde of little kids dressed in shorts and T-shirts stumbled up the steps, holding onto a long piece of red rope. Blair watched as the kids struggled to make it to the top of the steps, yelling and laughing, all moving together in a group. She remembered how in first grade, for whatever ridiculous reason, everyone in her class had decided that she had cooties. Serena was the only one who would talk to her. And then, of course, as soon as she had accepted Blair, everyone else had been quick to follow. Serena never had trouble finding people to worship her and copy her every move, even back when they could barely form sentences.

Serena exhaled a cloud of sweetly scented smoke. "Sometimes I can't believe we were ever that young."

Like they're so ancient now.

"I *know*." Blair pushed her glossy dark hair off her shoulders. "I can't believe we're going to college in a week." She looked at the group of kids again. Two girls were fighting over a place on the red rope. "I can't wait to get to Yale and just start over again. Can't you just picture it?" She closed her eyes, smiling happily as she conjured up the freshly-mowed green grass strewn with fall leaves and ivy-covered brick walls. Ah, Yale. She and Nate were going to move into a cozy colonial house and live happily ever after. They could even have Serena over for dinner sometimes. She'd regale them with stories about the single life, crazy frat parties, and silly hookups followed by morning walks of shame, and Blair and Nate would chuckle and smile at each other across the table, smugly happy that they'd found the *one* and weren't out there getting drunk and sloppy.

Serena closed her eyes too, and tried her best to put herself there, beside Blair and Nate at Yale in the fall. But behind her closed eyelids lay a mass of empty, undefined darkness. She frowned. She couldn't ignore the fact that every time she tried to imagine her life at college, she wound up drawing a complete blank. She snapped her eyes open and instantly felt comforted by the sight of Fifth Avenue, its sea of yellow taxis heading downtown, the stately green-awninged buildings with their impeccably dressed doormen who wore suits and white gloves no matter how hot it was.

Blair took a drag from her Galoise. "So, when I was saying I wanted to kill my family before . . . I'm kind of serious this time. They're moving to L.A. because Cyrus is building some golf course or mall or something putrid that the people out there like. Of course they *would* leave the city for the fucking natural-disaster capital of the world." She rolled her eyes, her bitterness starting to creep back in.

"*What?*" Serena angled her body toward Blair's, so that their knees were touching. "Are you serious?"

Blair crushed out the cigarette beneath the heel of her leopard-print Repetto ballet flats. "She gave me this whole sob story about how poor baby Yale needed to be raised in a place that had a *backyard.*"

"We didn't have backyards and we turned out okay," Serena replied, her normally smooth brow wrinkled in thought. *Had they turned out okay?* Another group of kids ran up the massive steps, screaming at the top of their lungs.

"That's what *I* said." Blair threw up her hands in exasperation. "I mean, we had the whole *city* to play in. Like those kids. *They* don't look unhappy." She gestured toward the group of five-year-olds, who were giggling as they raced each other up the giant stone steps. Blair straightened with a sudden thought. "But actually, maybe I won't have to kill my family now. Maybe an earthquake will just swallow them up. Except my baby sister, of course. She can stay." She tried to laugh but couldn't. Nothing was funny right now.

If picturing her family dead doesn't make her happy, maybe she should try something less violent, like meditation.

"Wow," Serena observed glumly, twirling a long piece of golden hair around one finger, suddenly feeling sad and serious. She looked out to Fifth Avenue again, just as a bus with the *Breakfast at Fred's* ad rolled by. She quickly turned away, not sure why seeing it made her feel jittery and unsettled. "I can't imagine you anywhere else but right here. I mean, we've lived, like, ten blocks away from each other our whole *lives.*"

Blair *had* always been here in the city, right by her side. Even when they weren't getting along—which was a lot of the time—it had made her feel better to know that Blair was just half a mile away, sleeping in the room Serena knew so well. What would Thanksgiving or Christmas break be like now with her in California? Or the summers, for that matter? Serena had always thought they'd be together forever, and now she wasn't so sure. She looked over at Blair, who was deep in thought.

"So, I told you about how the release date of my movie got pushed up, right? I'm totally stressed about the premiere," Serena said, deciding to change the subject for both their sakes. She pushed her mass of hair over her shoulder. "There's a press conference at the Soho House on Tuesday, and I'm really nervous."

Blair turned to her friend and took another swig of cold sweet coffee. Serena certainly *hadn't* told her the release date had been moved up, but that explained why she'd seen her face and the words "True Love Never Lies" pass by on three different buses since they'd sat down. Serena was staring straight ahead, and Blair couldn't tear her gaze away from her perfect profile. Even though her face was flushed and a little bit sweaty from the sun overhead, it should've been etched in glass and then minted onto a fucking coin. But however jealous she might be of the fact that Serena was going to be an overnight sensation, she had to admit she felt kind of proud, too. The only thing better than having fame and fortune happen to you was to have it happen to your best friend.

Excuse me, but what happened to the Blair we all know and love?

"Don't worry." Blair turned and gave Serena's knee a squeeze. "You're going to be fine."

"Thanks. That means a lot to me," Serena replied slowly, her voice soft. "Oh, and will you come shopping with me for the Met party?"

"Of course." Blair nodded. She remembered how much fun they used to have playing dress-up when they were little, trying on clothes in her room all afternoon and drinking Campari and sodas with lime, giggling together in the bathroom mirror as Serena expertly painted Blair's lids with black liner, or lacquered her nails with ballet slipper pink Essie polish.

Even if Serena had written Nate that stupid love letter, Blair was the one who was with him now. There really wasn't any reason they couldn't still be best friends. Serena would be the famous one and Blair would be . . . the happy one.

Right.

all n needs now is a peg leg

Nate crossed West Forty-fourth Street and headed toward the imposing beaux-arts limestone building that housed the New York Yacht Club. The large bay windows resembled the sterns of ships and made Nate wish desperately that he was still out at sea with Blair, her wet, sandy hair tickling his skin, nothing in the distance but blue sky and endless horizons. He only felt like himself when he was on board the *Charlotte*, far away from the city and the pressures of real life. Why did real life always have to be so *complicated*? He'd been back on dry land for one day, and he was already in serious trouble.

Story of his life.

He pushed open the front door and stepped inside the opulent interior of the old club. The paneling was all deep, rich mahogany, and everything in sight was gilded in gold. He pushed his shoulders back and tried to stand up a little straighter as he climbed the ornate, winding marble staircase toward an impeccably dressed attendant.

"I'm here to see . . . uh . . . Captain Chips," Nate said stupidly, realizing he couldn't even remember Chips's last name. "I'm Nate, um, Nathaniel Archibald." The attendant looked down at his metal clipboard and quickly found his name, placing a neat check mark right beside it.

"Right this way, Mr. Archibald. Captain *White* is expecting you in the Grill Room." The attendant emphasized the name White, as if implying that Nate ought to remember it. Nate gulped and followed him down the wooden stairs to a set of heavy oak doors.

The gracefully curved ceiling of the Grill Room was fashioned out of planks of oak, the floors and walls paneled in the dark wood. Round tables covered in white linen tablecloths were scattered around the cozy, underground space. It was like being in the belly of a tall ship, and Nate instantly felt a thousand times more comfortable. He could almost hear the wood creaking under his feet as he was led toward a man dressed in full navy uniform, gold medals shining on his lapels. His white hair was neatly combed back from a deeply tanned, severely lined face. A gold wedding band winked from his wrinkled, leathery hand. As Nate approached, the man stood and gripped Nate's palm.

"Nate Archibald. You're the spitting image of your father," Chips growled with a Scottish accent. He looked at Nate with crinkly-lidded blue eyes beneath bushy white brows, and motioned to the leather-cushioned chair across from his. "Sit. Have a drink."

Chips sat back down and gestured to the waiter, a man in his forties with neatly combed sandy hair falling over a wide forehead. Chips pointed at his glassful of amber-colored liquid and held up two wizened fingers. "You like scotch?" He cocked an eyebrow at Nate.

"Sure." Nate shuffled his legs under the table. "Anything's fine."

The waiter leaned in, speaking softly. "I'm sorry, sir," he whispered apologetically. "I'm going to need to see some ID." Nate paused for a second, feeling like he'd been trapped. He'd already agreed to have scotch, but now he'd have to show his fake ID. Was Chips setting him up? He gulped and reached into the back pocket of his cargo shorts, retrieving the battered brown leather wallet his dad had given him for his sixteenth birthday. He pulled out the fake ID he'd gotten off the Internet. It looked pretty good, and it usually worked—except for the fact they'd mixed up the hair and eyes categories, so if you read it closely it said "brown eyes, green hair."

The waiter peered at the ID for a long moment and Nate shifted in his chair guiltily. When the waiter looked up, he shot him a wry smile. "Very good, *sir*," he added, handing Nate back the laminated card.

"I always say," Chips declared, "that all it takes to cure life's woes is a bottle of good scotch and the open sea." He chuckled and slapped the tabletop with one hand as if to punctuate his speech.

Nate nodded lamely as he leaned back in his chair, trying to get comfortable. He glanced around the room. He was the youngest person there by at least forty years—clusters of wizened old men were gathered at every single oak table, each man gruffer and stonier than the next. One of them had an actual eye patch. The old cyclops squinted in Nate's direction with his one good eye. Before Nate could start to muse on what terrible sailing accident had caused him to lose his eyeball, the white-jacketed waiter returned and placed a glass of scotch in front of him.

"Thank you," he mumbled.

"Cheers, my boy." Chips lifted his tumbler and then took a huge swig. Nate quickly followed suit, gagging on the fiery amber liquid. The scotch was freaking strong—stronger than anything he'd ever had—and Chips was drinking it like lemonade. Who *was* this guy?

"You're nothing like what I thought," Nate blurted out, turning red and taking another small, tentative nip. From everything his dad had told him about Chips, Nate had thought he would be a total hard-ass who'd give him lecture on getting his shit together the second he sat down. But so far Chips couldn't have been *less* like Nate's father. He seemed almost *mellow.*

"Ha!" Chips laughed, slapping his stiff-looking extended leg. "You though you were going to be meeting Captain White, didn't you? Some cantankerous, salt-waterlogged old geezer who would read you the riot act? Maybe a hook for an arm? That it?"

Nate nodded, blushing. He looked over at the eye-patch man, hoping he hadn't heard Chips's little outburst. He'd probably be kind of offended. Who knew what these old sailor guys were like when they got angry? "Well, uh . . . yeah. I mean, my dad's pretty pissed at me right now and everything. I thought he'd send me to someone who knew how to . . . hunt."

Chips chuckled and drained his glass in one even swallow. He signaled the waiter for a refill. The waiter appeared at his side almost instantaneously, picking up the empty glass and whisking it quietly away. Nate couldn't help but notice that for a place called the Grill Room, they didn't seem to be serving much of anything grilled—or really anything to eat, period. Just booze.

Who's complaining?

Chips turned back to him and began again. "Well, Nate, let me tell you—that *was* me—a long, *long* time ago. Back when I was your dad's captain, I was the strictest, most serious sonofabitch you've ever laid eyes on. But it's been a lot of years since then, and I've learned quite a few things."

Chips leaned back in his chair, his blue eyes twinkling. "There's a certain kind of clarity that comes with old age. You really learn to put everything into perspective. You *have* to." The waiter appeared and set a fresh drink down in front of him, ice cubes rattling. Chips drummed his fingers on the snow white tablecloth. His eyes scanned the room, and he lifted a hand and gave a small wave to an old man in full white military dress who looked about a hundred and fifty years old. "What are your priorities, Nate? What do *you* want from life?"

Nate was silent for a moment and Chips continued. "For me, it's the open sea—the sun on my face, the sound of waves." He closed his eyes. "The simple things. The good stuff." He opened his eyes and raised his glass. Nate took another burning gulp.

The simple things sounded good to Nate. In fact, they sounded *right*. He was so tired of everything being so . . . challenging. Why couldn't things just be easy for a change?

Being the prince of the Upper East Side is *so* exhausting.

Chips opened the large white menu and perused it thoughtfully, humming softly to himself.

Nate looked at him over the top of his menu and suddenly wished there were a menu for real life—one that listed all of his options, and how much they cost. "I don't know what I want," he admitted, his voice echoing in the cavernous room. The minute he said it aloud, he knew it was true. He looked around again at all the old sailors, each and every one a man who'd chosen a path in life and stuck with it. One had even lost an eye over what he'd chosen. Or maybe they were just a bunch of old seaworthy fuckups.

"I'll tell you one thing." Chips closed his menu and leaned across the table. "You've got to think with your balls, not your dick." His breath smelled like applesauce laced with grain alcohol. "Because the men who think with their dicks are cowards," he finished, leaning back and nodding sagely.

Nate felt himself nodding back, even though he had no idea what Chips was talking about. Had he been thinking with his balls or his dick? Was he a coward? It *was* kind of cowardly not to have told Blair that he hadn't really graduated, that he wasn't going to Yale with her. . . .

Chips summoned the waiter again. "Two hard-boiled eggs and a shaker of salt," he commanded. "For both of us."

Nate surrendered his menu to the waiter. Chips seemed to think his "I don't know what I want" was about the food. Nate hated hard-boiled eggs, and all this talk of thinking with his dick and balls had kind of taken away his appetite for anything but that strong, barely drinkable scotch, anyway.

Well, drink up, honey. It might help you grow some.

v's tea party for two

Vanessa stepped through the doors of the Galapagos Art Space in Brooklyn and looked around. The room was cavernous and densely packed with Williamsburg hipsters wearing striped shirts and sporting asymmetrical haircuts. Bar-height tables were sprinkled haphazardly throughout the room like croutons on a salad, and the grating sounds of three-chord punk blasted from the loudspeakers. Vanessa spied Ruby's bandmates fussing with wires and plugs on a platform in the center of the room. The drum kit was adorned with the word SUGARDADDY, their band's name, in garish red letters. She scanned the stage for Ruby, but her sister was nowhere in sight.

As Vanessa maneuvered her way to the front of the room, protecting her camera from dirty art boys and their Jack-and-Cokes, she spotted Piotr sitting at a table right in front of the stage, a full pitcher of Coke sitting in front of him. When Piotr saw her, he waved her over. Vanessa sighed, wishing she were more excited about filming her sister's last gig as a single woman. She needed it to round out the Ruby

Retrospective she was making for her sister's wedding present, but the reality of shooting the shit with her future *brother-in-law*, whom her sister would be *marrying* in just five days, was kind of unbearable. Vanessa kept forcing herself to say wedding-related words over and over again in her head to make it more real.

She got closer to his table and tried to smile. Droplets of water beaded on the cold pitcher of Coke. Vanessa licked her lips. She was pretty thirsty—maybe she could put up with Piotr for a few minutes while she loaded her camera and set up. If he was going to be family soon, she'd have to learn to converse with him, right?

"What's up?" she asked, plunking her camera down on the table and almost knocking over the Coke.

"'Allo, Vanessa. You made it," Piotr said with an awkward, crooked-toothed smile. "You want?" He gestured to the glass on the table.

She took a seat, resisting her desire to push him onto the sticky floor and run. The guy could barely speak proper English and now he was about to be her brother-in-law? "That'd be great," she replied tensely.

Piotr walked to the bar to get her a glass, and Vanessa noticed that even though he was still wearing those gross leather pants, he really wasn't half-bad looking, with his shaggy blond hair and tight black T-shirt. Okay, so his crooked teeth and smoker's cough weren't exactly swoon-worthy, but at least they made him sort of . . . quirky.

Vanessa looked around the room, accidentally catching the eye of a frighteningly large man in a red T-shirt with cut-off sleeves that read GUNS DON'T KILL PEOPLE—*I* KILL

PEOPLE. His biceps were enormous and covered in tattoos. He saw her staring and gave a toothy smile, then started heading through the pack of people toward her table. Vanessa looked wildly around, hoping he was headed toward someone else. Just then Piotr swooped in and fell back into his seat, and the big guy scowled and backed off. Phew. Vanessa never thought she'd be so happy to see her sister's fiancé.

"So . . ." Piotr filled her glass, apparently unaware of the fate he'd just saved her from. "You film show tonight, yes?"

"Yes." Vanessa nodded like a maniac. "I film show." *Fuck.* It was hard not to talk like him once you got into a conversation. She took a sip of Coke, sputtering when she realized it wasn't Coke at all but Guinness.

"I am also making Ruby gift." Piotr moved his stool slightly closer to hers. "In my country,"—he tapped his chest with one finger—"it is customary for groom to give bride special gift." Piotr paused and took a sip of beer, licking his lips before continuing. "I shop all day for something I think she like."

"What did you get her?" Vanessa asked, curious now.

Piotr smiled again, his whole face lighting up. "When we met, she tell me when she was—how you say? Small?" He gestured with his hands to indicate someone short.

Vanessa nodded, taking a sip of the dark beer. "You mean when she was a little girl?"

"Yes!" Piotr said with relief. "Little girl. Anyway, she tell me how she and you"—he pointed at Vanessa with his full glass—"make tea party with apple juice?"

She burst out laughing, trying not to spit a mouthful of

Guinness all over the table. That was *not* what she'd been expecting Piotr to say. She remembered how she and Ruby used to play dress-up in their mother's closet for hours, putting together outrageous ensembles of feathers, beads, and long, tie-dyed hippie dresses before sitting down at the kitchen table to drink Red Cheek apple juice from their mother's special china cups. They'd sit there for hours, talking in fake British accents and giggling as they said things like "Pass the bloody crumpets!" and "Hand me me bloomin' bloomers!" even though that one didn't even make sense.

"So, I look all day," Piotr continued, refilling his and Vanessa's now-empty glasses, "for antique tea set for her, and I finally find one this afternoon." He looked up worriedly, his forehead a mass of wrinkles. "You think she will like?"

Vanessa looked at the concern in Piotr's blue eyes, the love that was so obviously there for her sister, and something inside her melted. He obviously loved Ruby—only a guy in love would run around New York all day to find a freaking tea set.

"Yes." Vanessa nodded, raising her camera to her face and pointing it toward the stage to check the exposure, but mostly to hide the fact that she was touched. "I think she will like *very* much."

Seeing Piotr so obviously in love made Vanessa feel kind of . . . romantic. She closed her eyes for a moment and pictured Dan at home, sprawled out on the lumpy brown leather sofa, writing poetry in his beat-up notebook. She knew he'd been having a hard time with the poem for Ruby and Piotr's wedding, and the idea of him trying so hard to find the right words for her sister warmed her chest.

You sure that isn't the booze?

Maybe when she got home later they could really talk. She'd tried to be supportive of Dan when he'd come out, but seeing how uncomfortable he was at his surprise party, she still had her doubts . . . not to mention her hopes about his supposed gayness. Maybe she'd be able to tell him how she felt . . . and try to help him figure out what he was really feeling.

Yes, and just exactly how would she do this? *Naked?*

Vanessa smiled as SugarDaddy took the stage in a clamor of guitars. Ruby wore her signature purple leather pants, her black, chin-length hair sticking out in every direction, like she'd blow-dried it upside down—or electrocuted herself with her blow-dryer. She spotted Vanessa and Piotr sitting together and waved. Then she stuck her tongue out between her pinky and pointer fingers. "What's happening, fuckers!?" she yelled into the microphone, and the crowd cheered, wildly.

Vanessa smiled. Everything was going to be okay. Her sister was still her sister, her brother-in-law-to-be was weird and European but also sort of sweet, and she'd talk to Dan tonight. He'd tell her he was just confused, that he wasn't gay, and that he'd been in love with her all along. And maybe someday, years from now, he'd be the one giving *her* an antique tea set.

She pointed her camera up at Ruby's smiling face as she leaned into the microphone and began to howl.

"You stole my *soooooooul*, you fucking ass-*hole!*"

Oh, how romantic.

Air Mail - Par Avion - August 17

obr_ den Dan!

I've been waiting to write, because I didn't want to ruin the surprise, but Mom must have gotten there by now and I couldn't wait any longer. I hope you don't mind that I told her about your recent gaylicious discovery. It was just so nice to get to know her again this summer—did you know that she and Dad met at a Russian bathhouse in Moscow!?— and I thought maybe she should know about you too. . . .

Anyway, Prague is amazing. Staying solo at Mom's flat (how very European of me, right?) is super-fun but a little lonely. I'll be back soon to pack for Waverly (yay!), but until then, *Na shledanou!* (That's "goodbye.")

I miss you guys and I miss New York. Have a cupcake from our favorite place on Amsterdam for me. Make it a pink one!

Love,

Jenny

this would be really funny if it wasn't happening to someone we know and love

Dan lay on the bed in Vanessa's room, his notebook open across his lap. The empty white page was practically blinding him. It was the same story every night—he would sit there staring at a blank page for hours, trying to write a poem about love for Ruby's wedding, until, completely dejected, he'd finally just pass out. He started to scribble.

Love. Above. Shove.

I love to shove you from above?

Kiss. Bliss. Piss.

Crap. This wasn't working. Every time he tried to write, visions of himself as a kid, dressing up in totally gay outfits, sprang into his head. What could he possibly know about love when the only time he'd ever been in love was with Vanessa, who apparently didn't qualify, since she wasn't even the right gender? He looked over at the clock. One a.m. It had been a long day of shelving dusty books at the Strand and trying to hide from Greg. Luckily, their shifts only overlapped for an hour, so Dan had managed to completely avoid crossing paths. He dreaded the "special talk" Greg said he wanted to have, though he wasn't sure how long he could put it off.

He sat up and a flash of gold text caught his eye. The anthology his mom had given him three nights ago was perched on top of the dresser. With its black cover, the book was almost camouflaged by the monochromatic, gray space—Vanessa had gotten permission from Jenny to redecorate, which for Vanessa meant making everything as dark as possible—but the gold title twinkled at him from afar, taunting him.

Oh, come now, you know you're curious.

He reached over and grabbed the large volume, plopping back down on the bed with it. Maybe reading some gay love poems would help inspire him to write a straight one? He cracked open its stiff binding. The first page was the introduction.

Homosexual love has been a part of every society throughout the history of mankind, from the Ancient Greeks to modern day.

What was this, a history lesson? Already bored, Dan scanned down toward the end.

Read the poems aloud to your lover, as the spoken word is even more powerful than those printed on the page. You will feel yourself transported by the undercurrent of beautiful, corporeal, HomoSensual love.

Huh. That was interesting. He'd always found it helpful to read his own poems aloud to get a sense of the rhythm, but he'd never tried doing it with other people's work. Maybe reading aloud would get the creative juices flowing, get him feeling the rhythm? Besides, he *did* have a great reading voice, as Greg had once pointed out.

He flipped the book open to a random place and chuckled when he realized he'd landed on page 69. No matter. He cleared his throat and began to read Shakespeare's Sonnet 18: *"Shall I compare thee to a summer's day? Thou art more lovely and more temperate: Rough winds do shake the darling buds of May. . . ."* Dan paused to read silently to himself for a few lines, and then again read aloud. *"So long as men can breathe or eyes can see, So long lives this and this gives life to thee."*

As he uttered the last lines of his poem, the door swung open and Vanessa burst into the room, her camera bag slung over her shoulder.

Whoopsie.

Her eyes widened with surprise. Clearly she'd heard everything—or at least, enough. Dan could only imagine what it looked like. He was in bed all alone, reciting one of Shakespeare's most romantic—and unquestionably gay—sonnets to himself.

Hello, awkward?

"Uh, sorry." Vanessa quickly turned around and stared at the floor as Dan frantically grabbed for the book and closed it with a loud smack. He stood and attempted to put it on the cluttered desk.

"It's not what it looks—*ow!*" The book fell off the side of the desk, all ten pounds of it landing directly on his little toe.

"No, no. I should have knocked." Vanessa's head was entirely red as she bent over her bag, not looking at him.

"So." Dan examined his cuticles as she continued to put away her camera equipment. "Where were you, anyway?" He tried to project an aura of calmness, grabbing a copy of

Dostoyevsky's *Crime and Punishment* from the nightstand and flipping aimlessly through its thick pages.

Like that's the only thing he's been reading.

Vanessa finally turned to face him. "I was filming Ruby's last gig as a single woman," she explained, stripping off a pair of expensive-looking wide-legged black sailor pants— likely something Blair had left behind during her brief tenure as Vanessa's roommate. She was wearing an old pair of Dan's green-and-white-striped boxers underneath. Then she pulled off her plain black T-shirt so that she was clad in only the boxers and a white Hanes tank top. Dan had always loved Vanessa's fashion sense—or lack of it—and he couldn't help noticing how sexy she looked. It was nice to see her wearing something of his. "Everyone was wasted. At the end of the set, Ruby's drummer puked onstage."

"Gross." Dan pulled off his army green Kafka T-shirt and scooted under the covers.

"Totally," she agreed, climbing under the sheets beside him and switching off the bedside light. Hopefully the darkness would hide her embarrassment and confusion. They lay in uncomfortable silence, and Vanessa couldn't help but give in to her feeling of total dejection. After her conversation with Piotr, she'd felt so . . . hopeful. She'd thought she might be able to work things out with Dan, but if he was spending his free time home alone reciting romantic gay poetry to himself, there really wasn't any question about his sexual status now. She sighed heavily, looking up at the dark ceiling.

Dan tried hard to think of something to say. He'd never had trouble talking to Vanessa before—she was his best friend. In fact, she was one of the only people he really *could* talk to. In less than a week he'd be driving out to Evergreen College in Washington State to start a new life—in a 1977 Buick Skylark, no less—and he had to figure all this out before he got into that car and drove away. Why couldn't he talk to her now, when he needed her the most?

Maybe because she just walked in on him reading in iambic pen-maneater.

"So . . ." he whispered into the dark. "Are you doing okay? I mean, with Ruby's wedding and everything?"

Vanessa snorted. Dan could picture the face she was almost certainly making—her eyes rolled to the ceiling, a wry twist turning up the corners of her lips.

"Yeah," she breathed. "I just have to film the clusterfuck." He heard her exhale heavily into the warm, humid air before she spoke again. "*You're* the one I feel sorry for—I mean, you have to come up with some meaningful, epic fucking *love* poem about those two morons."

"Thanks," Dan mumbled sarcastically. "You've filled me with confidence." He turned over to face her, wanting to look at her even though she was turned away. He could hear the small, quiet sound of her breathing in the dark room and could feel the warmth of her almost-naked body. She was always so warm at night. The ridiculously soft skin of her bare arm grazed his. One of the things he'd always loved about Vanessa's body were its contrasts—her stubbly scalp next to the softness of her skin. The pillowy feel of her lips and cheeks . . . Dan smiled and moved ever so slightly closer to her warm, sleepy flesh.

Vanessa felt Dan's hot breath tickle her neck as he lay inches from her on the bed. Being in such close quarters with him when all her hopes had been so recently dashed was killing her. "So, how's Greg?" she asked softly, hoping the note of rejection in her voice wasn't as clear to him as it sounded to her. She moved toward the edge of the bed, shifting so that her left foot hung off the side. Anything to escape the torture of feeling Dan's skin on hers.

"Umm . . . he's fine," Dan mumbled. Greg. Right. His boyfriend. As Vanessa inched further and further away from him on the bed, it became obvious that she wanted nothing to do with him. And why should she? He was a confused pink-disco-suit-wearing, cream-puff-eating, gay-poem-reading idiot who still seemed to be in love with his ex-girlfriend despite the fact that every person in his life had apparently been waiting for him to come out since he learned to use the potty. Dan sighed and flipped over onto his back dejectedly, more puzzled than ever as he slipped into a sweaty, troubled sleep.

To be or not to be . . . gay—that is the question.

Disclaimer: All the real names of places, people, and events have been altered or abbreviated to protect the innocent. Namely, me.

hey people!

You know what they say about New York—it's the city that never sleeps . . . and neither do I. Not when there's this much good gossip to keep me up at night! Okay, and there may have been that little end-of-summer bash at One keeping me out till the wee hours last night, but it's all in service to *you*. I'll have to trade my snakeskin Jimmy Choo stilettos for Gucci leather riding boots soon enough, so now's the time to stay out late, dance with a gorgeous stranger, and, most importantly, expose as much bare, sweaty flesh as possible. And the same goes for you girls and boys—as if you need a reminder!

hollywood shuffle

This morning, as I was walking to fetch my skinny vanilla latte and natural-grain bagel, I couldn't help but notice that a certain very blond actress's picture has been plastered *everywhere* overnight—bus stops, the sides of buildings. That's right, our very own **S** is poised to become a major Hollywood star—not that we ever doubted it for a second. **S** is being touted as a fair-haired, modern-day Audrey Hepburn. And that means, cats and kittens, that we'll soon be purring contentedly as we gaze up at **S**'s celestial face on the big screen. Either that, or we'll be clawing our plush velvet seats in envy. . . .

The word on the street is that, due to phenomenal early reviews in *Variety, Vanity Fair,* and *Esquire,* the release date for *Breakfast at Fred's* has been pushed up! The fun begins tomorrow at the luxurious **Soho House,** the part members-only club, part hotel, where they're holding a big *Breakfast at Fred's* press conference. **S** will be meeting up with her yummylicious co-star **T,** aka my new boyfriend (shhhhh . . . don't wake me up! If anyone can make him like girls, I can) who is, in case you've been residing on Mars, currently in possession of the hottest six-pack abs this side of the Hudson. Too bad he pitches for the other team. Anyone who's anyone on the gossip circuit will be there to watch as A Star is Born—our little **S** is all grown up!—and you know that means I'll find a way in. . . .

It's time to zip yourself into that purple tapestry Calypso sheath, don your Dior shades, raise one hand in protest to the glaring flashbulbs while exclaiming, "Gentlemen! No pictures, *please*!" For those of you who don't know the drill, some helpful advice from yours truly:

do's and don'ts for attending your first press junket

(1) Do bring sunglasses, preferably large Chanel or Gucci ones, even if the event takes place at night. *Especially* if it takes place at night. Those flashbulbs really are blinding! And besides, nothing creates an air of mystery like a pair of oversize shades.

(2) Do escape to the ladies' room for frequent makeup touch-ups—nobody likes a shiny nose on camera. Besides, where better to overhear the latest gossip about the premiere—and spread some of your own.

(3) Wear indelible lip color, or a sealant over your favorite shade: getting lipstick on your teeth during an interview is so gauche—and totally avoidable. Red-carpet red is *always* a classic choice.

(4) Do feel free to have a fling with your leading man—after all, the suite *is* booked for the night! And don't worry—we won't tell.

(5) And, most importantly, bring the hotness! After all, it's *all* about you!

sightings

N at the **NY Yacht Club** having cocktails with some old guy in a sailor suit. Does **N** have a new dealer? Odd. Whatever the case, we're guessing he won't be joining the navy anytime soon. . . . **D** at his home-away-from-home, **the Strand** bookstore, secluded in a dusty corner furiously turning the pages of *Queer Culture: A Way Out of the Closet.* From what I hear about a certain surprise party, he's already way, *way* out. . . . **V,** back in Williamsburg, filming her sister **R**'s show at the **Galapagos Art Space,** a leather-pants-wearing blond guy by her side . . . **S**'s picture in **Times Square** on a *huge* billboard featuring nothing but her flawless face and the words TRUE LOVE NEVER LIES. **S** herself, clad in all black, entering **N's Park Avenue** town house dressed like she's auditioning for a role in the next 007 film. **B** sitting outside, waiting for her. With all three supposedly going off to a certain ivy-covered cam-pus in just a few short days, it's certain that we'll have oodles of rumors to discuss—so keep those catty, info-packed e-mails coming!

Speaking of interesting e-mails, I hear roommate assignments are in the mail, so don't be surprised if you receive an introduction from your soon-to-be suitemate. My heart bleeds for all of you who'll inevitably get stuck with some freshman calculus major who wants nothing more than to wake up at 6 a.m. every morning to *study* while you're just nodding off and trying not to hurl last night's excess of keg beer (ah, college) all over your La Perla peignoir. My roommate will, of course, be my long-lost twin—perfect, just like me!

You know you love me.

gossip girl

don't hate her because she's perfect

"Serena! Serena, over here!"

Flashbulbs exploded in front of Serena's face like bursts of fierce white lightning. She smiled and plucked a perfectly ripe raspberry from the flute of Cristal she held in one hand, popping it into her mouth. She'd never expected the press conference for *Breakfast at Fred's* to involve so much pampering, or to be so breathtakingly fancy—not to mention so well attended. Throngs of reporters and photographers surrounded her and her totally yummy costar, Thaddeus Smith, as they sat out on the sun-drenched terrace of one of the SoHo House's top-floor penthouses. Maybe the life of a movie star *was* all it was cracked up to be.

Thad turned to smile at her from his matching white deck chair, the gold stubble on his razor-sharp jawline gleaming in the light. He wore a pair of severely distressed Marc Jacobs jeans, his tanned biceps startlingly dark against his crisp white polo shirt. Chrome Dior aviators hid his infamous blue eyes from view, and his evenly tanned feet were encased in a pair of blue-and-silver Michael Kors flip-flops.

Serena's crush on Thad had passed with the realization that Thad had a serious boyfriend, but it didn't stop her from admiring him.

There's just so much to admire.

As the sun began to set over the Manhattan skyline, bathing the terrace in an orange sherbet hue, a male reporter pushed through the crowd, thrusting a mini tape recorder toward Thad. "Thad!" he yelled, even though he was only a foot away. A camera swung from around his neck. "What was it like working with Serena van der Woodsen? This is her debut. Can she really act?"

"It was a rare privilege," Thad replied, grabbing Serena's hand and squeezing it tightly in his own. "Serena—as the whole world will soon see—is a pro. Plus, she's absolutely gorgeous."

Serena blushed, surveying the suite from her perch on the terrace. The penthouse suite gleamed with chrome, glass, and light, and the room was decorated in blue and cream. An enormous flat-screen TV hung from the sky blue wall. A giant oil painting of the night sky illuminated another. This would the perfect place to bring a guy—and by "guy" she meant Nate. They could take a bubble bath in the six-person tub and order chocolate-covered strawberries and champagne from room service. They could watch one of the many not-yet-released DVDs that Ken had stocked the room with when they got bored—which would be never.

"Serena!" a young female reporter yelled out, scribbling furiously on a small white pad, her rectangular crimson eyeglasses sliding down her tiny nose. "What are your plans? Any films in the near future?" The cameras clicked incessantly as Serena cleared her throat and prepared to speak.

Ken Mogul had said in his e-mail not to worry about the press conference, that he'd be there to take care of everything. But when Serena had arrived, she'd been met by Jade, Ken's assistant and wife, a stunning Afro-Asian ex-Ford model with straight black hair to her waist, who'd informed Serena coldly that Ken might be a little late.

"Actually," she answered with an apologetic smile, "I start college next week, so I don't think I'll be making any more movies for a while."

She crossed her legs and leaned back on the gray-and-beige-striped deck chair. She was glad she'd worn the black Bailey Winter sunglasses that were designed especially for Holly, the character she played in the movie. She'd thought they'd help her feel more in character, but she hadn't realized she'd need them to shade her eyes from the sun—not to mention the flashbulbs.

Serena folded her hands over the skirt of her simple white Marc Jacobs sheath dress and pulled a stray golden hair away from her face. With her white, Hermès lace-up sandals and the much-coveted cream-and-black Fendi B bag at her feet, she was the picture of New York glamour. Now she just needed to make sure she acted that way. She was okay with the sitting-there part. It felt sort of . . . *right* to be there, flashbulbs exploding in her face every five seconds. It was the speaking part—knowing that people were hanging on her every word, writing every syllable down and possibly hoping that she'd make a dumb-blond, spoiled-starlet mistake—that made her feel quivery inside. She'd grown up having people look at and talk about her, but this was the first time anyone had asked for her own original thoughts.

Agh!

"Which college, Serena?" another reporter yelled out, startling her from her moment of reverie.

"I'm heading to Yale on Sunday, actually," she replied, a bit more confidently than she actually felt. She pushed her hair off her shoulders and continued. "I just want to be a normal girl for a while. You know, go to school, be like everyone else."

As if that were even *remotely* possible.

"Normal girl? Ha! Not if I can help it!" a deep male voice rang out. Reporters turned to see Ken Mogul making his way toward the terrace through the suite, balancing a bottle of champagne and two crystal champagne flutes in his hands. His bulging blue eyes looked like they might rocket out of his face, and his shoulder-length, curly red hair had been smoothed down and pulled into a low ponytail. He was trailed by Jade, who towered over him in her ridiculously high gold snakeskin Jimmy Choos. Just when it seemed he was going to take a seat, Ken jumped onto the outdoor coffee table which was covered with champagne glasses, sending them crashing.

Serena shook her head slightly, feeling a little dazed. Between the constant snap and glitter of flashbulbs, the champagne, the close proximity of Thad, and now this weird performance, her head was spinning and she felt like she needed to go back into the AC.

Little Miss Demanding. She really is becoming a Hollywood star!

From his high perch, Ken poured Serena a flute of Veuve Clicquot and clinked his full glass against hers. "Serena van der Woodsen is the greatest talent of the twenty-first century, and though some of you may think I've sold out by shooting *Breakfast at Fred's* entirely inside the mainstream zeitgeist, it is Serena who is my greatest independent work of art."

Okay. What exactly did he just say?

He hopped off the table and laid himself flat on the ground at Serena's Hermès-sandaled feet, murmuring, "I'm not worthy," over and over again.

Serena blushed. She certainly didn't feel like an independent work of art—far from it. She was just a confused high school graduate who was going to college because she wasn't exactly sure what to do next. She looked up and saw Ken Mogul's gorgeous wife looking at her coldly, arms folded across her chest. Serena shrugged shyly, as if to let her know that she wasn't really into all this ass-kissing, star-worship stuff.

The cameras went crazy, clicking away like mad. Ken sat up abruptly and held his stubbly hand in front of his face. "Gentlemen, please!" he shouted. The flashes stopped as quickly as they'd started, and the crowd grew silent again, waiting for Ken to speak. "Not only do we begin shooting the sequel to *Breakfast at Fred's* next month, but I plan to shoot a new film this spring, in the style of the visionary director François Truffaut—a gritty, black-and-white exercise in emotional realism and the searing depravity of love and addiction." He put his glass of champagne down dramatically. "And both films will star Serena van der Woodsen, of course." Serena's mouth dropped open and

Ken met her wide-eyed gaze. He gave her a quick wink, his scary blue eyes twinkling. "Our little Serena is going to be a big, big star!"

"I told you!" Thad broke in, grabbing her hand and raising it in the air.

Serena sat there in stunned silence as the reporters went nuts around her. "Serena, Serena! Does that mean Yale is on hold?" a male broke through the shouting.

She looked at Ken and then at Thad, who both smiled back at her expectantly. She couldn't *not* go to Yale . . . *or* . . . could she? Blair and Nate would be fine—or better off—without her. But was she ready to leave them? The crowded terrace fell completely silent as Serena turned back to the cameras, squaring her shoulders. "No comment."

Ditto.

TO: bwaldorf@constancebillard.edu
FROM: caligirl90210@gmail.com
Subject: We're roomies!

Dear Blair,

I was *so* excited when I got my roommate
assignment in the mail this morning!
Aren't you just *dying* to get to Yale? I've
been shopping all week (make that all
summer!), since it'll be a pain once we're
on campus—doesn't it totally suck that
freshmen aren't allowed to have cars
anymore?!

I guess I better back up and tell you a
little about myself: I live in Beverly
Hills and my dad's a cosmetic dentist.
Which means my whole family has perfect
teeth. Anyway, I'm not sure what I'm going
to miss most about Cali—my parents, my
convertible, my swimming pool, or the
malls. But I guess Macy's is only a train
ride away.

I've been skating all my life. I went to
nationals in pairs skating with Ashton, my
partner, who was also my boyfriend until I
broke up with him last week. My favorite
store is the Build-A-Bear Workshop. I have
a *huge* teddy bear collection. My favorite
color is white, which technically isn't a
color, but it's the color of my ice skates
and ice when it's been skated on, plus my
birthstone is a pearl, which is also

white. When Ashton and I won regionals, I
wore the most beautiful peal tiara.

So, you're from New York? That's all the
housing slip said. Do you live in
Manhattan? I've never been there. What was
your high school like? Do you have a
boyfriend? I was going out with Ashton for
almost two years, but I thought it would be
better to break up before college. Long
distance relationships just don't last. . . .

Anyway, I'm beyond excited to meet you!
Please write back soon and tell me all
about yourself. We're going to have the
best time this fall, and I hope we'll
become lifelong friends. Oh and my stuffed
French bulldog CeeCee says hello too!

xoxoxo,
Alana

TO: caligirl90210@gmail.com
FROM: Bwaldorf@constancebillard.edu
Subject: re: We're roomies!

Dear Alana,

That's so weird—my family is actually
moving from New York to L.A. really soon.
It will be cool to know someone if I'm
forced to spend breaks there.

So . . . about me: I grew up in Manhattan
on the Upper East Side and attended an
all-girls school called Constance
Billard. My mom married a moron and had a
baby even though they're like ninety
years old. I named her Yale. My parents
are divorced and my dad lives in a
chateau on a vineyard in France. He and
his boyfriend just adopted Cambodian
twins. I can't even talk about it.

Yes, I have a boyfriend—his name is Nate,
and we've been together *forever*. This
past summer we borrowed his father's
yacht and sailed around for a month and
fell totally in love all over again, and
lucky for you he's coming to Yale, too.
Why so lucky? Because you'll get the room
all to yourself once Natie and I find a
house together off-campus. It's all
working out so perfectly I could just
scream with happiness.

See you soon!

Sincerely,
Blair

P.S. But seriously, we can't have cars on campus?

to err is human, to forgive is against b's rules

Blair surveyed the various Louis Vuitton trunks that surrounded her, the endless LV monograms multiplying and making her feel dizzy. She grabbed a stack of Fair Isle sweaters and held the soft material to her cheek for a minute before throwing them into an empty trunk. Looking around at the half-packed trunks and suitcases, at Aaron's old, smelly room in a state of total disarray, she still couldn't quite believe her family was really moving to California—or that she had to bring every single piece of winter clothing she owned to Yale with her, since she'd never be able to wear it in L.A. anyway. The whole process of packing some things for college and some things for California was made all the more obnoxious by the fact that she had to *ship* the trunks to Yale since she wouldn't be driving her beautiful bisque-colored BMW to school. Why the fuck did Yale have to change the rules about bringing a car the very year *she* was going there? Blair sighed, flopping down on the ugly hemp bedspread. She couldn't imagine anything more depressing than having to take the freaking *train* to school.

Well, she could hitchhike. That might be fun.

Blair closed her eyes and tried to picture what Thanksgiving and Christmas breaks would be like in Los Angeles. There would be no sledding in Central Park or walking up Fifth Avenue at Christmastime with Serena, making fun of the tourists gawking at the Saks windows. No more ice-skating at Rockefeller Center with Nate under the enormous tree, a cloudy December sky threatening snow overhead. It was painfully sunny almost every day of the year in Los Angeles, and there was practically no ozone layer, for God's sake. She'd have to slather herself in SPF 40 just to open a fucking window.

She sat up, grabbed a trunk, and began filling it with armloads of silk underwear. If she and Nate couldn't share New York anymore, at least they'd have the perfect home together in New Haven—maybe a little stone cottage close to campus with ivy climbing gaily up the gray stone walls. They would sit facing each other in front of a roaring fire, drinking gin and tonics and studying. She'd make flash cards to help him study for his economics exams, and they'd cook dinner together every night, moving carefully around each other in the cozy kitchen. Nate would stop in the middle of carving the venison from the deer he'd shot himself on last weekend's hunting trip and take her in his arms, covering her with kisses until, dinner forgotten, he would lay her down on the bearskin rug—from a bear he had killed and skinned— slowly peeling her clothes from her body. . . .

Blair dropped the pair of black cropped Gucci jodhpurs she was holding and grabbed her cell, hitting speed dial number 3. Nate's phone went straight to voice mail . . . again. She threw the phone onto the cat-pee-stained, sea-grass-mat-covered floor and it went skittering into the corner. Where *was* he?

Then the door opened and Nate walked in, as if on cue. Blair jumped to her feet and threw herself into his arms, purring against his chest. "I just called you!" She wrapped her arms around him and squeezed tight, breathing in the scent of summer and his slightly sweaty armpits. But Nate didn't seem to be hugging her back. She pulled back ever so slightly and looked up into his face. He looked serious—and Nate never looked serious.

Uh-oh.

"What's wrong?" Blair demanded, her brow furrowing. Without waiting for an answer she turned around and began folding pairs of jeans, working methodically. If she kept busy, maybe she wouldn't have an aneurysm. What the fuck was going on?

"I have to tell you something, Blair." Nate's voice was shaking. "There's something important I've been keeping from you."

Blair's heart bumped crazily in her chest. He looked so totally *white* under his tan. Seeing him so obviously upset made her even more nervous. She sat down on a closed trunk and waited. Had Serena finally told Nate she was in love with him? Did he love Serena back? Were *they* going to run off to France together to adopt Cambodian twins?

"I didn't get my diploma," Nate blurted in a rush, as if hoping she might not catch the words. "I have to repeat senior year at St. Jude's."

Blair grabbed the edge of the trunk she was sitting on with white fingers, staring at him uncomprehendingly.

"I can't go to Yale with you." He clarified. "I'm so sorry."

"What?" Blair screeched in disbelief. She stood up, fingers clenched into fists at her sides. "What did you say?"

Nate's face was an infuriating blank. The whole room seemed to go red. Seriously? Was this *seriously* happening? First her best friend betrayed her, then her family abandoned their fucking home, then her car was practically ripped away from her, and now the supposed love of her life was making her go off to college without him because he was *stuck in high school?* Was this seriously fucking *happening?*

"WHAT THE HELL, NATE!?" she screamed, throwing a pair of black alligator Manolos across the room, narrowly missing his head.

Love hurts!

Blair's head filled with static. Nate wasn't going to Yale with her—he was staying right here in New York—in the city where very soon she would no longer have a home. He might as well have told her that he *was* in love with Serena—the end result was still the same. She and Nate would be apart next year, living totally separate lives. How were they supposed to live happily ever after the way they were destined to if he was still in *high school?* Blair was breathing so fast her head felt light and dizzy.

"I'll, um . . . I'll call you later," Nate said uncomfortably, looking down at the carpet. His shoulders rose in a deep, shuddering sigh. "When you're a little more calm."

Which might be never.

"What do you want me to say, Nate? Congratu-freakinglations? Hey, at least you can call me to help you with your *homework?!*" Blair screamed as he opened the door and closed it softly behind him.

Don't go giving him any ideas. . . .

TO: caligirl90210@gmail.com
FROM: Bwaldorf@constancebillard.edu
Subject: re: We're Roomies!

Dear Alana,

P.P.S. Forget every fucking thing I just
said. I hope you're at least a semi-
fucking normal human being, because no
one else in my life is.

See you soon.

Blair

tangled up in s

Nate walked out of Blair's apartment building and onto Fifth Avenue, grateful for the anonymous noise and clamor of the busy street. At least no one was yelling at him out here. He knew that she wouldn't take the news that he wasn't going to Yale with her well or anything, but he hadn't expected it to be *that* bad. He stopped on the corner and pulled out a pack of cigarettes. He was tempted by the tightly rolled emergency joint he'd shoved in the back, but pulled out a Parliament instead and lit the tip, his hands shaking.

He was trying to think with his balls like Chips said. He'd thought that if he just came clean to her, everything would just fall into place. Sure, he'd be in Manhattan for an extra year, but they'd see each other every weekend. It wasn't like he *wanted* to stay behind in the city while Blair and Serena—his girls—were up in New Haven.

Nate exhaled a cloud of smoke and started walking uptown, not knowing or caring where he was headed. Thinking with his balls was totally overrated. All he really needed was to talk to someone who actually cared about him, someone who knew him better than anyone. The problem was, that person had just thrown a pair of shoes at his head.

He stopped in his tracks and looked up at the tall stone building in front of him at Eighty-first and Fifth Avenue, almost across from the Metropolitan Museum of Art. His feet had led him right to Serena's doorstep. As he stared up at the gauzy, white curtains covering the windows of the top-floor apartment, Nate wondered if she was home. He walked into the lobby and raised his hand to the doorman, who smiled and waved him through.

As he rode up in the wood-paneled elevator, Nate wasn't sure what he would say to Serena if she even *was* home. All he wanted was to chill for a while and forget everything that had just happened in the last torturous hour, but knowing Blair, she'd probably already told Serena the news. He strode purposefully to the van der Woodsens' door and knocked.

Serena opened the door to her apartment almost instantly, as if she'd been waiting for him. She was wearing a crisp white cotton dress, like she was about to go play tennis, except that her golden hair was messily piled on top of her head with a paintbrush sticking through it. "Hey." Nate grinned. "Want to hang out for a while?"

She smiled slowly, then opened the door wide, grabbing his T-shirt and pulling him inside.

A few minutes later they sat cross-legged on the floor by the edge of her frilly white bed, the leather photo album spread out in front of them. Serena leaned forward to turn to a new page, her hair falling across Nate's shoulder. He breathed deeply. His pulse was finally slowing. All it took was Serena's signature scent of patchouli and lilies to calm him down.

Nate looked around at her familiar room. There was the tiny glass ballerina atop her mahogany jewelry chest. The kilt-wearing teddy bear from Scotland he used to make say dirty things until Serena squealed at him to stop, even though she was laughing hysterically. The giant mahogany armoire with crazily printed underwear spilling out of it. The little silver box on her night table that he knew was full of her baby teeth.

"Did Blair call you?" Nate asked, resting his head on the bed behind him. He looked up at the white eyelet canopy overhead and recognized the little brown burn mark he'd made in ninth grade.

She shook her head. "Why?"

He squirmed uncomfortably on the carpet. "I don't know."

Serena just smiled and turned back to the album. An eight-by-ten photo of her in the fifth grade, dressed up as a fairy, peered up at them. "My hair is green." She blushed and tried to turn the page.

"No." Nate sat forward and reached for the album, flipping the page back so he could study the picture. Little Serena trapped underneath the clear plastic, wearing a pink satin gown and wings, a sparkling silver wand in her hand. "You look beautiful."

Serena rolled her eyes. "Anyway . . ." she said, turning the pages, "why did you come over here again?"

Nate shrugged, Chips's words still echoing in his brain. If he could only figure out what thinking with his balls actually meant, maybe he could figure some shit out. "I was in the neighborhood." He looked down at a picture of him and

Serena. He didn't remember taking this one. Their cheeks were pressed close together, flushed and smiling, and it was taken from above, his arm holding the camera out in front of their faces.

"Is that—" he heard the words tumble out of his mouth.

"It's from the day I came down from Ridgefield," she said quietly, finishing his thoughts. Serena swallowed hard, looking down at the page. "The day we . . ."

Nate knew before she'd even said the words. It was a photograph from the night they'd lost their virginity to each other, more than two years ago. He couldn't help thinking about her soft skin and the fun they'd had. Some documentary about the Ten Commandments was on TV that night, and when they'd turned it on after they'd made love for the very first time, Serena had yelled out, "You parted my red sea!" He smiled, remembering how happy they were, how they'd stayed in each other's arms until the sun rose.

"I don't even remember taking it," Serena added with a shrug of her shoulders before she reached out and started to flip to another page in the album.

"Me neither," Nate said, reluctant to let go of the page. Why couldn't happiness just stay like that—trapped under plastic and hermetically sealed? Why did everything have to get so *complicated*? He wished more than anything that he could just go back in time to that night and start all over again.

Serena grabbed the book away from him, closed it, and sat up, crossing her legs Indian style. She was wearing a pair of ridiculously tiny white shorts under her cotton dress. It almost hurt Nate's eyes to look at her.

Sounds like he was thinking with, ahem, *something* now.

"Nate," she began, taking a deep breath, "I need to ask you something. I . . . I really need to know the truth."

"What?" His heart stopped for a second. Serena's almost navy blue eyes were so serious that he found himself reaching over and grabbing her hand, squeezing her soft palm in his own to comfort her.

She squirmed uncomfortably and swallowed hard. "Did you ever get my letter?"

Letter? Nate shook his head slowly.

Serena took another deep breath and looked straight at him. "I wrote you a letter to tell you that I love you," she said quietly. "I always have."

The room was so quiet that Nate didn't know whether the sound of breathing in his ears was his or hers. Sitting there with Serena, on the floor of her room, everything felt right. And *simple*. In fact, when he really thought about it, things between him and Serena had always been simple—it was *life* that had complicated them.

And somehow it felt totally right for him to kiss her. He leaned forward, his bare knees sinking into the carpet, and pressed his lips to hers. As he breathed in the scent of her, he felt his limbs relax, his body going limp with relief and happiness.

Kissing Serena was the exact *opposite* of having a pair of stilettos thrown at his head—it was absolutely effortless. They staggered to their feet and she pushed him down on the bed, kissing him back eagerly.

And the rest is history, repeating itself.

TO: DHump18@gmail.com
FROM: perma_green420@hotmail.com
Subject: Changes

Hey Dan,

Dude. I guess you and me are going to be
roommates at Evergreen. I don't know about
you, but I'm totally stoked on going out
to Washington. I'm from this shit-ass town
in the boondocks of Idaho, and after
eighteen goddamn years here I *need* to get
the fuck out.

It's not just that living here bores me to
tears, but the people here just have no
respect for the earth, right? If the kids
I grew up with spent a quarter of the time
they spend cooking meth in their basements
focusing on the fucking earth, we'd have
solved global warming by now. Honestly.
It's like with smokers—why do they do it?
I can't stand people who damage themselves
and others for no fucking reason, you
know? It's all about respect.

So what about you, bro? You stoked for
school? I hope you're not bringing too
much stuff, 'cause I hear our rooms are
pretty small. I'm pretty neat, mostly
because I don't have a lot—I try to
simplify, stick to the basics, you know.
The only thing about me that's high
maintenance is my allergies—I'm allergic
to coffee beans and will go into

anaphylactic shock if I'm even near a
coffee ground. Trust me, it's not as
cool as it sounds.

Are you signing up for that frosh
orientation camping trip? Sounds pretty
fucking sweet to me. Getting to know our
classmates, spending some time out in the
open country, living off the earth—way it
should be, man. Way it should be.

Peace, love, and unity,
Urth Greenberg

breaking up isn't all that hard to do

Dan sat on the curb outside the Strand, a cigarette in one hand and a cup of weak, tepid black coffee in the other. Taxis rumbled down Broadway, pouring black smoke out of their tailpipes. A stream of tourists flooded the sidewalks, mopping their sweaty brows and looking questioningly into the musty old bookstore as if trying to gauge the strength of its air-conditioning. The heat shimmered off the pavement in waves and Dan pushed his long, straggly brown hair back from his forehead with one hand.

For the past few days, he'd bailed on the shifts that overlapped with Greg's in an attempt to postpone their inevitable talk. He just didn't know what to *say* when Greg told him he wanted to be more serious, more *official*. Avoidance had seemed like a good plan, but then this morning his boss had threatened to fire him if he didn't come in, so he'd spent the day in stealth mode, hiding out in the gardening section and ducking behind bookshelves whenever he heard footsteps approaching.

"Hello Daniel." An unfamiliar, elderly voice startled him.

He looked up from his perch on the sidewalk and recognized Aggie, the seventysomething receptionist at Riverside Prep who wore a different wig every day. Today it was black and curly, sort of like Ernie's hair from *Sesame Street*.

"Hello Aggie," Dan mumbled. This was the problem with New York—you couldn't get a second of peace and quiet without running into someone you knew. Aggie would probably want to have tea with him now, maybe get in one last heart-to-heart before he left for college.

Or take him wig shopping?

"Well, Daniel, it's lovely to run into you like this, though I can't stay and chat. Congratulations on your recent announcement, and I'm sorry I missed your party!" Dan watched in shock as Aggie smiled, patting her wig, and then shuffled off in the direction of the discount books racks.

Dan gave her a slight wave and then sighed, pressing his back against the brick wall, which felt like it was searing his flesh through his damp T-shirt. Well, that was weird. Did his mom invite the *entire* world to his coming-out party? He adjusted his butt on the hot pavement and pulled a notebook from his ratty black Timbuk2 messenger bag. If he didn't get something written for the wedding soon, he'd be seriously screwed. But the trouble was, nothing was coming to him. What did he know about marriage anyway? How was he supposed to write about loving someone for the rest of your life when he couldn't even figure out his *own* love life?

Good point.

As he looked up from the blank white page, he saw Greg stroll around the corner, wearing a white button-down shirt and stiff white jeans. Oh God. Greg stopped when he saw

Dan sitting there and smiled. Then he smiled and hurried over.

"Hey." He touched Dan on the shoulder. "Where've you been? I've been wanting to talk to you." His voice sounded genuinely concerned.

Dan looked at the cement. He could feel his T-shirt sticking to his back with sweat. "I've been sick," he mumbled, coughing into one fist and looking away. He noticed a group of tourists approaching en masse and he wondered if he could duck in with them and make his escape. "Really sick." His gaze shifted tentatively to Greg, who was staring at him with something like amusement, his blue eyes creasing at the corners. "I just didn't want to give it to you—I think I'm still pretty contagious and—"

Greg cut him off with a wave of his hand. "Listen, I really wanted to talk to you about something." He sat down next to Dan on the sidewalk.

Dan stayed silent, fiddling with the pen in his hand. The throng of tourists came and went, but he knew he had to sit there and stick it out. He dreaded the words that were sure to fall from Greg's lips any second now, *Let's do this thing. I want you to meet my parents. I want to show you things only another man can.*

Greg cleared his throat and continued. "I thought that me and you had a pretty good thing going." He stopped, his words hanging in the air above their heads. "But . . . I've kind of met someone else."

Huh? Dan stared at Greg, his mouth open. He felt like he'd just been smacked in the head with a two-by-four. Two girls dressed all in black stepped around them, practically trampling them with their combat boots and giving them a dirty look for blocking the sidewalk.

"I met this amazing guy at . . . um . . ." Greg looked down at the pavement, his cheeks flushing bright red, and ran a hand through his hair before continuing. "A party . . . and, well, we kind of just had this really intense *connection*." He put his hand on Dan's forearm, squeezing hard—but in a brotherly, reassuring way. "I'm sorry."

This time, Dan didn't squirm at his touch. "Don't worry about it." He patted Greg's hand. "It's totally fine." He sighed, breathing in the heavy August air, which suddenly felt a whole lot less oppressive.

A look of relief swept over Greg's face. "I know you'll find somebody special," he declared in a rush, removing his hand from Dan's arm. "And I hope we can still be friends," he added, pushing his glasses up on his nose.

"Absolutely," Dan enthused. "Totally." He looked out at the bustling city traffic and wondered briefly whether his "somebody special" could be right here, before his very eyes, among the masses. Two girls sat at an outdoor table in front of the Così restaurant across the street, sipping lemonade as they surveyed the passersby from behind huge sunglasses. Across from them sat a guy in a baseball cap, iced coffee in hand, reading a magazine. He looked up and caught Dan staring, and Dan quickly averted his eyes.

"Soooo . . ." Greg looked over at his closed notebook. "What are you working on? Another future *New Yorker* poem?"

"Hah." Dan snorted, opening the notebook and holding up the blank page. "I'm supposed to be working on a poem for Vanessa's sister's wedding, but I can't think of a thing to say. I mean, what do I know about marriage?"

Greg wiped his hands on his jeans. "All you have to do is envision the person you love most in the world—the person you want to wake up with in the morning and go to sleep with at night." He paused, blushing deeply and running his hands through his hair. "Even if you haven't met that person yet—you just have to *imagine* them! I mean, with me and . . ." Greg looked sheepishly at the ground. "I can't imagine wanting to do those things with *anyone* else, you know?"

"I guess." Dan stared at the cracks in the cement. "I just don't know if there's anyone I feel like that about . . . anymore." He closed his notebook and tucked it back inside his messenger bag.

Looking at Greg's feet, Dan noticed he was wearing black socks with little white Paul Frank monkey faces on them. Dan didn't know exactly what his type of guy—er, person— was yet, but he was pretty darn sure his soul mate didn't wear monkey socks.

"I mean," he started again, looking over at Greg, who was listening intently, "how will I know when it's the right person?"

Greg held Dan's gaze for a moment before standing up. He slapped the back of his white jeans with both hands. "You'll just . . . know," he said quietly. "You'll know when you know."

Dan looked out again at the sea of people on the street— the wide-eyed tourists with their cameras, the skater kids who flocked to Union Square in the summer, the NYU students who were moving into their apartments a few weeks early, lugging hand-me-down furniture, arms loaded with boxes. In the few minutes that he and Greg had been sitting here, hundreds of people must have walked past. If he stayed a little longer, those hundreds would soon be thousands. How could you find one out of thousands? Wouldn't it take forever?

Greg stuck his hands into his pockets. "You'll know when you can't imagine seeing anyone else after the day's over, and even though you just saw them a few hours ago, you can't wait to see them again that night."

Dan nodded mutely, still dizzily watching the crowd on the sidewalk as if it held all of life's answers.

"Well, I'd better get back to work," Greg said, pushing his glasses up on his nose. "I'm not even on break yet—I just snuck out to talk to you." Dan remembered himself and stood up, slinging his messenger bag over one shoulder. He grabbed Greg's arm before he walked away.

"Hey," he said, moving closer. "Thanks . . . for everything."

Greg smiled. He wrapped his arms around Dan's back and squeezed tight, clapping him on the shoulders before they both pulled back.

As Dan watched him walk away, he couldn't help feeling a little sad. Not about Greg, but about love in general. He wanted what Greg had described: someone to sit around and drink coffee with in the morning. Someone he could do all those dopey, ridiculously romantic New York things with before he left for Evergreen—like watch every Woody Allen movie filmed in Manhattan, or take a carriage ride through Central Park under a full moon. Someone to wake up with every morning, the light covering their bare skin like a golden blanket . . .

Pale fury. Why did you leave me?

He pulled out his notebook and scribbled furiously, unsure of what he was writing.

Eyes closed, our bones ache.
This isn't chemistry or geography.
It's physics. Pure physics.

Dan still wasn't sure what he was trying to say, but it was something to do with friction, and friction caused heat, and when he thought about heat he couldn't help but think about a certain prickly-headed girl lying next to him in bed. His hands began to sweat as he continued to write.

Not feeling so gay anymore, eh?

maybe a leopard *can* change her spots

"Watch where you're going, man!"

A yellow cab swerved on the shimmering black asphalt, almost grazing Vanessa's arm as she crossed Broadway, squinting into the annihilating afternoon sunlight. The cabbie's rude, grating voice lingered in her ears. Did he say *man*? Vanessa smiled smugly to herself. *Well*, she thought, picking up the pace, *that's what you get for having such a sleek, aerodynamic hairstyle.*

Doesn't she mean androgynous?

She'd gone downtown around noon to film some of Ruby's East Village hangouts in the daylight, but now, faced with the sweltering heat of the day, she was ready for a break. She rubbed her stubbly head with one hand as she waited for the light to change.

The Strand bookstore was half a block away, its carts of moldy discount books parked out front. Vanessa wondered if Dan was working—she'd been avoiding him the last few days after the whole romantic-gay-poetry incident, but maybe she'd just stop by and say hi. She watched the little red hand warning her to stay put.

College was just around the corner, and soon Dan— along with just about everyone else—would be gone. Well, Ruby would be around, but it wasn't exactly the same between them anymore—now that she spent every waking second with Piotr. Vanessa couldn't help feeling kind of . . . obsolete. Maybe it had been a mistake to stay in the city, but she'd wanted to study film at NYU for as long as she could remember, and now she finally had her chance. Plus, she loved New York. The trouble was, it was going to be a whole different city without Dan.

The light was taking forever to change, and she could feel the sweat running down the insides of her legs and into the black patent-leather platform Mary Janes on her feet. As she shaded her eyes from the glare, she suddenly noticed Dan across the street, standing near the carts of used books, with Greg.

They were talking, and then Dan opened his arms and Greg stepped into them, squeezing tightly. Even from where she was standing Vanessa could see that Dan's eyes were closed as he hugged Greg, his body totally relaxed in a way she hadn't seen him in ages. She'd seen them talking at his coming-out party, but Dan had looked so uncomfortable it had been hard to believe they were actually together. Now it was more than obvious that they were a happy couple, totally in love.

Vanessa turned around and began walking quickly back down Broadway, pulling a pair of vintage white sunglasses from her battered army bag to cover her eyes—which were rapidly filling with tears. The poem had been one thing—after all, Dan's poems were always a little strange—but to actually see him embrace another guy was something else—it was *real*. Had he always been gay? How had she never known?

She wiped the tears from under the dark lenses and ran her hands over her head the way she always did when she was upset. As her fingers touched her prickly scalp, she stopped dead in her tracks. The most disastrous thought of all bubbled up in her brain, and before she could stop it, it spilled out. Did Dan only go out with her in the first place because of her shaved head? Was it possible that he only liked her hair because it made her look . . . *manly?*

Vanessa suddenly felt like she was going to be sick all over the corner of Eleventh and Broadway. Almost before she knew what she was doing, she grabbed her cell and began punching keys in total panic. She needed to feel feminine and sexy immediately, and there was only one person who could really help her.

"Helllllooo?" Blair's voice sounded like it was trapped in a wind tunnel or something.

"Hey Blair—it's Vanessa." There was a pause in which Vanessa could hear the sound of giggling in the background, and then a loud whooshing noise. "I need . . . help." Vanessa took a deep breath, wondering why the next words were so hard for her to say. "I need . . . a makeover," she blurted out, putting her index finger in her mouth and gnawing violently on her nail.

"Actually, you've got perfect timing. I'm at Warren

Tricomi getting extensions right this very minute" Blair responded enthusiastically. Vanessa realized that the wind was the sound of hair-dryers in the background. "Come on over immediamente."

Twenty minutes later Vanessa sat in a stylist's chair next to Blair, watching as a thin Frenchman named Louis with a pointy nose and sleek chin-length black hair threaded strands of golden brown hair into Blair's already thick mane.

"Iz like a buuuuutifffffful mermaaaaid," Louis told Blair, who looked back at him in the gold-framed salon mirror approvingly. "*Et pour ton ami*"—Louis pointed at Vanessa with a long, skinny finger—"vee vill make mageek! I vill return!"

Vanessa looked around. The spa looked like a European palace, its dark oak floors covered with Persian carpets and walls with filigreed gold mirrors. The chair she sat in was plush burgundy velvet. She crossed her legs uncomfortably, placing her hands on her calves to hide their prickliness. Light streamed in through the giant plate-glass windows at the front, and a row of copper sinks and shampoo chairs lined the far wall. The salon was filled with tanned, manicured, designer-clad ladies-who-lunch types, reading *Vogue* or leaning back with their eyes closed as stylists pampered them with head massages. Places like this always made Vanessa feel like she had three heads—all of them begging for a makeover. Blair, of course, looked right at home as she sat there, a stack of magazines on her lap, her tanned legs crossed high on her thigh, barking orders to the assistants flitting around her.

"So what *happened*?" she turned to Vanessa as soon as Louis walked away.

"I just need to look more like a girl." Vanessa mumbled, slouching in her chair.

"Well, obviously." Blair wrinkled her perfect little nose and gestured at Vanessa's slumped form with her perfectly pink fingernails. "Finally you realize you *are* a girl."

Vanessa looked in the mirror at her sweaty bald head and dusty black boots. Then she looked over at Blair's completely feminine form: her pink toes peeped out of a pair of light aqua espadrilles and gold bracelets tinkled on her slender, graceful arm. Vanessa sighed heavily, slumping down even further in her chair. She was absolutely hopeless.

"I *know* I'm a girl," she finally answered. "But I need to be a girl that's more like . . ." She gestured at Blair's body. "More like *you*."

"Done and done." Blair smiled. She was starting to feel more like herself again. After Nate's little announcement, she had come to the one place she knew would make her feel better—the salon. And it had worked, of course. The only thing that had kept her from losing her mind was Louis's soothing murmur as he threaded new long locks into her roots and told her how lucky she was to have such healthy, strong hair. There was just something totally calming about sitting in a stylist's chair. It was like Audrey Hepburn said about Tiffany—nothing very bad could ever happen to you there.

Now that she had calmed down, Blair wanted to talk to Nate and make sure he didn't do anything stupid, like think they were broken up and throw himself off the Brooklyn Bridge or take some poison to end his suffering—although to be honest, Nate had never been much of a Romeo.

She began punching the keys on her cell. She'd been calling his phone every five minutes but had gotten voice mail every time. She tried Serena's, too, hoping for someone to commiserate with, but she wasn't there either. Where were they, anyway?

She *really* doesn't want to know. . . .

Blair surveyed Vanessa's dusty black shorts and grit streaked army green tank top. She could definitely benefit from some quality time in the stylist's chair. Blair was happy to help—she'd always liked a challenge, and God knew she could use the distraction.

Vanessa was beginning to wonder who Blair thought it was so important to call every five seconds when a cell phone started to blast Madonna's "Like a Virgin." Vanessa turned around and spotted Isabel Coates and Kati Farkas seated next to each other under the dryers, their heads sporting matching strips of aluminum foil. Kati talked loudly on her cell, holding her palm against her other ear to block out the roar of wind. She was wearing some kind of frilly pink sundress that hung from her body like a sack, and Isabel wore the exact same thing—but in a bilious shade of green. Isabel looked up and spotted Vanessa sitting in a stylist's chair. She elbowed Kati, who burst into a fit of laughter.

"Getting a new look?" Kati yelled out, holding the phone away from her head.

"Obviously," Vanessa mumbled, before turning back around and facing the dreaded mirror. Blair was leaving yet another message.

". . . so I'm *still* here at the spa, and you need to call me when you get this. Just don't do anything stupid, okay?" She crankily snapped her cell shut and sighed.

"Where's Nate?" Vanessa asked as a perky blond assistant dressed entirely in white spandex placed a glass of ice water with lemon slices on the countertop in front of her. Vanessa grabbed the glass, swallowing the cold water greedily.

"Fuck if I know." Blair sighed. "And it's not like I don't need help, getting ready for Yale and everything."

"I know what you mean," Vanessa said sympathetically, placing the empty glass back on the countertop. "It's not like I'm spending a lot of time with Ruby now that she's getting married. Or Dan," she added. "He's so busy with his job and his new boyfriend that I might as well not even exist."

Blair turned to her in surprise, a smile moving across her lips. "I'm going to ignore the Dan-being-gay info in favor of the much more interesting news here—your sister's getting *married*?" she asked, her eyes lighting up. "When, when, *when*?"

Shit. Vanessa should have known better than to mention the M-word in front of a girl like Blair. "Um, the bachelorette party is tonight and the wedding's on Saturday afternoon."

"Okay, this is more serious than I thought." Blair sat up in her chair as if energized with the mission, her posture stick-straight. "You *have* to look amazing for the wedding." Blair pointed at Vanessa's bald head. "Louis! Louis! Give her something really dramatic. Blond to her waist!" She turned to Vanessa again. "Oh, and by the way, after the wedding you should come by the Met—my mom's throwing a goodbye party for me. Plus you'll already be all dolled up from the wedding. Bring whoever." She waved a hand as if renting out one of the largest and most opulent museums in the world wasn't a big deal at all.

Vanessa nodded. "Oh, okay. Maybe I will. Thanks."

Louis quietly circled Vanessa's chair, touching her scalp with his long, cool fingers. "Zer iz not too muuch to vork vith," he observed, foraging in the roots of Vanessa's troubled head.

"That's okay," Vanessa replied dejectedly. "I'm beyond hope," she added dramatically.

"Ah!" he cried, snapping his fingers. "Ve have some fabooluuuuuuus hummus-har wigs—long and blond."

Long blond hummus hair? Vanessa stared at her bald scalp in the mirror and tilted her head to the side.

"Very Ashlee Simpson." Blair held up the *Us Weekly* on her lap and pointed at the cover. "Brilliant!" She clapped her hands together excitedly.

Normally, the mere thought of trying to look like someone on the cover of *Us Weekly* would force Vanessa to dry heave. But these were desperate times. Another eruption of giggles emitted from Kati and Isabel's end of the salon. Vanessa peered thoughtfully at herself in the mirror. She was ready for a change.

"Bring it on," she nodded confidently to Louis, smiling into the mirror.

Oh dear. Remember girls, it's always better to stick to what you were born with—anything stuck on might . . . fall off.

the more things change, the more they stay the same

Serena purred happily, snuggling closer to Nate's warm, naked body. Lying in his arms felt so incredibly right. When they'd lost their virginity to each other, more than two years ago, it had been amazing, their every curve a perfect fit. This time was no different—they'd sunk into the soft sheets and each other's bodies like they had been made for one another. Serena couldn't believe how comfortable she felt with Nate—how comfortable she'd always been with him. She never, ever wanted to get out of bed. Couldn't they just stay wrapped in each other's arms forever, ordering Chinese takeout every few hours and feeding each other greasy spareribs?

Nothing says romance like pork-fried rice!

She buried her nose in his ear and he pulled her close, wrapping the sheet around their naked, sweaty bodies. Serena reached up, twining her arms around Nate's neck.

The minute his lips had touched hers and their clothes had fallen away, Serena knew she'd been right all along—she really loved him. She felt like she was going to burst with it, and had been holding the words in for so long that all she wanted to do now was repeat them over and over again.

"Serena?" Nate asked, rolling on his side and propping his head up on one hand.

"Yes, Natie?" She rolled him back over and placed her head on his chest, snuggling under his armpit. She loved the sound of her name when he said it.

"I have something to tell you." He traced his fingertips along her bare shoulders. It felt electric.

Serena sat up, pulling the sheet with her to cover her smooth skin, her blond hair falling over her bare back. "What?" She whispered, trying to stay calm.

"I didn't get my diploma," he said quietly. He grabbed her kilted teddy bear from the corner of her all-white canopy bed and hugged it. "I'm not going to Yale next year—I'm going to have to stay here in New York and repeat senior year."

Serena opened her eyes wide with surprise. Not going to Yale? Did Blair know? She looked at her teddy, as if he might convey some answers, and pulled the covers up higher around her torso, shrugging off the thought of Blair, because with it would come guilt, masses and masses of guilt.

"I wish I could just take off." Nate pulled a faded green T-shirt over his head, his voice muffled inside the soft cotton. "Just sail away and never come back." His head popped through the cloth, and he pulled the material over his tanned chest.

He ran his hands through his hair and flopped back down next to her. Her eyes were so brilliantly, deeply blue that it was hard for him to imagine ever looking anywhere else. He looked at her tanned, lightly freckled face, and he knew that he'd never forget the way she looked right now—her cheeks flushed pink, her long body wrapped up in white sheets—as long as he lived.

If Blair finds out, that might not be for long.

"What are you going to do?" Serena asked, pushing her hair from her face.

"Stay here, I guess," Nate answered dejectedly. "It's not like I've got much of a choice."

Serena stroked his hand, wishing she could kiss him and make this all better. The late-afternoon sunlight filtered in through the open windows, and she looked out at the wide blue sky outside. She could hear the faint sounds of the city below, the buses rumbling by with the posters of her face on their sides. Suddenly her pulse began to race. "You know . . . I'm not so sure about going to Yale either," she said quietly.

"What?" Nate demanded, his green eyes glittering. "Why?"

"Well, I keep trying to picture it . . . but I just can't." She had been about to say, *whenever Blair talks about it*, but then she stopped herself. "And then at that press conference yesterday, the director announced that he's filming the sequel to *Breakfast at Fred's* in New York in a month and . . . I don't know. I just . . . I think I need to stay here."

The minute the words left her lips, Serena knew they were true. She wasn't sure if she'd ever really wanted to go to Yale, but she knew for certain she didn't want to go to Yale without Nate. And from the way he was staring at her, it looked like the feeling was completely mutual.

"Really?" Nate asked. He'd been picturing himself as the

only guy with a five o'clock shadow taking Algebra I at St. Jude's. But with Serena here, maybe he wouldn't feel so out of place after all. It would be just like always—except without Blair. Wait, Blair.

Remember her?

But maybe he could still go visit Blair on weekends. People did that, didn't they? Like having an apartment in the city and a house in the country. When he thought about it that way, it all seemed so simple. Why hadn't he thought of it before? He could spend weekdays with Serena and weekends and holidays with Blair, and everyone would be happy.

Sounds like he's thinking with the whole package.

"Really." She smiled and he pulled her closer.

Then, with his breath tickling her ear, he whispered, "I love you too."

Aw. So cute. Unless you're a certain girl with newly implanted Warren Tricomi extensions.

v gets in touch with her wild side

"Yeeeeehaaaaaaaw!"

Vanessa shook the golden hair from her face and squared her shoulders before opening the bar's heavy black door. Coyote Ugly was basically a frat-boy bar ruled by domina-trixlike, Amazonian female bartenders in cowboy hats. The bartenders were also fond of line dancing across the surface of the heavy wooden bar, dousing the crowd with water—or beer. It wasn't exactly Vanessa's kind of place, but it was the perfect location for Ruby's bachelorette party. Ruby thought the bar, which had been made legendary in the totally watered-down film bearing its name, was hilarious—in a totally ironic way, of course.

Of course.

The bar was packed with people, elbow to elbow, mainly drunken frat guys in pastel polo shirts and loafers. Three stunning female bartenders worked the crowd furiously, throwing bottles in the air and knocking back shots along with the guys. The screech of country music filled the room. Vanessa stomped across the sawdust-covered floor in her black Prada platforms—Blair cast-offs—and looked around. Ruby was leaning against the wall wearing a short red dress and combat boots, doing shots with a group of obviously intoxicated girls. Vanessa walked up and elbowed her sister in the ribs.

"Watch it!" Ruby yelled, an annoyed look on her face. "Bitch," she muttered.

Vanessa grabbed her sister's arm and leaned in closer. "Ruby, it's *me*."

Ruby's face went blank with shock. She reached up, touching the strands of long blond hair framing Vanessa's face, staring at her eyes, carefully outlined with brown pencil and expertly shadowed—courtesy of Ms. Blair Cornelia Waldorf, of course—and promptly began laughing like a lunatic.

"Oh my God," she laughed, downing another shot of amber liquid, "I really *am* wasted." As soon as she drained the glass, shivering slightly as the liquor hit her chest, she grabbed Vanessa's arms again, looking her up and down and taking in the short black Anna Sui skirt and tight, beaded charcoal gray Chloé corset top Blair had practically shoved into Vanessa's messenger bag. "Seriously, Vanessa, you look ridiculous. But also kind of . . . hot!"

"Really?" Vanessa reached up to touch the wig. She was still a little uncomfortable in this getup—not to mention sweltering. The room was the temperature of a sauna, and her cascading wig of human hair wasn't helping any.

"Do a shot!" Ruby yelled, shoving a glass in her hand.

Vanessa tilted her head back, momentarily afraid her wig might fall off in the process, and downed the shot, which tasted like gasoline. She shook her head from side to side like she was trying to chase her impending hangover away.

Fat chance.

"What the hell are you guys drinking?" she croaked, wiping her mouth with the back of her hand.

"J&BwithaJ&Bback!" A girl Vanessa recognized as one of the bartenders from the Five and Dime, one of Ruby's favorite Brooklyn hangouts, slurred, shoving another shot glass into Vanessa's hand. "Drink it!"

As if she had a choice.

The liquor burned Vanessa's throat. She shook her shoulders and tried to regain her eyesight. "C'mon, sissy, I want to talk!" Ruby yelled into her ear.

"You want to walk?" Vanessa asked, pointing to a bartender wearing a tight Western shirt unbuttoned to her belly button, ridiculously short jean shorts, and red stilettos, strutting on top of the bar as though it were a catwalk.

"No!" Ruby pulled her into a darkened corner near the ladies' room. At least it was slightly quieter. She clutched Vanessa's arm like a drowning woman.

"I *said*, I need to *talk*." Ruby had to shout over the frantic fiddle of the Charlie Daniels Band's "The Devil Went Down to Georgia." "I don't think I can do this!"

"Do what?" Vanessa asked, pouring another shot into her glass from the half-empty bottle of J&B Ruby clutched in her hand. "Drink?" She held up the bottle to her sister's face. "'Cause you seem pretty good at it to me."

Ruby waved the bottle away impatiently. "I don't think I can marry Piotr. I don't know if I can go through with it." Ruby's face crumpled like a used Kleenex.

"Wait—what?" Vanessa bent down to place the bottle of J&B on the floor, then she stood back up to put her arms around her sister. "Why? What's going on?"

"Well," Ruby sniffed, "he gave me this gift today—he said it was in honor of our future life together or some bullshit."

Vanessa wrinkled her brow in confusion. "Soooo?"

"V, he bought me this Suzy Homemaker antique tea set for a fucking wedding present. He doesn't fucking know me at all. I mean, if that's what he's expecting . . ." She trailed off and poured herself another shot, knocking it back expertly and wiping her mouth with the back of her hand. "Does he think I'm going to be this perfect, stay-at-home Stepford Wife? Because that's not what I'm about at all, and he should *know* that!" Ruby filled her shot glass again, and this time Vanessa held her own glass out for a refill.

When in Rome . . .

"I mean, how can I marry a guy who obviously doesn't even know who the hell I *am*?" Ruby shook her head in sadness and disgust. Behind them a couple stumbled out of the ladies' room, looking around guiltily.

"He knows who you are," Vanessa heard herself saying— much to her surprise. "And I think he really loves you."

"Why do you say that?" Ruby asked suspiciously.

"Listen." Vanessa took her by the arm and was grateful when the music changed to a less noisy Bonnie Raitt ballad. "I had a long talk with Piotr the other night at your gig."

"You did?" Ruby asked. "I mean, so what?" she added, as if reminding herself to be bitter and angry.

"Just stay with me here," Vanessa said impatiently. "He mentioned that, back when you guys first met, you'd told him about how we used to have tea parties when we were little. Remember?" Ruby nodded and Vanessa kept going. "You told him that we'd drink apple juice out of those pretty china cups mom had and pretend it was tea? Well, *that's* where he got the idea to buy you an antique tea set."

Up on the bar, the red-stilettoed bartender was lining up one polo-shirted guy after another and forcing them to do shots, then dousing them with water as a chaser. "That's the sweetest thing I've ever heard," Ruby responded quietly, filling her shot glass again—along with Vanessa's. "I'm an asshole," she declared, one lone tear spilling over her cheek. "I can't believe I ever doubted him."

Vanessa brushed the tear away with her fingers, and Ruby held her glass in the air, her drunken brown eyes shining in the dim light. "A toast?"

"To your wedding!" Vanessa yelled, clinking glasses with her sister and then downing the contents of the glass.

Twenty minutes and another shot later, the room was spinning. The Coyote Ugly girls were up on the bar line dancing, screaming insults into a megaphone, and Vanessa found herself unable to tear her eyes away as the girls worked the room. They were so *confident*. One gorgeous brunette in a tight black wifebeater, rhinestone-studded jeans, and a cowboy hat danced furiously on top of the bar, her body shaking with the music. A guy in front of the bar in a pink Izod shirt with the collar popped grabbed her leg. The brunette bent down, smiling wickedly, and doused him with a pitcher of water hidden behind the bar. The crowd erupted in cheers.

Ruby grabbed Vanessa's arm and slurred, "You should be

up there, V. You're hotter than *any* of those girls!" Then she pushed her from behind, shoving her toward the bar. "Get up there and show them how it's done!"

Vanessa looked down at her hot outfit, enjoying the feel of the blond hair swinging around her face as she moved. She pushed up to the front of the crowd and extended her hand toward the Daisy Duke brunette, who whooped and pulled her up onto the bar. Vanessa surveyed the crowd, feeling a sudden surge of power. She started swinging her hips, her platforms kicking shot glasses off the bar as she moved her feet.

If only that cab driver who'd mistaken her for a guy could see her now—he'd beg for forgiveness. So what if Dan, the guy she'd thought was the love of her life, only liked her for her bald head? She was as much of a woman as anyone else in here. And now she freaking *looked* like it.

"What's up, hot stuff?" the bartender purred, grabbing her by the waist, pulling her close. The crowd went wild, cheering and whooping with raucous, liquor-soaked shouts.

"Hey baby!" A guy up front tried to get Vanessa's attention while someone else shouted, "Shake it, girl!"

Vanessa shook her hips and two-stepped her way down the slick surface of the bar, winking at frat guys and flipping her long blond hair as she went. Okay, so maybe this wasn't the most mature way to deal with Dan rejecting her, but hearing all the encouraging whoops and hollers sure as hell felt therapeutic.

So *that's* what those *Girls Gone Wild* videos are about—healing. As if!

A drunken guy with a blond buzz cut held out a fistful of

dollar bills in his hand, gesturing to her and shouting loudly. Without a moment's thought, Vanessa bent at the waist and grabbed the sleeve of his blue Abercrombie T-shirt, pulling him closer as if she were about to kiss him. Then she grabbed a pitcher of water from behind the bar and dumped it over the poor guy's head. She wasn't just doing this for herself—she was doing it for girls with gay ex-boyfriends everywhere.

The crowd went wild, screaming and cheering, and through her alcoholic haze Vanessa could hear her sister's drunken voice holler over the din—

"*Yeah*! That's my *sister*!"

Aw. Wouldn't mom be proud?

FROM: trentdawg_87@yahoo.com
TO: narchibald@st.judes.edu
Subject: Whassup?

Nate dawg!

Looks like it's going to be you and me
next year, dawg. And you know our room
will be the place to be for all the hot
bitches. I can't wait to get me some of
that Ivy League tail—some kinky librarian
shit. Yeeeeeeh, dawg!

Truth is, dawg, I won't be round the crib
too much this fall, so you can hit the
library honeys in peace. What up! See, I'm
a swimmer and coach makes us eat, like,
all of our meals together and practice
until players start dying. Seriously. And
if that ain't enough, there are all sorts
of wicked brutal pranks and shit the sen-
iors pull on us freshies. It's going to be
gnarly.

So here's the dizzle: you get the girls
through November, and then you're going to
have to fork over some of those hotties.
Hook it up, dawg!

Holla back,
T

TO: <u>trentdawg_87@gmail.com</u>
FROM: <u>narchibald@stjudes.edu</u>
Subject: re: Whassup?

Hey T,

Enjoy the single, dude—I'm not coming.

Later,
Nate (dawg)

it's a family affaaaaaair

Dan sat on the lumpy brown leather sofa, resting his arms on his knees and staring pensively at the night sky framed by the open window. The cool thing about the city was that the sky was never really totally dark—the glare of streetlights cast a glow on the whole city no matter what time it was—so that even if you were awake at say, three in the morning, like he was now, you didn't feel so lonely. Dan was usually comforted by the city lights and sounds of people out and about, but tonight it was having the opposite effect—it was as if everyone else was out doing something fun while he was stuck here all alone. His mom and dad had gone to bed at nine-thirty after drinking two bottles of wine and looking through his mom's slide show of her life with her count. Dan had decided to skip that one, thanks very much. Six hours later he was still wide awake, his laptop open across his knees, the screen blank. It was weird that Vanessa hadn't come home yet, and he was starting to get a little worried— not that he was waiting up for her or anything.

Uh-huh. Sure he wasn't.

He had tried to go to bed just after midnight, but he just couldn't seem to fall asleep. After a couple hours of staring at the ceiling, he'd decided sleep was out of the question and that the couch was a better bet. Too many unanswered questions were floating around in his head, and they were starting to make him dizzy.

Dan was glad he'd figured stuff out with Greg, but after realizing that *Vanessa* was the inspiration for his poem, he was more confused than ever. If he was gay, then why was he writing a love poem inspired by a girl? Maybe when Vanessa came home, he'd nonchalantly ask her what she thought about this whole gay thing as she was getting ready for bed, and then he could let it slip that he wasn't too sure of it. Then he'd hug her and they'd sit down and really *talk*—just the way they used to. If she ever *came* home, that is . . . His chest ached thinking of the possibility that Vanessa had met someone else and was at this very moment in some hipster's smoky, messy apartment, doing bong hits and peeling off her clothes in front of some indie band asshole with too much wax in his hair and not enough rocks tumbling around in his head.

Just then Dan heard the scraping sound of a key in the lock and the creaking noise the front door always made as it opened. *Finally.* His heart buoyed, but he didn't want Vanessa to think he'd been up waiting for her. He closed the laptop and lay down flat, trying to look like he had simply fallen asleep on the couch, writing. He heard the sound of footsteps tiptoeing across the room and felt a pair of warm hands on his face. He smiled sleepily, turning over. Vanessa's hands were so soft . . . but she kind of smelled like those peanuts, the ones you get on airplanes.

Dan opened his eyes and yelped, sitting up quickly as he focused on his sister's freckled face just inches from his own. Jenny Humphrey stood above him, wearing a purple Juicy Couture sweat suit and navy Pumas.

"Surprise!" She whispered loudly, reaching over and messing up his hair. He swatted her hand away.

"You know I hate when you do that," Dan hissed. Despite his rude welcome, he found himself grinning stupidly. He was glad to see his sister—it felt like ages ago since she'd left for Europe to study art for the summer. He'd missed having her around to talk to.

"I know you hate it. That's why I do it." Jenny grinned and sat down on the couch, shaking her curly brown hair back from her round cheeks. She leaned back in for a hug, and Dan wrapped his arms around his little sister, breathing in her familiar, comforting scent of bubble gum and Dolce & Gabbana Light Blue perfume.

"Seriously, though, what are you *doing* here? You almost gave me a heart attack." Dan leaned back on the couch and gazed at his sister, still unable to believe she was really here.

"Hello, I'm going to school in a few days too." She dropped a bulging, dark green Coach duffel bag on the floor. "And, besides, it was kind of sad to be so far away when the family was all together for the first time in, like, *years*. I wanted to come home and be here while Mom was around."

"So how was Europe?" Dan ran his hands through his hair so that it stuck up in mousy brown clumps all over his head. He knew he should be mad at Jenny for telling his mom he was gay, but all of his anger dissolved the second he saw his little sister's sweet, angelic face. "Have any beret-wearing European *lovaaaahs*?"

Jenny stuck her tongue out at her brother and reached down to pull off her sneakers. "Nope, but if I meet anyone who fits that description I'll be sure to pass him along to you," she retorted. "I didn't know that was your type." She smirked at her own wit. "Seriously though—how's it feel to be gay?"

Dan, realizing he was naked to the waist, grabbed a dirty gray sweatshirt from the other side of the couch and pulled it on. "It's . . . I'm not sure," he said, his head getting stuck in an armhole. "I'm kind of confused about the whole thing," he added once he finally got his head out.

"Well, duh!" Jenny exclaimed, repositioning herself on the couch. "Shove over!" She pushed his body with her hip. Dan noticed that her face seemed a little more grown-up to him—or maybe it was just that he hadn't seen her in a while. It seemed less . . . round. "I mean, that's normal, right?" she asked.

"How should I know?" Dan flopped back against the arm of the couch, exasperated. "It's not like I have a lot of experience with this whole thing." He turned his head toward the window, his voice wistful. "I just wish I could find someone to just *be* with, you know?" He wasn't even sure what he meant by that—he was with people all the time. All he knew was that he'd felt really . . . lonely lately. Sure, every man was an island, but this was getting ridiculous.

"Don't worry," Jenny said quietly, reaching over and patting her brother's hand. "You'll find someone. I mean, any guy would be totally lucky to have you."

It was sweet of her to say that, but Dan wasn't entirely sure it was true. "Yeah, I guess," he mumbled.

"Well, what kind of guys do you like, anyway?" Jenny reached up and pulled her relentlessly curly hair into a knot. "I'm pretty sure it's not the ones who wear berets."

Dan laughed despite himself. "I don't know." He picked up the TV remote from the floor and fiddled with it. "How many kinds *are* there, anyway?"

"Uh, *a lot*," she giggled, pulling off a thin purple sock, balling it up and throwing it at his face. "What about the hip-hop guys who hang out by the Christopher Street PATH station?" Jenny held up a hand as if she was going to start counting the types on her fingers. "Or the Chelsea dudes with too many hair products who always wear those fantastic Marc Jacobs shirts? Or the nerdy intellectual-but-still-hot-hipster Brooklyn guys girls always wish were straight? That's probably more your scene." She smiled knowingly and stretched her arms over her head.

Dan shook his head in disbelief. He felt like he'd just landed on Planet Strange. Who was this person pretending to be his baby sister? "Since when do you hang out on *Christopher Street*?" he muttered, completely astonished. Even his little sister knew more about being gay than he did. It was totally depressing.

"Never mind about that." Jenny giggled, reaching down and unzipping her bursting-at-the-seams L.L. Bean duffel bag. "Is Mom in your room?" She whispered, gesturing toward the closed bedroom doors on the other end of the apartment.

"Yeah," Dan replied, sitting up and scratching his arms

sleepily. Jenny had apparently cured his insomnia. "Vanessa and I are sharing your old room."

"Then I guess it's sofa city for me." His sister sighed, pulling out a bulging floral toiletry case from her bag. Dan stood up, raising his arms over his head and yawning loudly. As weird and unexpected as it was to have both his mother and Jenny home, it felt kind of nice to have everybody under one roof.

Well, *almost* everybody . . . there's one roommate still missing.

Just then, the door to his room creaked open, and their mom shuffled out, picking sleep from the corners of her eyes. Her voluminous pink robe billowed out behind her as she moved, her fuzzy slippers scraping the floor. Dan watched as her eyes focused on her youngest child, and her face lit up with surprise.

"Jenny!" she exclaimed rushing over and folding her daughter into her tentlike arms, "You're here! You didn't burn my apartment down, did you?"

"Nope. I just wanted to be with you guys." She squeezed her mother back. Dan watched as his mom smoothed back Jenny's unruly nest of hair and kissed her on the forehead. He couldn't help but be touched at Jenny's optimistic, girlish enthusiasm. If his being gay had brought his family together, maybe it wasn't such a bad thing after all.

"Such a sweetheart." Jeanette touched Jenny's face with her palm. "I'll make some oolong." She breezed past Dan, stopping to smooth his hair like a mother who'd been smoothing hair all her life.

Tea? That probably meant girl talk. And Dan wasn't sure

he was ready to be one of the girls. "I'm going to bed," he announced, shuffling toward his room.

"See you in a few hours," Jenny replied with a yawn, stretching as she followed their mom into the kitchen.

"'Night, baby!" Jeanette called out from the kitchen sink, where she was busily filling the kettle with water.

Dan walked into his room and shut the door, then climbed into the empty bed. He could hear his mom and sister chattering away in the kitchen, whispers interspersed with the occasional giggle. How could they have so much energy this late at night? He'd never understand women. But then again, he barely understood himself. Dan sighed and watched the night change from purple to gray in the early morning light as he finally drifted into sleep, still wondering sleepily where Vanessa was and if she was okay.

Aren't we all.

Disclaimer: All the real names of places, people, and events have been altered or abbreviated to protect the innocent. Namely, me.

hey people!

The end of summer is almost here, and the Waldorf Rose farewell party at the Met is rapidly approaching. If you haven't heard—if you've been, say, camping in Siberia, for instance—Davita Fjorde, public relations guru to the crème de la crème (otherwise known as you and me), is planning the party and probably clicking her rhinestone-heeled Jimmy Choos right at this very moment, making amazing things happen. So break out those spanking new Christian Louboutins and a barely-there Zac Posen cocktail dress and book your hair and makeup appointments at Fekkai. After all, it's your last chance to satisfy that secret crush on the cute boy you never had the nerve to talk to. It'll be the last time you'll see your fellow classmates—thank God. (Hey, I'm just being honest— so sue me.) And it's your last chance to gossip about the people you love the least—or most! So let's get to it, people, because it's been one hell of an exciting week.

your e-mail

Dear GG,
So I e-mailed my new roomie, and she told me she's from NYC and graduated from Constance Billard, and that got me thinking, OMG maybe she knows Serena van der Woodsen from *Breakfast at Fred's*—my favorite movie of all time! My best friend's movie producer dad screened it at their house a

Q: few weeks ago, and we've watched it, like, twenty-two times already! Did you hear that Serena is going to Yale? Guess what? Me too!! I so can't wait to meet her.

—Crazy for Serena

A: Dear CFS,

Constance Billard is a pretty small school, and, on top of that, Manhattan is a pretty small island. Everyone knows *everyone* here—or at least, everyone worth knowing! You can be sure that your new roomie knows **S,** or at the very least has been at a party with her once or twice. Here's a thought that might just make you pee your pants: maybe your new roomie *is* **S**?!

—GG

Q: Dear GG,

I just got back from Europe and I *really* want to score an invite to **B**'s party at the Met! Can you help? How can I get invited at the last minute?

Missing Out

A: Dear MO,

Ah, the pain of not getting an invite—not something I can personally relate to, but I'm sure it really sucks. What I have to say won't make you feel any better—but at least it's honest: there's always next year! So invite some friends over and spend the night watching *Lost* reruns. Your time will come—and sooner than you think.

—GG

sightings

A group of totally bizarro Brooklyn hipsters, doing a run-through of their "Ode to Love" in **Prospect Park** at sunrise. Practicing for something?

There's one invite we're glad we didn't get! And speaking of sunrise, a very intoxicated **V** and her soon-to-be-betrothed sister, **R,** were seen falling all over each other on their way up the stairs to **R**'s **Williamsburg apartment**—a long blonde . . . something . . . dragging behind them. **C** and some spectacled, cute geek at the **Magnolia Bakery** in the West Village, licking frosting off of each other's pink cupcakes, and feeding C's monkey spoonfuls of banana pudding, looking very smug and practically married.

pre-party planning

And you know what that means: it's time to hit the stores. I'm off to stroll Fifth and take in more of Manhattan's finest than my American Express black card can possibly hold. But, then again, it has no limits—and neither do I!

You know you love me.

gossip girl

s and b shop till they drop

Serena held an ivory Calvin Klein silk dress up to her slender shoulders, her blond hair falling over her back in a beautiful, tangled mess. The slick material draped over her perfect body like running water. Blair had tried that dress on earlier in the week, but it had looked like shit on her.

Jealous much?

"What do you think?" Serena turned to face Blair, her face flushed and glowing despite the unspeakably horrible fluorescent light of the dressing room. Blair didn't answer. Shouldn't Serena know by now that *everything* looked good on her? If she didn't, Blair certainly wasn't going to tell her.

"Ugh." Serena placed the dress back on the hanger. "It'd probably look better on you anyway."

Blair rolled her eyes and stomped out of the dressing room. Serena had been tiptoeing around her since they'd met up in front of Barneys half an hour ago. First of all, she had brought her an iced latte and a fudge brownie—Blair's favorite combination—and now there was all this ass-kissing talk about the dress. Why was Serena being so *nice* all of a sudden? Not that she wasn't always nice—but this was overly, cloyingly nice.

Blair grabbed a Milly NY green-and-gold brocade print dress and held it up to her body, fluffing her newly extensioned hair with one hand. Her new golden streaks looked amazing against the metallic thread of the dress. Serena came thwacking out of the dressing room, her tanned legs extending from a short white miniskirt, turquoise flip-flops on her feet.

"Hey!" she exclaimed, walking up to Blair. "That'll look incredible on you!"

Blair stayed silent as she hung the dress back on the rack with a snap of her wrist and began manically flipping through a rack of Stella McCartney tunics.

"So," she began, her voice casual as she turned to face her friend, "where were you yesterday? I called to see if you wanted to get your hair done with me, but I kept getting your voice mail."

Serena looked at the floor, the windows, at the rows of shining, expensive dresses surrounding them—anywhere but Blair's face. Did Blair know what had happened between her and Nate? Had Nate said something? Serena didn't think so, but she couldn't be sure either. She'd thought that if she and Blair went shopping the way they used to, that everything would somehow magically go back to normal—in spite of the fact that absolutely *nothing* was normal anymore.

Blair had been in love with Nate for as long as Serena could remember. The problem was, *so had she*. And after spending the entire day and night in bed together yesterday, Serena was positive Nate loved her too. She tried to hide the ridiculous smile that was in grave danger of spreading across her face. She and Nate were finally, really, *seriously* going to be together soon—just as soon as Blair left for Yale on Sunday. Serena didn't want to hurt her—that was the *last* thing she wanted to do—but she was ecstatic to have finally won Nate's heart. Even if it meant breaking Blair's. Ugh. Why did she always have to choose between her best friend and her boyfriend?

Um . . . because technically he's *Blair's* boyfriend?

"Yesterday? I don't remember what I was doing," she finally answered, looking up into Blair's impassive face and narrowed eyes. Blair grabbed a black satin Dior dress and fingered the price tag. "I think I just forgot to turn my phone back on—and then by the time I got your messages, it was too late."

The haute couture department of Barneys was spare and intimidating. Light wafted in through floor-to-ceiling windows, warming the dark wood floor. Not a salesperson was in sight—Barneys prided themselves on their aloof, unpushy sales staff who turned out to be enormously helpful, but only when called upon. That was one of the reasons the girls liked the store so much. It was their home away from home.

"Huh." Blair turned and walked at a brisk clip across the floor, her flat, delicate Dolce & Gabbana silver sandals barely making a sound. "Talk to Nate lately?"

"No," Serena answered quickly. "Not at all."

Blair ran her hands along a pile of electric-orange-and-robin's-egg-blue TSE cashmere sweaters. Was it just her, or was Serena acting a little jumpy? She wondered if Nate had told Serena about not graduating and not going to Yale and otherwise ruining Blair's life. "You sure?" She pushed.

"Not since, um, we did the slide-show stuff that day you caught us." Serena laughed awkwardly and turned to rifle through the colorful Missoni knit dresses behind her.

Blair squinted distrustfully at the back of Serena's blond head, trying to read her possibly evil, maybe lying, definitely-in-love with Nate thoughts. "Well, you missed Vanessa Abrams getting one hot makeover yesterday. You should really keep your phone on," she finally said to her back. "I'm going back to look at the Prada dresses."

Serena followed Blair, trying to match her quick steps. "Vanessa got a makeover? How come?" Serena asked, grateful for the opportunity to change the subject. She stopped on the opposite side of the rack from Blair and started flipping through the chocolate- and mocha-colored Prada bubble dresses Blair had already passed over.

"Her sister's getting married this weekend." Blair lifted her eyes from the white silk Prada dress she was fingering. "And, you know—sometimes people just need a change."

Serena bent down and tried to make eye contact through a gap in the dresses. There was something else she was feeling guilty about not telling Blair. "Speaking of changes—there's something I need to tell you," she said quietly.

Blair pushed her hair off her shoulders and straightened the straps of her white Nation tank top. "I already know about Nate," she snapped. "You don't have to hide it from me."

"You *do*?" Serena gripped a plush hanger with both hands. *Blair knew about her and Nate?*

"Of course I do." Blair squinted, irritated that Serena would think for a second that Nate would not tell *her*, his girlfriend. "I cannot fucking believe he's not going to Yale. Repeating senior year. He's totally retarded," she spat.

"Oh." Serena looked at Blair, her navy blue eyes wide. That was a close call. "Oh! I mean that's . . . that is awful. But that's not what I was going to say. . . ." Her voice trailed off, her heart thumping hard against her rib cage.

Blair pulled a Lauren Moffatt houndstooth-print tunic over her head and looked at her reflection in the mirror. Serena stood behind her, standing almost a full head taller and looking nervous. She twirled a long blond lock around her finger. Blair wondered if Serena was finally going to confess to her about her love letter to Nate. Well, it was about time. Then Blair could forgive her and they could go off to Yale, best friends forever, and put all this behind them. Even if Nate had to stay in the city, at least she'd have Serena—and at least Serena would be far, far away from him. Blair took a deep breath and prepared herself to try and forgive her best friend.

"What is it then?" She moved on to the Diane von Furstenberg dresses Serena was practically hiding behind.

"I'm not going to Yale either," Serena admitted sheepishly as she fingered a wildly patterned wrap dress, avoiding Blair's eyes. "I'm going to defer for a year so I can do some more acting."

Excuse me? Blair felt like her brain was on fire. *Not going to Yale, not going to Yale*—the words spun around and around in her head until she thought she might pass out. First Nate, now Serena? She dropped the yellow DVF chiffon gown she'd been holding. The light silk fluttered soundlessly to the floor.

"You're *what*?" Blair demanded in disbelief, shaking her head from side to side like she had water in her ears.

"I'm just . . . not going." Serena shrugged. "I'm going to stay in New York and shoot the sequel to *Breakfast at Fred's.*"

Serena was staying in New York? *With Nate?* Blair felt the ground start to wobble beneath her.

Just then a group of tourists passed by, squealing and pointing at Serena, cameras hanging around their necks. The crowd engulfed both girls, and Blair was rudely shoved out of the way by a sharp, jabby elbow. They surrounded Serena in a mob.

"Thank you." Serena blushed as she signed one of the tourist's matchbooks from Fred's, Barneys' ninth-floor restaurant, about to become even more famous because of her new film.

Blair watched as Serena signed one autograph after another, bowing her head humbly and graciously without so much as a glance in Blair's direction. How could Serena drop a bomb like that and then move onto her worshippers, completely ignoring her? Blair seethed, manically twirling her ruby ring around her middle finger, as the crowd around Serena grew. A man dressed in an avocado-and-vermillion seersucker suit kissed Serena's hand, and a suburban mom took her picture with her Nikon Elph. Next year Blair would be just another freshman at college, and Serena would be . . . a movie star. A movie star living in the same city as *her* boyfriend. How could she ever compete?

Her sandals hit the floor with a rude slapping sound as

she turned her back on Serena and her idiotic adoring fans. Damn Barneys. Damn Serena. She was getting the hell out of town, but no fucking way was she leaving Nate behind.

That's what we've always loved about her—the angrier she gets, the more ingenious she is.

who's your daddy?

Blair sat in the half-packed bedroom, surrounded by over-stuffed trunks and clutter so deep that the pee-stained sea-grass mats on the floor were only a faint memory. She stared at the mess, her whole body shaking. Serena wasn't going to Yale with her. She was staying here in New York for another year with . . . Nate? No way was Blair was going to leave both of them alone in the same city next year—she'd rather stab herself in the eye with the stiletto heel of one of her new Fendi boots.

Ouch.

A pile of T-shirts fell off of the bed and landed on the floor with a soft thud as she angrily flailed around. She yanked her shoes off and threw them angrily at the wall, needing to hear an even louder sound. How could Nate resist Serena when she was a huge star, and right here in the same city with him? *No.* It simply could not happen.

She reached for her cell and held down speed dial number 4. Number 1 was 911 for an emergency, which this was, but whatever; number 2 was for Serena—definitely not who she was looking for right now; and number 3 was for Nate, the completely effed-up love of her life.

"H-Hello?" the male voice sounded waterlogged with sleep.

"Daddy, it's me." Blair spoke tentatively. If she was going to get what she wanted from him, she'd need to tread lightly. "I'm sorry—did I wake you?" She made her voice small. There was a long pause, and she could hear sheets rustling and the click of a light being turned on halfway around the world.

"Of course you woke me, Blair-Bear—it's four a.m. here." Her father sounded slightly annoyed—not to mention sleep-deprived. The sound of the two babies wailing in the background reached her ear. She rolled her eyes in disdain.

"Well, it's *important*," she whined.

"I'm sure that it is," Harold Waldorf said with a sigh. "But important things are happening over here too. Giles has been up all night with the twins—just the nastiest case of colic. We tried this fabulous new vaporizer, but nothing is working." There was a pause, and Blair could hear the guttural cooing of a baby over the line.

"I'm sorry I didn't tell you about the twins before now, honey. But it was kind of a spur-of-the-moment acquisition." He chuckled, and Blair could hear one of the sniveling brats cooing again. "But let me tell you, it was the best one I've ever made."

Burberry baby bib: fifty dollars. Hermès Pacifier: six hundred dollars. Cambodian babies: priceless.

"Blair," her father cooed over the din of baby-speak, "Ping would like to say hello—say hi to your new little brother!" She heard a rustling sound as the little monster was held up to the phone, and then a series of gurgling noises that sounded like the baby was drowning in its own spit. "Pong is still sleeping, but when she wakes up she'll say hi too." Blair rolled her eyes. Ping and Pong?

Isn't it technically called table tennis?

"Daddy," she snapped. *"I need to talk to you!"*

What happened to treading lightly?

"There's no need to get *snippy* about it," her father replied, rather snippily himself. "Just let me put the baby down." Good. Maybe now he could pay some attention to his firstborn.

"You know how Nate and I were going to Yale together?" Blair plowed ahead, not waiting for her father to respond. She could hear the sound of him whispering in French to someone in the background. "Well, Nate didn't get his diploma from St. Jude's, and now it looks like he can't go to Yale in the fall—they want him to repeat senior year instead."

"Oh, honey." Her father's voice was sympathetic now. "I'm so sorry. You must be devastated."

"Well, I *was*." Blair picked up her Mason-Pearson hairbrush and whipped it through her smooth, chestnut-and-gold locks. "Until I remembered that you're on the board of trustees. Isn't there something you can do about it? Maybe talk to the dean of admissions and put in a good word for Nate or something? Everyone respects you *so* much, Daddy," she said, back to her original plan of kissing ass. Her father sighed, and then there was more rustling.

"It's not so easy, Blair-Bear. . . . I can't just make a

diploma magically appear." He whispered something in French to Giles, and Blair momentarily wished she'd actually learned the language in her AP French class. "I'd really like to help, but I can't just snap my fingers and make Nate's problems go away. Besides, with the new twins and all, this isn't the best—"

"Daddy, you *owe* me." Blair cut him off midsentence with an exasperated sigh. "First you move to France during my *formative* years, and now you've replaced me with these twins." She took a deep breath and tried to stop herself from completely losing it. Had everyone gone totally insane? First her mother had announced the family was moving to Los Angeles, next Serena and Nate had told her they were staying in New York, and now her dad was going to bail on her when she needed him most?

Blair heard footsteps in the hall, and suddenly the door swung open to reveal her stepbrother, Aaron, wearing electric yellow Quicksilver board shorts and a burgundy Harvard T-shirt, followed by his disgusting boxer, Mookie—who immediately bounded up to Blair and began covering her crotch in dog drool.

"Get off me!" she yelled, rubbing the wet, goopy places on her legs where Mookie had licked her. The dog trotted over to the corner where Blair had tossed her dirty laundry, picked out one of her pink Cosabella thongs, and lay down, the lace hanging from his jowls.

Well, at least *someone's* interested in getting in her pants these days.

Blair rolled her eyes to the ceiling and threw a pillow at Aaron. He sat down on the floor next to the boxer and lit one of his foul herbal cigarettes, chuckling as Mookie ripped Blair's expensive underwear to shreds. His normally pale face was tan, and his dark, short dreadlocks were streaked with copper, like he'd been living on a beach all summer. Aaron was annoying, but at least he didn't look anything like his dad, Cyrus, who was the most revolting human specimen of a stepfather Blair had ever encountered.

"Daddy, are you still there?"

"I'm here, Blair-Bear—and I'll try. But no promises, okay? I want you to be realistic about the situation. If it's meant to be, it's meant to be." The babies started wailing again, and her dad offered a quick "Love you, see you in a few days!" before signing off.

Oh, it was meant to be, all right, Blair thought as she tossed her phone down on the bed. You couldn't stop destiny—and she and Nate were *destined* to be together forever.

"Thanks for the friendly welcome, Sis." Aaron grinned and leaned up against Mookie, throwing his arm around the dog's neck in a half nelson. Good. Maybe he'd strangle the thing by accident. Mookie offered him a wet lick across his face.

"Oh, right. Welcome back," she said irritably. "And I told you to stop calling me that. Just because my mom married your dad doesn't mean I'm your sister."

"Uh, no offense, Sis, but that's exactly what it means." Aaron smoothed down Mookie's gross, slobbery fur with one hand and chuckled.

"Whatever." Blair inspected her French manicure, which was now chipped. As if she needed one more fucked up thing in her life.

Poor baby!

"So, you getting psyched for Yale?" Aaron asked, lying back on the floor. Mookie promptly got up and sat on his chest, obscuring his face so that all Blair could see was his dreadlocks, and Mookie's grinning, drooling muzzle. It was like they'd become one giant dog-dreadlock monster. Before Blair could answer, Aaron's muffled voice continued. "Remember when I drove you up for your interview, and we stayed at that gross motel?"

"Oh God—how could I forget?" Blair laughed bitterly. At the time, she'd thought her luck couldn't get any worse. After a night of drinking too much beer and eating too much junk food from their motel vending machine, she'd overslept for her Yale interview, which had wound up being a total disaster. Now that she was into Yale, she could look back and laugh. If she hadn't gotten in, Aaron wouldn't be alive now to remind her of the story. "Anyway, how was your road trip? Pick up any interesting, homicidal hitchhikers?"

He laughed. "No hitchhikers. It was good—I pretty much didn't want to come back. But I guess I should probably pack up a few things before I leave for Harvard."

"Yeah, before the movers come and we become homeless," Blair added angrily. She kicked the trunk at the foot of her bed for emphasis.

"Well, I guess that tells me how you're feeling about the move." Aaron inched a little farther away, as if afraid she was going to kick him next. "What, are you worried you'll miss all the good sales at Barneys?"

"Yeah, actually." Blair crossed her arms over her chest.

He nodded his dreadlocked head sympathetically and

took another puff from his herbal cigarette, which smelled like boiled broccoli and Lysol. "So, how's everybody been while I was gone?" His voice was muffled by Mookie, who was practically sitting on his face at this point. "How's Vanessa?"

"Can you move that disgusting mutt so I can see you?" Blair pulled her newly long hair back into a ponytail. Aaron shoved Mookie off of his chest. The dog whimpered and slid reluctantly onto the floor.

"So, how's Vanessa?" He asked again, sitting up and crossing his legs Indian style. "Is she coming to the Met party?"

"I think so." Blair picked up a nail file from the floor and began furiously filing away at her ring finger. "But she'll be coming from her sister's wedding in Brooklyn, so she'll probably get there late. Why do you care anyway?"

"Who said I care?" Aaron raised one eyebrow and grinned mischievously. "Maybe I'm just curious."

True love never lies, part deux?

summertime, and the living's easy . . .

"Your lemonade, Miss van der Woodsen."

A crisp, British-accented voice woke Serena from her light slumber. She looked up to see a handsome waiter leaning over her, a gleaming silver tray with a tall, frosted glass of lemonade balanced perfectly on one hand. The turquoise water of the SoHo House pool sparkled behind him, casting a tint of blue on his entirely white uniform.

Serena sat up in her deck chair, tying up the straps of her white, barely there Marni bikini so that she wouldn't flash him by accident.

That's one way to tip!

"Thank you." She smiled, pushing her white Chanel sunglasses to the top of her head. This was the life.

"Please let me know if you desire anything else," the waiter offered with a polite little bow before leaving.

Serena smiled to herself as she leaned back on her pristine white deck chair, taking in the scene around her. The entire poolside area was furnished in white, with white lounge chairs, oversize white umbrellas, and white monogrammed SoHo

House towels. The stylish guests had taken it upon themselves to match the scenery, clad entirely in white bikinis, wraps, and linen pants. The pool was strikingly turquoise against the bright white, and the tops of Manhattan's Financial District skyscrapers glittered in the distance.

She sighed, feeling the hot August sun warm every inch of her smooth skin. This really was the life. After their press conference at the Soho House on Tuesday, Ken Mogul had handed Serena and Thad the jet-black key cards to the penthouse and let them know the room was rented for a week. Since Thad had his own apartment in the city, he'd told her she could stay in the room the whole time if she wanted to. Serena preferred to stay in her own room at home—her parents were hardly ever home, though they wouldn't exactly approve of her living in a hotel room on her own—but access to the exclusive, Meatpacking District, members-only rooftop pool came with the card, and she certainly wasn't going to say no to that. The only thing missing was someone special to enjoy it with.

She picked up her cell and dialed a number she knew as well as her own.

"Hey stranger." Nate picked up on the first ring, his slightly sleepy voice sending shivers up her spine. She pictured him still lazing in bed, no shirt on, just waking up from a dream—about her, of course.

"Hey yourself." She grinned into the phone. "What are you up to right now?"

Twenty minutes later Nate bounded out onto the deck of the SoHo House pool, his brown leather flip-flops thwacking against the stone tiles, oblivious to the ogling female eyes that were fixed on his perfect body. In his green Billabong swim trunks and faded gray T-shirt, Nate was the only person on the entire roof deck not wearing white.

"Hey." He smiled widely as he reached her deck chair, his golden brown hair falling into his eyes. A shiver of nervous goose bumps spread over her skin. He sank down into the chair beside her. "You look . . . comfortable."

"Cheerio, old chap," Serena responded in a playful, mock-British accent, and held up the black key card, marked with only four letters—SHPH. "Soho House Penthouse," she explained with a flirtatious wink.

Nate reached for the card to get a closer look, but she playfully swatted his hand away.

He shrugged and took off his shirt, settling into the plush white lounge-chair cushion. "Your British accent sounds faker than Madonna's." He picked up her glass of lemonade and took a long swig, smacking his lips in satisfaction as he put the half-empty glass back down.

"First you insult my accent, and then you drink my lemonade? You're in for it, buddy." She stood and grabbed his arm, dragging him toward the pool. They tumbled over the edge and hit the water with a loud splash, narrowly missing an Elizabeth Taylor look-alike in a white one-piece swimsuit and matching head turban doing water calisthenics in the shallow end. Maybe it really *was* Elizabeth Taylor.

"Excuse me." The woman scowled, moving away from Serena and Nate as they stood in the water dripping and panting.

Serena took a deep breath and plunged underneath the

surface of the water. For as long as she could remember, she'd loved being underwater, the whole world drowned out, only the sound of gently rushing water in her ears. She opened her eyes, the chlorine stinging them slightly, and saw Nate underwater right in front of her, his green eyes wide open too. His hair was standing straight up, and he waved his hand, a liquid "hello" escaping his lips with a rush of bubbles.

She giggled, nearly choking, and suddenly thought of the games of Marco Polo she and Nate and Blair had played when they were younger. Nate would always cheat, shouting "Marco!" and then opening his eyes for a moment to see where they were. Then he'd grab the girls with huge splashing lunges, pretending he'd just found them by accident. Nate never seemed to care which girl he caught, he'd just grab whomever was in front of him and held on. Serena closed her eyes, the sting of the chlorine now too much to bear, and shot up to the surface.

Nate sidestroked into the shallow end and hopped up onto the edge of the pool, letting his legs dangle in the water. Serena looked so peaceful floating on her back in the calm water, her blond hair forming a halo around her head, an angelic smile on her face. *Being* with Serena was so much less stressful than being with Blair. Immediately he thought of his last, highly stressful interaction with Blair, whom he'd been avoiding since the day before yesterday, when she'd thrown her shoes at him.

Blair had left him hundreds of voice mails, but Nate thought he should wait to speak with her until she'd had a little more time to cool off.

Just not in this particular pool.

He knew that Blair was angry, but he also knew that she'd eventually forgive him, just like she always did. He could still visit her at Yale on the weekends. And Serena would be here with him in New York. He'd always thought he'd have to choose between the two girls, but now it seemed he could have them both. That was pretty ballsy, if he did say so himself.

Serena opened one eye and discovered Nate staring at her. With a rush of water, she stood up, her wet hair falling down her back in a slick mass. Winding it around her hand, she squeezed the water out and then tied her hair into a neat knot. Her swimsuit straps had fallen down again, and she hitched them up before anything embarrassing happened.

Not that it's anything Nate hasn't seen before. . . .

"Impressive." He smiled, kicking a little water up at her with one golden foot. "Um, putting your hair up without a barrette or whatever," he stammered, turning pink. "Not the swimsuit-almost-falling-off part. Not that I'd mind that," he added.

"Really now?" she hopped up on the ledge beside him, her hair promptly falling out of its not-so-secure bun and draping messily over her shoulders. "Because along with that key card comes a very beautiful, very *empty* hotel suite." She inched a little closer to him on the pool ledge.

Nate grinned, the sun bouncing off the water and making his green eyes glitter even more than usual. He opened his mouth to speak but was interrupted by a voice behind them.

"Serena van der Woodsen!" a syrupy, high-pitched voice exclaimed. They both turned to see Bailey Winter, all five feet of the famous designer, dressed in a white linen suit, a hot pink handkerchief in his pocket and an enormous pair of white sunglasses perched on his head. His houseboy, Stefan, was behind him, manning the leashes of Bailey's five pugs. "You remember Stefan," he chirped with a wave behind him. "And of course you remember Azzedine, Coco, Cristobal, Gianni, and Madame Gres." He tittered, gesturing at the dogs.

How could *anyone* forget?

"Of course!" Serena jumped up and gave Bailey a damp hug. "It's so good to see you!" she exclaimed affectionately.

After Bailey had designed the costumes for *Breakfast at Fred's*, he'd invited Serena and Blair to be live-in muses at his East Hampton summer home. Their stay had had its share of problems, mainly due to a pair of skinny Eastern European models determined to make their life there a living hell. In a horrendous scene at one of Bailey's famous parties, they'd ruined his furniture, horrified the guests, and then run out of the party—and away from the Hamptons—without so much as a goodbye. Serena had felt so guilty for leaving on such bad terms that she'd written Bailey a note later on in the summer, apologizing for their behavior and thanking him for their stay. He'd written back saying that he couldn't possibly hold a grudge against someone so lovely and talented, and that she was welcome any time.

"What are you doing back in the city?" She grabbed a white towel and wrapped it around her midriff.

The little man folded up his sunglasses and put them into his pocket. "The Hamptons get so dull at the end of the summer. All the fun's here in the city!" He waved his petite hands in the air. "You certainly are at the center of all the action—I can't believe my little Serena is becoming a big, big movie star!" He shrieked and grabbed her hands. "I just went to a screening of *Breakfast at Fred's,* and of course the costumes are *to die for,* if I do say so myself, but you, my dear, are the icing on the German chocolate cake!" he added, pinching Stefan's toned behind, apropos of nothing.

Liz Taylor was lounging on a deck chair a few feet away with a little white Chihuahua curled at her feet. She looked up from her copy of Italian *Vogue,* and her dog jumped down to sniff Cristobal's butt curiously.

That's one way to say hello.

"Serena van der Woodsen, from *Breakfast at Fred's?*" the woman demanded loudly in an imperious Spanish accent. So she wasn't Liz Taylor after all. "I thought you looked familiar. I absolutely *adored* that movie. . . ."

A crowd began to form around Serena. Suddenly it hit Nate that she was starring in a big-time film, and that she was about to become really famous, a movie star. He wondered if from now on it was going to be like this all the time, getting stopped on the street, mobbed by fans, paparazzi following them everywhere. Serena smiled shyly as she autographed someone's towel. He could already see the gossip columns, wondering why the accomplished young starlet was hanging out with a loser still stuck in high school. Not that he cared what other people thought, but still. It would be . . . weird. He ran his fingers through his hair, wishing he had a joint with him, and then remembered that he did—in the pocket of his now-soaking shorts. Oops.

He picked up his towel and started to dry off. Then he heard his phone's muffled ring and found it underneath his T-shirt. He flipped it open, grateful for something to do besides watching Serena and feeling dumb and useless. "Hello?"

"Long time no see. What are you up to right now?" Blair's voice surprised him. She sounded downright chipper, and not angry at all.

"Hey . . . ," he mumbled, wandering to the very edge of the roof. The city was sprawled out beneath him, the low town houses of the Meatpacking District giving way to new Chelsea condos and the midtown high-rises beyond.

Serena noticed him wander away and hoped he was talking to Blair, perhaps calmly explaining that he and Serena would both be staying in the city this year . . . *together*. Of course she felt slightly guilty stealing Nate away, but once Blair was happily ensconced at Yale—her dream school—she'd forget all about them.

"Thank you soo much." The Spanish woman's voice broke into her thoughts. She proudly waved her autographed Italian *Vogue*. "Binky and I are such fans. Aren't we, Binky?" She swept up the tiny dog with one arm. Binky strained in her arms, reaching for Cristobal's wiggling and whimpering form at his owner's feet.

"Of course." Serena nodded. "My pleasure." Bailey grabbed her arm and began to whisper in her ear. "You must be my only muse. I'll dress you exclusively in my designs, just like Audrey Hepburn and Givenchy!" But Serena barely heard him, distracted by the sight of Nate putting his T-shirt back on. He waved, mouthing, "I'll talk to you later," as he backed toward the exit. She sighed. So much for taking advantage of her hotel suite.

That's okay—they have the rest of their lives to spend together. Don't they?

b can barely contain herself

Nate rounded the corner of Nineteenth Street and crossed Sixth Avenue, without waiting for the walk signal. The Container Store loomed up ahead, its huge display windows and royal blue awnings a little too showy for a store that sold plastic storage bins and shower racks. Nate pushed through the glass doors and into the enormous store, taking in the high ceilings and fake Romanesque columns. He searched for a familiar chestnut-brown head of hair as he strode down the wide central path, glancing down endless aisles with labels like SHELVING, CLEANING, HOME OFFICE, KITCHEN, and BATH. The store was heavily air-conditioned, and he could feel goose bumps forming all over his still-damp body. He'd felt bad running out on Serena like that, but he'd been so relieved when Blair had called and invited him to come dorm-room shopping. She sounded almost normal—a thousand times calmer than she'd been when he'd last seen her—and he wanted to take advantage of her being in a good mood. At least she couldn't kill him in such a public place.

Don't be so sure—that girl loves to make a scene.

Finally he spotted her, looking radiant in a sea-green cotton sundress—not the most practical outfit for dorm room shopping, but then Blair was never practical. Her hair was a little longer than he last remembered it, and streaked with strands of gold. He blinked, wondering if the chlorine had done something to his eyes. She was standing by a desk that advertised custom-made closets, arguing with a harried-looking salesgirl in a dark blue apron that read CONTAIN YOURSELF! A long line of people stood behind her, shuffling their feet impatiently and checking their watches. Of course, Blair could have cared less.

Of course.

Her little brother Tyler and stepbrother, Aaron, were with her, piles of oddly shaped bins stacked at their feet as they waited for Blair, their faces slack with boredom. Tyler pulled a set of plastic clips out of the packaging and stuck them all over his clothing, clipping the last one over the bridge of his nose. Aaron was reading a book covered in ribbed cardboard, one of the display books that stores used to make the living room displays look lived-in. Nate had always assumed those books were blank inside. Given the glazed look in Aaron's eyes, maybe they were.

"Hey guys," Nate called over to them. Aaron and Tyler looked up and smiled relieved smiles. Now that Nate was there, they could be excused from Her Highness's service.

"Oh, good, you're here," Blair observed. "One sec." She turned back to the salesgirl. "Thanks for your *help*," she snapped icily, stepping away from the desk.

"They're all morons," she announced loudly when she got closer to Nate. "They won't design a special storage system for my dorm's closet just because I don't have the exact dimensions. Isn't that, like, what they get paid for?" She rolled her eyes and turned to Aaron and Tyler. "Well, what are you two waiting for?" They sighed and grabbed the piles of stuff from off the floor, following her as she strode purposefully to the back of the store.

Nate lingered behind them, fingering the wet joint still in his pocket. Blair could be a little scary when she got into decorating mode, but at least she wasn't unleashing her, um, *energy* in his direction. He felt sorry for Aaron and Tyler, though. Aaron had piled everything into a big laundry basket and was struggling to hold it upright. "Hey man. I saw some carts by the front of the store—want me to go grab one?" he offered.

Aaron shook his head, his short dreadlocks knocking back and forth. "Sis refuses to use a shopping cart," he told Nate helplessly.

"I heard that," Blair snapped without turning around. "Shopping carts are for old ladies," she declared, continuing at her manic pace. She stopped at the kitchen section, touching a steel wine rack. She turned and smiled mischievously at the three boys. "Besides, who needs a cart when you've got three strapping young men to carry your things for you?" She raised one perfectly arched eyebrow, grabbing the wine rack with one hand and placing it on top of Aaron's mounting pile.

"This is child abuse," Tyler complained from behind a lacquered baby-blue-and-white polka-dot hatbox, his voice nasal from the clip on his nose. Tyler's pageboy helmet of light brown, stick-straight hair had grown out so that it nearly reached his chin, and his Brooks Brothers khakis were torn at the knees. Who knew what he would look like after four years of high school in L.A.? He placed the hatbox on the floor and grabbed the white wire easy-glide bin on the shelf in front of him, which was filled with boxes of snacks. He passed over the Carr's crackers and Pringles, pulling out a box of Le Petite Écolier cookies.

"Tyler, those are display items—you know, to show how much you can fit in the bins?" Blair scolded, now holding up a set of glass measuring cups.

"He's hungry. I should take him home," Aaron offered eagerly. "I mean, uh, since you and Nate probably want some alone time and all," he added, already putting the overloaded laundry basket at Nate's feet.

"Fine." Blair sighed, returning the measuring cups to their shelf. "Nate and I can handle this ourselves."

"Thanks," Aaron nodded quickly. He grabbed the bag of cookies from Tyler. "I'll make sure we pay for these. Later!" They made a dash for the front of the store, as if they were trying to outrun a tornado.

Hurricane Blair?

"Hey," Nate murmured. Blair was reading the instructions on a speed mixer. He was suddenly aware of how *alone* they were—and remembered what had happened the last time they'd been alone together.

At lease she's wearing soft rubber flip-flops.

Blair seemed calm now, but maybe she'd just been waiting for Aaron and Tyler to leave. If that mixer was plugged in, it could really do some damage to his face. But, then, to his utter relief, she smiled.

"Hey, yourself," she responded, her blue eyes shining.

"Natie, I'm glad you came. I just wanted to tell you that I'm sorry about the other day. I got . . . carried away. And I've been thinking about it. We can totally make this work." She gave his hand a squeeze and then dropped the mixer back on the shelf with a loud thump. "You never know what surprises the future may bring."

Nate felt his body sag with relief. He hadn't even realized how tense he'd been.

"Let's go to Bedroom." Blair suggested. Then she giggled. "I said to bed*room*, not to bed. Don't get your hopes up, horndog." She turned on her heel and started walking down the gleaming white aisle, an extra flirtatious swish in her step.

Nate bent down and picked up the massive laundry bin stuffed with carefully selected items. "Seriously, Blair, why do you need all this stuff? Where are you going to put it?" he asked when he'd caught up with her, his arms sagging under the bin's weight. Suddenly he remembered the description of hell in Dante's *Inferno* from eleventh-grade English class. There were different circles of hell, and everyone suffered according to their crimes. Was carrying the leaden bin his penance for sleeping with Serena? Was he doomed to carry that guilt for all eternity?

The Curse of the Container Store—coming to a Blockbuster near you.

"I admit, fitting everything into a tiny dorm room is going to be a challenge." Blair paused at a shelf filled with clear plastic boxes and bins of every shape and color. She ran her hands over a huge set of colorful, stackable drawers, opening each drawer one by one. "But I had the Yale housing office fax me a floor plan this morning. If we loft my room-mate's bed way up close to the ceiling, we should have just enough space for a double bed and a dresser and maybe even a small love seat."

We?

"And it'll only be for a few weeks, anyway—before we find a cute little colonial house with ivy and one of those claw-footed bathtubs and a woodstove. That's what the kitchen stuff is for."

"But you don't cook," Nate pointed out. Suddenly the rest of what she'd said hit him in a rush. "And wait—we? But I'm going to be here in the city. . . ."

Blair tossed the set of drawers on top of the stack in the overflowing laundry bin. "Well, you could just take the train into the city in the morning and come back to New Haven at night. You get out of school at, like, three anyway."

She moved down the aisle and held up a yellow-and-white-striped pillow with attached lap desk, contemplating its usefulness.

Right, because she only buys useful things. Like wine racks.

After talking to her father and realizing there was a distinct possibility he might *not* be able to get Nate back into Yale—apparently colleges took those diploma things pretty seriously—Blair had gone into full contingency-plan mode. Nate would take the train into Manhattan in the morning and come home to her at night. They would be like one of those suburban families, where the dad commutes to the city every day and then comes back to his cozy home—not to mention his horny wife—at night. He would walk in the door, loosening his tie as he made his way toward the kitchen, and she'd be waiting for him in nothing but a red-and-white polka-dot apron and bright red toenail polish. Then they'd stay blissfully in each other's arms all night, kissing nonstop until dawn broke in the morning and Nate had to leave again—already pining for her as he waited for the morning train.

Okay, so it wouldn't be the most glamorous thing in the world to tell her new Yale friends that her boyfriend was still in high school, but she could easily tell them he had a great banking job and was going to work for a year before starting college. Or maybe he was just so smart he didn't need a college degree at all, he was one of those stock market prodigies she'd seen in the news.

The Prodigal Stoner?

Nate frowned. "Take the train every day? But doesn't it take like an hour and a half each way? Why don't I just stay here in the city during the week and visit you on weekends?"

"And leave you here all by yourself, with those slutty L'École girls? I don't think so," Blair responded tersely.

Nate shifted his eyes to the floor beneath her icy blue stare. "You can trust me," he mumbled. Besides, he wouldn't be with any L'École girls. He'd be with Serena. Not that he could actually say that out loud.

"You can do your *homework* on the train," she added decisively. Seriously, he was lucky she was even talking to him. Yale had been her dream her whole life, and for years now Nate had been a part of that dream, too. He'd pretty much shat all over her plans with his no-diploma bullshit. Maybe he could be a little more conscious of the fact that she was giving him a second chance, that she *needed* to keep her dreams intact.

She shook the lap desk up and down, trying to figure out what was in it, and then sat down cross-legged on the floor, placing it on her lap and mock-writing on it. Nate couldn't help but smile, watching her fake-scribble so intently like a little kid.

Blair signed her pretend letter with a flourish and then tossed the lap desk back on a shelf. Nate had never met anyone who knew so clearly what she wanted or didn't want. Each object she tossed into that laundry basket somehow fit perfectly into the life she had mapped out for herself years ago. But to him the color-coordinated pencil holders, the shower totes, and the dry-erase message boards looked like a bunch of useless junk, stuff he'd never use in a place he couldn't even picture. Yale was Blair's dream, not his.

"Okay, I think we're done here." She pulled a list out of her oversize brown leather Chloé bag and examined it carefully to make sure she hadn't forgotten anything.

Unlikely.

She led the way to the register, where she snatched up a little metal hook attached to a suction cup. "For your razor," she explained. Nate nodded in silence, his shoulders slouching under the weight of the heavy laundry basket. As crazy as Blair was, the fact that she was trying to squeeze him into her tiny dorm room made him fall in love with her all over again. Jesus, life was confusing.

If only those people in their neat blue aprons could help.

speak your mind, and the rest will follow

It was a ridiculously hot day in Prospect Park. Picnickers found shade underneath leafy green trees, and small children ran around wearing as little clothing as possible. The lake in the middle of the park was surrounded by people looking longingly at the water, wishing it were swimmable, and the dog beach was filled with wet pooches splashing and slobbering as their owners tried to keep up with them, leashes tangling into one huge knot.

Tiny beads of sweat trickled down Vanessa's back as she unloaded food from coolers onto a picnic table near the lake, its white tablecloth flapping in the breeze. She wiped a hand across her brow, wishing the wind were stronger. At least she'd ditched that hot, itchy blond wig. Her crazy night of table dancing at Coyote Ugly had been a lot of fun, but her wicked hangover the next morning, combined with her reflection in the mirror, was positively sobering. With black mascara streaked all over her face, red lipstick smeared clownlike around her mouth, and the blond wig hanging off her head like a dead animal, Vanessa hadn't felt sexy anymore—she'd just felt like roadkill. Today, she was back to her trademark shorn scalp and black combat boots, though she had worn a sky blue Betsey Johnson party dress for the occasion—Blair's influence, of course.

Of course.

She pulled a tray covered in tinfoil from the last cooler and peeked inside. Her sister's famous soy-tempeh lasagna. Of course the wedding food was gross—other than Vanessa, the entire Abrams family was vegetarian. It would be the first time she'd seen her parents since their visit in March, when their "found art" exhibit was on display at a gallery in the city. The exhibit had rather memorably included a chain of metal cheese graters tacked to a wall and a live horse, eating Caesar salad from a wooden bowl and pooping freely on the floor. During her parents' short stay, her father had even worn his full-length hemp skirt to a fancy party on Fifth Avenue.

So that's what started the men-in-skirts trend.

"Eggplant!" Vanessa's mother's voice rang out, calling her by her childhood nickname. Gabriela Abrams wore a brown-and-yellow African tribal robe despite the heat, and white ribbons tied at the ends of her long braided gray pigtails. She looked like a cross between Gandhi and Little Bo Peep.

"Hey Mom," Vanessa mumbled as her mother threw her arms around her. The robe was stiff and scratched Vanessa's bare arms.

Arlo Abrams appeared from behind Gabriela and joined in on the hug. "This place has good chi," he noted approvingly, pecking Vanessa quickly on the cheek. His long gray hair was braided down his back with another white ribbon tied in a bow at the bottom, and his body was cloaked in what appeared to be a white linen bathrobe. It was no surprise that Vanessa's parents had similar clothes and hairstyles. If Gabriela didn't dress Arlo, he'd simply walk around naked.

Let's hope nothing ever happens to her.

Vanessa fidgeted, smothered by her parents' embrace. Vanessa looked over her dad's shoulder and spotted Dan approaching from a distance, wearing a stiff blue button-down shirt and tie. She didn't even know he *owned* a tie. Her stomach flip-flopped when she saw him, and she suddenly wished she'd eaten breakfast that morning instead of drinking the Humphreys' gross instant coffee.

Don't worry—there's plenty of tempeh lasagna to go around.

"Mom, Dad, why don't you sit over here?" She ushered her parents toward one of the picnic tables arranged alongside the grass aisle, wiping the sweat off her brow. "I have to talk to Ruby and Piotr." She glanced at the two lovebirds who were standing at the makeshift altar/oak tree, trying to keep their hands off each other and not doing a very good job. In their usual unconventional manner, her parents chose to perch on top of the picnic table rather than sit on the bench.

"Our little girl's a maid of honor!" her mother cried, pulling a woven burlap handkerchief out from between her breasts.

Her father put his hand on his wife's knee and squeezed it. "Now, Gabriela, save your juices for the wedding!"

Vanessa made her way down the aisle, wondering if that's

what happened to you when you stayed in the woods of Vermont for too long.

Dan wove his way around picnic tables decorated with white balloons, hoping he'd have time to stick napkins in his armpits to sop up the sweat trickling down his sides and staining his light blue oxford shirt before reading his poem.

"Isn't this romantic?" Jenny's voice broke through his thoughts. She gazed up at the trees as she walked, a dreamy expression on her round, freckled face. She was wearing a pink, gauzy sundress that looked a heck of a lot more comfortable than the long-sleeve button-down shirt and tie Dan had worn for the occasion. "Easy for you to say, little Miss Barely There Sundress." He grunted and tried to unstick his shirt from his sweaty back.

"Oh, come *on*, Dan," Jenny scoffed. "Don't you just think weddings are the most amazing things?"

Actually, he did. There was something really romantic about watching two people stand up in front of their friends and family and promise to stay together forever. It was almost . . . noble. What would it be like to have someone who loved him enough to want to be with him forever? "Yeah, I guess so," Dan mumbled, weaving around a suspicious-looking clod of dirt.

They approached a large oak tree with rose petals sprinkled at its roots. Piotr stood beneath the tree, wearing a canary-yellow tuxedo and holding onto Ruby's hand. She wore an antique-looking ivory-colored dress with a hot-pink sash around the middle. And next to her was Vanessa, looking beautiful in a slinky blue slip dress. Dan looked down at her feet—

she was wearing her trademark combat boots. At least some things never changed. Dan dropped Jenny's arm and moved closer, taking in the curve of Vanessa's hips swaying under the thin material of the dress. He felt his pulse start to race.

"Hey." Vanessa's throaty voice broke into his thoughts, and he realized his feet had brought him directly in front of her. Ruby stood behind her, madly kissing Piotr even though there had been no "You may kiss the bride" yet. The ceremony hadn't even begun.

"Hey." Dan smiled shyly. "You look . . . uh, nice." Damn. He was a poet, and he couldn't come up with anything better than "nice"?

Roses are red, violets are blue, your lips are real nice, and so are you!

She smiled back shyly. "Um . . . just trying something new for the wedding."

"He means gorgeous." Jenny threw her arms around Vanessa. "I love your dress!"

"You guys can sit here if you want." Vanessa pointed at an empty bench, and Dan and Jenny sat down. "I have to go cue up the music and get my camera ready. You're up after Piotr's friends, okay?" she told Dan and then quickly made her way to a picnic table farther down the aisle, where one of Piotr's friends, wearing a white T-shirt with a black skull and crossbones printed on it, was fiddling with an iBook.

Dan inspected the other partygoers, who were mostly dressed in casual clothes—except for Piotr's friends, who were wearing black-, white-, and red-striped suits. They resembled a pack of hipster clowns just released from some bizarre Czech prison.

Just then a Czech ballad struck up, and Ruby and Piotr began skipping backwards hand in hand around the giant oak tree. Some guy in one of those weird striped suits whom Dan could only assume was Piotr's best man joined in the skipping and the crowd cheered.

Whatever happened to "Here Comes the Bride"?

They stopped skipping and stood off to the side as the Czech ballad quieted and a group of four striped-suited guys made their way over to the tree. One guy stuck out his tongue and wagged it obscenely.

"I am animal!" he yelled. "Filled with lust of carnivore!"

"I am love," the group behind him began to chant, crouching down on the ground. "I am love, I am love, I am love. . . ."

Ruby and Piotr held hands, entranced by their friends' display. Behind them, a yellow Lab chased a squirrel up a tree, barking loudly.

". . . love, love, love, love . . ."

Jenny's brow was wrinkled in thought, as if she were trying to decode the symbolism. Dan could barely contain his giggles—and there was only one other person who probably felt the same way. He glanced at Vanessa, who was standing off to the side, her camera trained on the altar as she desperately tried to keep a straight face. He caught her eye and grinned; then he stuck out his tongue and wiggled it, imitating Piotr's crazy friends.

The striped-suited guys finally stopped screaming and bowed to a confused smattering of polite applause. Jenny elbowed Dan in the ribs. "You're up."

He smiled nervously. He didn't even know if this poem

was any good, and now he was going to have to test-drive it in front of Ruby's entire wedding party—not to mention his ex-girlfriend.

No pressure.

Dan walked to the front of the crowd and opened his notebook. He cleared his throat and began to read, his voice wavering.

> *Open the fridge and put*
> *My heart on a plate.*
> *I'm just as you left*
> *me, and I taste even better*
> *leftover.*

He kept his eyes on the page. It took all his effort to decipher his own scrawl. As he focused on the white paper, he couldn't help feeling moved by what he'd written. He looked up and locked eyes with Vanessa.

> *Pale fury, why did you leave me?*
> *You're prickly*
> *in the morning. So*
> *prickly.*
> *This isn't a cooking show.*
> *This isn't chemistry or geography.*
> *It's physics. Pure physics,*
> *I'm falling fast and faster still.*
> *So fall with me. Fall down with me.*
> *And stay.*

Vanessa blushed deeply, her cheeks turning bright pink, and Dan found it hard to tear his gaze away from her. She looked so beautiful in her light blue dress, her skin glowing white against the sky blue fabric. . . .

The sound of clapping woke him from his reverie. "Um, thank you," he mumbled as he headed back to his seat in a daze. He sat back down, and Jenny grabbed his arm. "That was really great. But we've *got* to talk about something later," she whispered loudly in his ear.

"Um, okay," Dan whispered back. He patted his damp forehead with a paper napkin, just as Ruby's bandmates began cartwheeling down the rose-petaled aisle.

Guess someone didn't hire a wedding planner.

chips ahoy!

Nate leaned out over the bow of the boat and dipped his hand in the white froth of the waves. Chips stood in the *Belinda*'s stern—named for his late wife—as he simultaneously steered the huge wheel of the forty-foot yacht and nursed a scotch on the rocks. The white sails billowed in the wind. It was a perfect, cloudless summer day, but after his afternoon with both Blair and Serena yesterday, Nate's thoughts were more muddled than ever. When Chips had called this morning and invited him out for a sail on the Hudson, he'd jumped at the chance to get back out on the water and as far away from the girls as possible. A little scotch wouldn't hurt either.

Wearing a pair of white Ralph Lauren sailing pants and a navy blue cashmere sweater, Chips looked sophisticated and stately manning the wheel of the pristine yacht.

"This is the life," he boomed, his wizened hands resting lightly on the wheel. "The open sea, the sun, and the wind." He took a deep breath and tilted his head toward the sky, breathing the clear, warm air deep into his lungs.

"I guess." Nate scuffed the toe of his sneakers against the planks of the deck. He was waiting for a big lecture on thinking with his balls, Chips's favorite topic.

The old man's stubby white beard sparkled in the late afternoon sunshine. "So, what's crawled up your arse, then?" he asked, his Scottish accent rolling around in his mouth like marbles.

"Oh. I'm—I'm fine," Nate answered quickly. "Sort of."

Chips looked at him knowingly, waiting for Nate to continue. Nate took a deep breath, inhaling the briny air into his lungs, and, for the first time in days, felt his head start to clear. When he was out on the ocean, everything just felt so much simpler. The whole world was reduced to its essentials: sun, sky, and water.

"I have to repeat my senior year of high school," he heard himself say. "I'm not going to Yale. I'm sure my dad told you, right?"

Chips nodded. "Apparently you stole Viagra from your coach because you thought it would make you more of a man?" He raised an eyebrow.

"Uh, yeah," Nate mumbled, turning a little red. "But that's not the only problem. There are these two girls. . . ." his voice trailed off into the breeze. "I think I have to choose between them, and I don't know who to pick." The boat hit a rough patch of water and Nate staggered backward.

"Whoa, there, Natie!" Chips laughed out loud and grabbed hold of Nate's arm. He steered him toward the bench behind the wheel, indicating that he should steer. Chips sat down heavily beside him and placed a large blue pillow behind his back for support. He pulled out a fat brown cigar from his pants pocket and rolled it around between his lips. Then he lit the tip and puffed away until the end glowed amber and the stench of cigar smoke filled the air, sweet and acrid. Nate looked out at the water, steering the boat and fretting over what he'd just said. Talking about it meant thinking about it, and that was the last thing he wanted to do.

"Now." Chips blew a ring of smoke over his head. "Let's start from the beginning."

"Well . . . first there's Blair," Nate began tentatively as he steered the boat expertly between the green and red buoys marking the entrance to Manhattan's harbor. "We've been together forever, and I really love her. She likes getting her way, and she just . . . wants everything to be perfect. She's leaving for Yale tomorrow, and she wants me to come live in New Haven with her." He reached into his pocket and ran his finger over the smooth surface of the silver lighter Blair had given him two years ago. "But I've always loved Serena, too. She's . . . the complete opposite of Blair. All light and mystery and laughter, but hard to pin down."

Chips nodded, listening carefully.

"And to make things even more complicated, they've been best friends forever, and I'm always kind of messing things up between them."

Kind of?

He took a deep breath, and Chips passed him his glass of scotch. "I know it's idiotic, but I just can't make up my mind." Nate took a deep swallow and handed the glass gratefully back to Chips. "About *anything*." He glanced out at the water again, hoping for a sign—a *B*-shaped cloud in the sky or an *S* reflected on the water's surface. Instead, all he could see was the two girls' faces winking at him. *You know you love me*, each one was saying.

Chips took a sip of scotch and looked thoughtfully at Nate, his gold wedding band glinting in the light. "Well, Nate, I've always believed that honesty is an essential component to happiness—along with all of this," he said, gesturing with his hand at the boat. "But there's also something to be said for protecting someone you love from unnecessary pain." He stood and tapped the ashes of his cigar over the side of the yacht before sitting back down again. Nate noticed for the first time that Chips's left leg looked a little stiff as he walked.

"You're right," Nate mused aloud. He leaned his head back to take in the warmth of the sun on his face, and closed his eyes for a minute. "I mean, what good would it do to tell Blair about Serena anyway? She's going to Yale tomorrow. And maybe she'll go, and I'll miss her so much I'll be on the Metro-North every freaking Friday. Or maybe me and Serena will be together—so why decide now, right?"

"Nate . . ." Chips turned and looked at Nate thoughtfully, one hand resting on his stiff leg. "Don't twist my words to your own convenience. There's a difference between protecting someone else and protecting yourself. And it doesn't sound to me like you've done much thinking about what's really best for those two girls you claim to love so much."

"Yeah?" Nate stared glumly down at the wide-planked floor. He knew how hurt Serena would be if he told her he was going to see Blair every weekend at Yale. He also knew that if he told Blair what had happened with Serena, that shoe-throwing scene would look like a trip to the circus.

Step right up to see the man-eating Manolo-thrower!

"But there's this other thing," Nate went on, struggling with his thoughts. "Blair and Serena . . . they both know exactly what they want. They've got all these *plans*. . . . Everyone else knows what they want, but I just . . . *don't*. And even if I did, I feel like everything's been decided for me." The sparkling water seemed to laugh at him. Weeks before, the water had been full of promise. Now he just felt like he was sinking.

"That's the biggest pile of bullshit I've ever heard in all my living days," Chips growled. He leaned forward so that his face was inches from Nate's. "Look at me—I'm sixty-five years old, I've got a bad leg, and on Sunday morning, I'm setting sail around the world." He tapped his shin and it made a weird knocking sound. "Knock on wood, it'll be the best thing I ever did."

Knock on wood?

Nate's eyes widened in surprise at Chips's announcement—sail around the world? Damn.

Chips tossed the cigar overboard with a flourish. "Boy,"— his voice was grave—"I'm going to give you the exact same advice I gave your father twenty-five years ago." He paused, looking Nate dead in the eye. "You need to figure out what you really want—no more of this pussyfooting around. Remember, you've got to think with your balls, not with your dick."

Here we go again.

Nate nodded, looking at the floor, starting to understand

what Chips's perverse little saying really meant. He was right—all this going back and forth about Serena and Blair wasn't helping anyone. It was all about his dick, but there was nothing brave or manly about lying to the two people he loved most in the world.

"Every boy has to become a man sometime." Chips drained his glass and placed it on the teak plank floor. "Now's your turn."

Is that Scottish-old-man-speak for "Grow a sack"?

Disclaimer: All the real names of places, people, and events have been altered or abbreviated to protect the innocent. Namely, me.

hey people!

The Met party is finally here, and I've spent all day at Bliss in preparation for tonight's festivities, having every gorgeous inch of me waxed, buffed, and painted for the occasion. It's time to slide my kissably smooth body into my favorite new silk Gucci dress and paint the town pink—if I can ever get away from my mirror, that is. Translation: Better make this a quickie.

Tonight **B**'s kooky family will attempt to out-fête every fête ever held at the Met, so be sure to wear your end-of-summer-blowout-best. If you weren't invited, don't feel too bad. While you're stuck at home watching reruns of *Grey's Anatomy,* I'll be doing the exhausting work of keeping tabs on everyone who's anyone, which is clearly *everyone* at this particular party. Cheer up, wallflowers—I'll be sure to give you all the juicy gossip and gory details next time. Stay tuned!

And for those of you folks at home packing up for your big off-to-college bon voyage tomorrow morning, I've put together a handy checklist of what to pack. I know most of you are too busy fantasizing about your own personal, tear-filled goodbye scenarios, so let me assist you with the dorm-room basics:

(1) A pair of horn-rimmed glasses—Armani or Chanel—whether you really need them or not. Every college boy has a sexy-librarian fantasy—trust me.

(2) One leather-bound notebook and a silver Montblanc pen—perfect for passing notes to the hottie who sits in front of you every Tuesday/Thursday.

(3) A new iBook. Take notes in class while checking your e-mail—and send some irresistible messages to your latest fling. It's called multi-tasking, people, and I should know.

(4) A noise machine set to City Sounds. There's no place like home. . . .

(5) Your wits and charm! College is all about red tape, rules, and reg-ulations. You're all about breaking them! So remember, you'll catch more flies with honey than vinegar. A tub of actual honey might also be useful for smearing on all those cute boys in Econ 202—not that I'm actually advocating such behavior. . . .

sightings

N in **Times Square,** staring longingly at a Polo billboard featuring a guy on a sailboat, flanked by two gorgeous models—a blonde and a brunette. Wishful thinking? Well, if anyone can make it happen, it's our friend **N**. . . . **S** at **Barnes & Noble** in Union Square, hidden behind an enormous pair of white sunglasses as she leafed through *The Idiot's Guide to Finding an Agent*. Sounds like someone's got a new project! **B** yelling at an employee in the bedding section of **ABC Carpet and Home** because they don't carry Pratesi sheets in size extra-long . . . **K** and **I** at **Chloé,** trying on identical party dresses—will they be bringing identical dates? **C** buying a tuxedo at **Armani** (doesn't he already *own* one? Or ten?), harassing the sales staff with his requests for a tailor to make a matching one in primate size XS. Please. **V** making the trek from Prospect Park toward the Upper East Side via subway with some weirdos wearing red, black, and white seersucker suits . . . Newlyweds **R** and **P** kissing madly in a taxi on their way to **JFK.** Word is they're headed to . . . Iceland for the honeymoon. That's one way to get cool. **A,** looking surprisingly dapper, buying a tux at Barneys and flirting madly with the dreadlocked salesgirl—though rumor has it he only has eyes for a certain sometimes-bald, sometime-wigged party invitee . . . **B's** mom, **E**, at **Bang & Olufsen** electronics store on the Upper East Side, buying the biggest flat screen in the place, and then later on at **Marquee** in the Meatpacking District, rocking out in the DJ booth to the Black Eyed Peas. Uh-oh. Tonight is definitely going to be . . . entertaining.

Well, people, I need to go fix myself a pre-party Grey Goose martini with just a *splash* of vermouth, relax on the new pink velvet chaise lounge I bought myself for school (so Marie Antoinette goes to college!), and try to calm my nerves for the big, big night ahead. It's kind of hard to pay attention to writing to you kittens when my freshly painted fingernails in Chanel's Black Satin (yes, I have it and you don't) are *so* totally distracting. See you at the party.

You know you love me.

gossip girl

the gift that keeps on giving

Blair glided through the arched entry to the Met's newly reopened Greek and Roman exhibition space and glanced around the enormous limestone room. Corinthian columns propped up the forty-foot ceiling, where a domed skylight opened up to the night sky. Ancient war scenes emerged from gold-veined marble walls, and dozens of marble pillars propped up the very anatomically correct Greek statues. Waiters in gold togas with silver trays wove expertly through the throngs of superbly dressed revelers.

The party was a who's who of Blair's life. Standing in little clusters were the elegantly dressed parents of almost everyone she had grown up with, delicately sipping champagne and smiling politely while gossiping furiously under their breath. Serena's parents looked as tall, blond, and poised as ever, her mother, Lillian van der Woodsen, looking statuesque in a stunning silver Oscar de la Renta strapless gown that even most girls Blair's age couldn't pull off. Chatting with Mrs. van der Woodsen was Misty Bass, Chuck's mother, her hair piled high on her head like a sad imitation of Marie Antoinette.

Let them eat cake!

Next to Misty was her husband, Bartholomew, trying to get a peep down Isabel's mother, Titi Coates's low-cut black chiffon Badgley Mischka dress.

Like father, like son . . .

Mr. Coates, Isabel's middle-aged movie-star has-been father, was in a crisp black tuxedo, looking even more distinguished than usual standing next to the bulbous, sweaty Cyrus Rose, who was patting his pot belly and grabbing fistfuls of appetizers from every platter within reach. Blair shuddered in disgust but was comforted by the fact that she'd be seeing her real father tonight—if he ever made it. He'd called from the Charles de Gaulle airport in Paris eight hours ago to tell them they'd missed their flight because Ping was having a bit of fit, projectile vomiting all over the place, and that they might only catch the tail end of the party. They'd have to drop the twins off with the Waldorf Roses' nanny and then hurry over. Well, at least baby Yale could teach the little brats some manners.

The classical Greek statues crowding the walls made the party seem even more packed than it already was. Blair bent down to fix the strap of her cerulean patent-leather Manolos. The shoes were a perfect match to her night-sky blue Viktor & Rolf strapless party frock, and they gleamed like they'd been candy-coated, glistening in the candlelight. Something moved behind her and Blair whipped her head around, losing her balance and nearly toppling onto the cool marble floor. Did one of those Adonises just *move*? The chiseled statue gave her a wink as he changed from one classical pose to another. Blair looked closer and realized that mixed in with the classical Greek and Roman sculptures were models covered in chalky clay-colored paint.

"Blair-Bear!" A voice broke into Blair's thoughts and she looked up to see her father, looking dapper and handsome in a jet-black Gucci tux. His sandy brown hair was spiked up like a kid's, and the distinguished-looking laugh lines at the corners of his bright blue eyes were the only signs of his real age.

"Daddy!" She ran to her father's outstretched arms and instantly felt comforted. "I was sure you weren't coming." She buried her head in his crisp white shirt.

"I wouldn't dream of missing your big night, Blair-Bear. And you're going to be even happier when I give you your gift." Her father pulled back and stroked her cheek. He was wearing his emerald green cuff links that Blair had always thought were the same color as Nate's eyes. His tanned fingers were manicured, and his hand smelled of some new, powdery cologne.

Johnson & Johnson's Eau de Bebe Ass?

"What gift?" Blair liked the sound of that. "You already got me a car for graduation." She looked up at him expectantly. What could be better than a car? A plane? A horse? Her own New York apartment? Her own New Haven town house?

Way to think small.

Her father leaned in to whisper in her ear. "I talked to the dean of admissions at Yale." He paused, his bronzed face crinkled into his trademark case-winning grin.

Blair threw her arms around his neck. "Oh, Daddy!" She hugged him tightly. She didn't even need to hear the rest. "Thank you, thank you, thank you, thank you!"

A handsome, tall, tuxedoed man approached, streaks of gray in his dark, fashionably long, combed-back hair. "Giles!" Harold Waldorf called out to him. "Finally, you get to meet my little angel, Blair!"

"Enchanté!" Giles exclaimed, grabbing Blair's hand and kissing it. His teeth were blindingly white and his chocolate-brown eyes warm. "She is *magnifique*!" he exclaimed in a heavy French accent.

Blair blushed and gave him a little curtsy. She was finally starting to feel like the belle of the ball. About time.

Didn't she *just* arrive?

"Blair, dear, we have to check on the babies." Her father gave her a quick hug. "We'll be back soon though. I think you've got some good news to share with someone anyway."

Giles kissed Blair first on one cheek, and then the other. *"Au revoir, jolie mademoiselle,"* he bid her graciously.

Blair grinned, not even caring that her father had just arrived and was now leaving again. Nate was back into Yale, handsome French men were kissing her hands, and this was *her* party. All was right with the world. "Say hi to Ping and Pong for me," she called after them, feeling particularly generous.

After her father and Giles left, Blair scanned the room for Nate. Instead, she found Serena standing by the bar, her elegant silver Valentino silk cocktail dress shining in the light, thin silver bands cinching her tiny waist. Blair walked toward her, her cobalt blue Viktor & Rolf gown with its intricately beaded bodice trailing silkily behind her like an inky pool of water. She smiled giddily to herself. Serena might look stunning, but next year she'd be stuck in the dirty old city while

Blair and Nate were miles away in their cozy New Haven love nest, feeding each other cornichons and oysters and all sorts of other cute, couple-y foods. Her father might not have given her a town house yet, but her birthday was coming up in November. . . .

Well, her mom did buy her an island.

"Hey." Blair kissed the air near Serena's cheeks.

Mwah! Mwah!

"Isn't this wild? Check out the naked guys in body paint over there!"

Serena set her empty champagne flute down on the faux-marble bar behind her and grabbed a full one. She hated how nervous she felt around Blair. How much did Blair know about her and Nate? How much would Serena be brave enough to tell her? "It's *beyond.* Your mom really outdid herself." Maybe it was best just to act cheerfully, casual, like she wasn't about to steal her best friend's boyfriend right out from under her nose.

Blair pushed closer to the bar, practically knocking over Rain Hoffstetter. Rain's chestnut brown hair was usually sweaty from soccer and pulled back in a lopsided ponytail, but tonight she was wearing it in loose waves around her face, and a black-and-silver Calvin Klein gown made her athletic body look slightly less manly.

But only slightly.

Next to Rain stood Nicki Button, famous for her two nose jobs—which Blair didn't think had done her all that much good. Rain and Nicki fought more than Serena and Blair did, mostly over clothes, not boys, but since both were headed to Vassar, maybe they'd made their peace.

Until five minutes from now, when they both realize they're wearing the same Prada slingbacks in silver and white. Totally last spring.

"Excuse me, ladies." Both girls practically jumped backwards as Blair reached past them and grabbed a flute of champagne. She turned back to Serena and clinked her glass against her friend's. "To us," she toasted heartily. She could afford to be a little magnanimous. She'd gotten exactly what she wanted—as usual.

The two girls downed the contents of their glasses in one gulp. Then Blair put a delicate hand on her hip. "Have you seen Nate?" she asked, raising one perfectly arched dark eyebrow. "I need to talk to him."

Serena grabbed another glass of champagne. She wished there were some simple solution to this, but there wasn't. Blair looked so happy tonight, she didn't want to ruin the party for her. She and Nate would just have to wait to tell her that they were together when Blair was happily settled in at Yale, and then maybe she wouldn't even mind that much. Finally she took the flute of champagne away from her lips. "I haven't seen him yet," she admitted.

Blair had noticed Serena stiffen at the sound of Nate's name, and for a second she almost felt sorry for her—what with that desperate love letter and all. She was dying to tell Serena about getting Nate into Yale, but it just seemed wrong to tell her before telling Nate himself. After all, Serena probably still harbored some desperate dream that she and Nate would live happily ever in the city together while Blair was up in New Haven. Like that would *ever* happen.

"Well, I'm off to find him," Blair chirped gaily.

As soon as she sauntered away, Rain and Nicki quickly filled the spot next to Serena. Rain held a cocktail napkin in her hand, and Nicki held a pen as they awkwardly tripped over themselves to get Serena's attention. So that was it— they wanted Serena's autograph. To Blair's surprise, she didn't even feel jealous. People were always drooling over Serena, and they always would be. What did she care? She had everything she'd ever wanted.

And by "everything," she meant a living, breathing person, right?

Blair was about to check the neighboring European sculpture room when she spotted Nate out of the corner of her eye. He was leaning against a tall Romanesque column near the dance floor, looking glum. Jeremy Scott Tompkinson, Nate's skinny, sideburned friend from school and Anthony Avuldsen, looking incredibly blond and athletic, were periodically punching him in the arm, clearly trying to pry him away from the column and get him to dance or drink or at least smile. Nate just waved his hand at them, so they shuffled off to the dance floor alone, dancing like idiots three feet apart from each other. Well, if the sight of his stoner friends jerking their arms and legs spastically on the dance floor couldn't cheer up Nate, Blair knew something that would. She pushed through the dancing crowd, practically trampling over Laura Salmon, dressed in a salmon-colored silk Dior dress that sagged in the chest and was way too old for her.

Salmon in salmon. How appropriate.

Blair bounded up to Nate, throwing her arms around

him. "Guess what?" she demanded, her blue eyes sparkling. "I have really big news." Nate smiled at her wordlessly, but his eyes were a million miles away. She plowed ahead anyway, grabbing his black bow tie and forcing him to pay attention. "So I told my dad about your little problem, and he talked to Yale, and *I got you in!*" She threw her arms tightly around him again and whispered in his ear. "Now we can be together at Yale—*just like we planned!*" Her whole body shook with excitement, but Nate just stood there, stock-still. He'd hardly even hugged her back. She pulled back and looked into his stunning green eyes, searching them questioningly.

"Wow." Nate shook his head slowly. "I don't know what to say." He blinked, trying to process what she'd just said. Go to Yale, for real? Not just take the train to New Haven twice a day and pretend he went there? "Blair . . . you're amazing."

Now that was more like it. "I know."

Blair was about to give Nate a kiss he'd never forget when she spotted her mother approaching from across the room, wearing an ivory-colored floor-length Versace gown encrusted with millions of tiny gold sequins, and Gucci stilettos that looked like they were made of twenty-four-carat gold ropes. Ever since Eleanor had lost all her baby weight, she'd been wearing tacky look-at-me outfits, but Blair was too happy to be annoyed with her crazy mother tonight.

Davita Fjorde strode alongside Eleanor, wearing a black Miu Miu minidress and hot pink satin Miu Miu peep-toe platforms, barking orders into her headset. "No, no, no!" she hissed. "Just wash him off and get him out there as a regular waiter. *Nonflammable* paint only! I don't need a human torch streaking through my party!" She smiled tightly at Eleanor and then murmured into her headset, "Okay, photo one, you're up once we find Blair."

Blair knew that her mom and Davita were preparing to drag her off somewhere so she could pose for some god-awful pictures her mother would no doubt blow up so large you'd be able to see every one of Blair's pores.

Knowing they'd be separated momentarily, she leaned in to whisper in Nate's ear. "Our train leaves at 10 A.M. tomorrow morning from Grand Central," she told him softly, loving the smell of Acqua Di Parma on his skin—a fresh, lemony scent she knew he only used on special occasions. "I know we could drive, but this will be so much more romantic!" She drew back and smiled sweetly up at him again.

Nate had never seen Blair look so beautiful—or so happy. Her skin was golden brown, her face rosy against her bright blue dress. The diamond studs in her tiny earlobes shone in the light. Across the room, Serena was standing at the bar, wearing a long, gauzy silver dress, her golden hair falling in gleaming tendrils down her bare back. Her face was in pro-file, and her features were so unbelievably gorgeous his breath caught in his chest. He forced himself to shift his attention back to Blair—his beautiful girlfriend, still wrapped in his arms. The sight of her glowing, hopeful face tore at his heart. Yale. He was going to Yale. He should have been ecstatic, but he didn't know what to say or even what to feel. He pulled her close and breathed in the familiar honey-almond scent of her hair. His chest felt tight, and suddenly it was hard to breathe. Blair nestled into him like there was no place she'd rather be. "I love you," he whispered into her hair, hoping the words would ground him. But now, more than ever before, Nate felt like a small wooden dinghy set adrift.

Better start rowing, boy.

what goes around comes around. . . .

Serena's chest felt hollow as she watched Nate bury his face in Blair's perfumed neck. They looked so ecstatic and in love that she had to turn away. What was going on? She'd thought they were barely even speaking anymore. Serena grabbed a flute of champagne and downed it, reaching for another. The golden bubbles tickled her nose and she sneezed twice. If she had to watch them practically do it right in front of her, she'd better drink herself silly.

Of course all she had to do was wait, but the waiting was killing her. Blair was would be off to Yale in the morning and Nate would be staying right here in New York. Finally, she'd have him all to herself, and years from now, when Blair came home from Yale with her perfect collegiate investment banker fiancé and Nate and Serena were in love—true, spend-the-rest-of-your-life-together love—they'd laugh at the idea that Blair and Nate had ever even been together. It would be some warm but distant memory, like Buck Naked or the alligator costume. Blair would be her maid of honor, and just before walking down the aisle she'd whisper in Serena's ear that she was sorry she'd stood in their way all those years. *Of course* Serena and Nate were meant to be together.

Right. Because it's just like Blair to do that.

Kati Farkas and Isabel Coates stumbled by, teetering on their obscenely high Manolos and clutching each other's arms to keep from falling down, their eyes glassy and bright.

"Hey Serena!" Kati giggled, her zebra-striped Norma Kamali dress sliding down her nonexistent chest. "You don't have a date either? You should come with us—we're going to snag some Greek gods!"

Isabel erupted in a fit of giggles. "How about that one?" She pointed across the room at a painted figure wearing a barely there loincloth made entirely out of silvery olive branches. Kati started to hiccup uncontrollably, which made both girls laugh even harder. The painted god grinned at Isabel, his white-plaster curls falling over his painted and powdered angular features.

"Hold this," Isabel slurred, handing her drink to Kati. She staggered over to the god and climbed up on the small dais supporting him. Without so much as a hello, she grabbed the male statue and kissed him, white paint smearing her black crepe D&G Grecian gown.

Way to leave town with a bang.

Serena turned away and checked her reflection in the long mirror hanging behind the bar. After much deliberation—though not nearly as much as Blair—she'd chosen a low-cut silvery Valentino cocktail dress with silver trim around the waist. Her legs looked endless beneath the midlength skirt, finished off with a pair of gold Christian Louboutin sandals with their trademark red soles. Normally she preferred one of her brother's old BROWN T-shirts and her ratty Sevens, but tonight she felt a bit like Cinderella, hoping to win the prince's heart. She glanced back at where Nate and Blair had been standing. Nate was now alone, leaning against the wall and staring pensively out into the crowd, with Blair nowhere in sight.

Serena pushed through the throng of revelers, waving at Blair's little brother Tyler and his girlfriend, Jasmine, who were ballroom dancing rather adorably, despite the fact that Gwen Stefani's "Hollaback Girl" was playing. Tyler just tipped his head at her, clearly engrossed in his waltz. Serena kept walking until she was standing right where she belonged—directly in front of Nate. Her breath caught in her throat as she looked at him. In his black Hugo Boss tux, crisp white shirt, and shiny dark Prada loafers, he really did look princely.

"Hey." His face broke into a wide grin when he saw her.

"Hey, yourself." She stepped a little closer and reached for his hand. He closed his fingers around hers, and Serena breathed a sigh of relief at the warm touch of his skin. "You okay?"

"Yeah." Nate shrugged his shoulders. "I guess." He dropped her hand, his eyes shifting nervously away and then back again.

"It'll be easier tomorrow, after Blair leaves." She took his hand again and squeezed it tightly in her own. It was torture to have to stand next to him like this and not really be able to touch him. All she wanted was to pull him close and kiss him, until Blair, the party, and the whole world fell away, leaving just the two of them.

"Yeah." Nate's eyes were shiny with emotion. "You look

really beautiful tonight." His voice trembled. Was he struggling to keep his hands off her, just like she was?

She tossed her long blond hair over one shoulder. "My hair does look a little better when I brush it," she joked. Behind them Tyler spun Jasmine around and around. Jasmine looked like she was about to puke all over her cute purple plaid satin Marc Jacobs halter dress.

Nate bit his lip nervously. "Blair wants me to meet her at Grand Central tomorrow at ten." He wanted to tell her the rest—that Blair wanted to meet him there because she'd gotten him back into Yale, that he wasn't sure whether to go or not go. But Serena looked so beautiful and trusting, he didn't have the heart.

Or the balls.

"Well, we should both go—I want to see her off too." Serena squeezed his arm. One more day and they'd be together forever.

Nate wrapped his arms around her and held her close, breathing in the familiar scent of patchouli and lilies—a scent he knew as well as his own. He'd loved her ever since he could remember, but he'd loved Blair too. And he wanted to be with both girls, always and forever.

So why don't they all move to Utah?

"I love you," Serena said, her voice catching in her throat.

Nate held her, squeezing her tight. "I love you too."

And true love never lies.

v is a femme fatale

Vanessa leaned against a podium, sipping champagne as she tried to subtly rearrange her light blue silk Betsey Johnson party dress. She tugged at the ridiculously short hem and wished for the hundredth time that night that she'd chosen something more comfortable—and in her usual shade of pure black—instead of something so girly. She'd changed into a pair of ridiculously uncomfortable heels after the wedding, worried the bouncers would take one look at her combat boots and kick her out of Blair's fancy party. Maybe she'd find a table and coax Dan into giving her a foot massage. If he ever got here.

She glanced around the wildly extravagant Roman-themed party, searching for his mop of unruly brown hair. After their intense eye-lock while he read his poem aloud at the wedding, Vanessa was dying to talk to him. But she'd lost him during Ruby's crazy reception and could only hope that Jenny would drag him up to the party sometime soon. Vanessa had made sure both their names were added to the list; it was only a matter of waiting. In the meantime, she was going to enjoy herself.

She tried to look sultry, throwing her shoulders back and arching her back the way Blair had taught her. But then she felt a little splash on her leg—of course, she'd spilled her drink. She bent down and tried to wipe the droplets off her bare calf with her cocktail napkin, her dress riding dangerously high. She straightened. It hadn't occurred to that she couldn't do the same things in a dress that she did in jeans. She quickly scanned the room to make sure no one had seen her privates.

But damn if some dude wasn't headed straight toward her. No, not some dude, *Aaron.* Of course he was here, he was Blair's stepbrother—why hadn't she thought of that? But when did he get so . . . *hot?* His hair was knotted in dreadlocks that tumbled messily over his forehead, and his brown eyes sparkled against his tanned skin. He wore a dark green, three-button suit, and a green silk tie hung loosely around his neck. She stood up straight and tried to look composed, but as she did the pedestal she'd been leaning against shook. She looked up to see the female nude statue above her move suddenly, before it struck a new pose.

Vanessa hadn't seen Aaron since they'd broken up at the beginning of the summer. After they'd been together for only a few weeks, Aaron had given her a silver friendship ring, which was totally corny—and, for Vanessa, a total dealbreaker. She'd immediately thrown it in a drawer. Considering she hadn't been able to stop sleeping with Dan at the time, it was probably for the best.

"Hey, stranger!" Aaron grabbed her hand, pulling her into a hug. He finally released her, stepping back to look her up and down with obvious approval. "You look gorgeous. I was hoping to see you tonight." His red lips curved into a big smile.

Vanessa raised her eyebrows. "It's good to see you too. Want to trade shoes?" Aaron laughed. "I'd look pretty hot in those," he agreed, pointing at her light blue

Robert Clergerie heels.

"So, how was your road trip?" she asked, remembering that a couple of months ago she was supposed to be on that trip. She'd stayed behind to be with Dan, and now he was gay.

Good call on that one.

"It was great." Aaron kept his eyes on Vanessa's décolletage as the busty statue above them rearranged her position, leaning forward annoyingly as if she were part of their conversation. "But Mookie and I missed you."

Vanessa felt herself blush. "So, um, when are you leaving for Harvard?"

"Tomorrow. I can't believe I'm leaving town. Sometimes I think it'd be great to be in the city, go to Columbia or NYU—like you." He pushed a stray dreadlock behind his ear.

"I don't know," Vanessa mused. "Lately it's felt weird, knowing everyone is going to leave to try out new places and I'll still be here, all on my own." She took a sip of her vodka tonic—she couldn't believe she was pouring her heart out to Aaron, of all people, whom she hadn't seen in months. Still, it felt nice to finally voice what had been weighing on her for so long. Between Ruby's marriage and Dan's coming out, nobody had thought to ask how *she* was doing in a while.

"If I know one thing about you, Vanessa Abrams, it's that

you'll be fine on your own." Aaron grinned. "Though I can't imagine you'll be on your own for very long. Kind of makes me wish I was staying all over again."

As soon as he said the word *stay*, the spell of Aaron's warm brown eyes was broken. Yes, he was gorgeous, and yes, he obviously still liked her, but all Vanessa could hear was Dan's poem. *Fall down with me. And stay.* She kept replaying the way he'd looked deep into her eyes as he'd uttered those lines—as if he'd written them just for her. But if that were true, then where the hell was he?

Forget Greek gods. The theme for this party should have been "Love Stinks."

hands off my lady, bob marley

Dan ducked around a Greek sculpture, vodka gimlet in one hand, feeling particularly small and insignificant beneath the giant marble statues looming over him. They were just the right height that their, um, anatomy was practically being shoved in his face. And it wasn't exactly a turn-on.

Jenny sipped from her glass of champagne, her eyes wide with excitement. "Don't you want to dance?" she demanded. "Come on, there are enough cute guys here for both of us."

"You've got to be kidding me." Dan gulped his drink, the ice clinking against his teeth and numbing his tongue. "I wouldn't even know how to *ask* another guy to dance, much less dance with him."

Why couldn't everyone just leave him alone? After the intense moment at the wedding, locking eyes with Vanessa while he read his poem, Dan wasn't sure what to think. It was like something was still . . . *there* between them. But then, just as he was about to finally talk to her, five different Williamsburg guys had come up to him to personally let him know how "touched" they were by his words. Before he knew it, he'd ended up with five phone numbers in his pocket . . . and five more assurances that he was gay.

Jenny rolled her eyes. "That's the easy part. You just sort of mush your bodies together and grind." She gave her hips a slight wiggle. Dan glanced nervously at one of the almost-naked man statues. He was so not ready for grinding.

"Hey, look, it's Vanessa." Jenny pointed toward the far corner of the immense hall. Dan craned his neck to get a good look, peering through the mass of beautifully dressed moving bodies. He finally spied her prickly head bobbing excitedly as she spoke to a handsome, dreadlocked Bob Marley wannabe. It was Blair's stepbrother, Aaron, who had nearly succeeded in stealing Vanessa away from him once before. "Who's the guy she's talking to?" Jenny asked, her voice full of admiration. "He's *cute*!"

Dan slouched, completely dejected. Vanessa and Aaron were laughing and flirting, and they'd probably get back together before the night was even over. Looking so beautiful and confident in her sky blue sheath dress, it was hard to believe Vanessa had ever been his girlfriend. Dan was a sexually confused, cream-puff-eating geek who was about to drive cross-country in a car that was practically extinct. What had she ever seen in him, anyway?

"What's wrong?" Jenny demanded, titling her head in concern when Dan didn't respond. He could feel her examining him closely. She definitely seemed more self-assured after her summer away, and in a couple of days she was headed to boarding school.

Kids. They grow up so fast.

"Nothing's wrong," he snapped, gazing forlornly into his

glass. He wished Jenny would just dance away into the night so he could sit by himself and be as morose as his poetry.

Life of the party, isn't he?

"Oh my God!" Jenny shouted excitedly. "You're *jealous*!"

She put her hand on his arm and looked earnestly up in his face. "This is exactly what I wanted to talk to you about. I've tried to be supportive all along, and stop me if what I'm about to say is totally off base but—"

Dan looked up into his sister's big brown eyes. He was reminded of the hundreds of times they'd sat in their crumbling apartment eating Rufus's disgusting leftovers and talking in half-sentences but understanding exactly what the other was saying.

"Honestly," Jenny went on, "you don't seem very gay to me."

"I *don't*?" Dan grabbed her freckled shoulder.

"Sorry." She shrugged.

Across the room Aaron and Vanessa were flirting mercilessly. Dan was practically dying to go over there and punch the guy out. Jenny was right—he *was* jealous. He wasn't gay, despite what his mom and everyone else in the world seemed to think. When he'd kissed Greg, he'd been drunk and confused. Actually he hadn't even been *awake* for part of it.

He frowned, not sure what to do now that he wasn't gay anymore.

Jenny poked him in the gut. "So talk to her, you idiot!" she squealed excitedly. "Get her away from that boy so I can flirt with him."

Dan gave his brilliant little sister a quick kiss on the cheek. Across the room, Vanessa's face was flushed and gorgeous in the museum's soft light. Despite the vodka sloshing around in his head, everything was finally completely clear. He didn't want to just *talk* to Vanessa, he wanted to *be* with her. He loved her because she was *Vanessa—his* Vanessa. And he was going to get her back.

Dan crossed the room determinedly, his gaze fixed on her. She looked so beautiful, teetering unsteadily in her glittery blue heels. He wanted to be there to catch her if she fell. He marched past table after table, knocking over drinks and stepping on people's toes.

It felt like it took years for him to finally reach her. "So, how about a dance?" Aaron was saying, holding his hand out to her.

Dan reached out and grabbed her hand instead. "Excuse me, but if she's going to dance, I'd rather it was with me."

Vanessa's chocolate brown eyes grew huge. "Dan—you're here."

"I'm sorry, Aaron," Dan apologized with a slow smile, his eyes never leaving Vanessa's face. "But I need her for a minute. Actually, longer than that."

Aaron stared momentarily and then kissed Vanessa wistfully on the cheek. "Take care." He nodded to both of them as he took off for the bar.

Dan's arms circled Vanessa's waist. *You're beautiful, I'm not gay, I love you, I want you back.* He was about to say all of it in a big, confused rush, but then Vanessa kissed him on the lips, a long, lingering, very ungay kiss full of promises and apologies.

"I know," she murmured, holding him. He brushed his chin over the top of her prickly head and smiled happily. The best part was, they were still roommates, if only for one more night.

Looks like someone's not going to get much sleep tonight.

nothing like a little father-son bonding

Nate stood at the mostly undiscovered bar under the enormous main staircase, as far from the other partygoers as he could get. A toga-toting bartender poured amber liquid into his empty glass for the hundredth time that night. Things were crazy tonight, so he might as well make them even crazier. And if drinking didn't work, he was going to go out and sit on the steps of the Met and smoke all six of the emergency joints in his pocket.

Old habits die hard.

He raised his glass to take another slug and felt a big slap on his back, causing him to nearly choke. He turned to see his father standing right beside him.

"There you are." The Captain was wearing his custom-made English double-breasted tuxedo, a black satin bow tie set at his throat, his gray hair neatly combed back from his aristocratic face. He set his empty champagne glass down on the bar next to Nate's.

"Well, I hear someone's bailed you out—as usual," the Captain proclaimed. "You're one lucky boy. Do you know that?"

Nate ran his hands through his hair, nodding mechanically. Leave it to his dad to reduce him to a drunken asshole with no dick.

"Though I suppose I shouldn't give Lady Luck all the credit for your good fortune. You've got one industrious girlfriend," his father remarked. "You don't deserve her."

Nate blushed and looked at his feet. He knew his dad was right—he *hadn't* done a goddamn thing to deserve getting back into Yale—he'd simply been lucky. Lucky that he had a girlfriend who didn't give up until she got her way. Lucky that *she* had a father who was on the board of trustees.

Blair sidestepped one of the Adonises as she walked over, her azure dress floating around her like waves. Through the window behind her, Nate could see the cars flying down Fifth Avenue, some of them slowing as they passed the gala happening inside.

"Blair, darling." The Captain slipped an arm around Blair's tiny shoulders. "I was just telling my ungrateful son here that he doesn't deserve you." He cracked a smile. Nate hated it when his father tried to be charming—especially when it was at his expense.

"That's true." Blair's blue eyes sparkled with mischief. "But he knows that." She slipped her arm through Nate's and rested her head on his shoulder. It occurred to Nate that she'd come to rescue him from his father. He really *didn't* deserve her.

"This calls for a toast," Captain Archibald announced jovially, picking up two champagne flutes filled with golden liquid from the bar and handing one each to Nate and Blair before raising his own glass. "You're Yalies now." The

Captain motioned in their direction with his full glass. "Here's to the navy blue!"

Nate opened his mouth to say something, anything, but nothing came out. A Yalie? He certainly didn't feel like one. "You know, Dad," he began, choosing his words carefully, "I wanted to thank you for introducing me to Chips—er, Captain Chips." He paused to swallow a gulp of champagne. "He really taught me a lot about being a man . . . and uh . . . thinking with your . . . you know."

Blair nodded distractedly, and Nate followed her gaze— she was staring at Chuck Bass, of all people. Nate was about to be jealous when he noticed that Chuck was standing with a nerdy blond spectacled kid in a too-small tux, his orange-and-blue monkey-patterned socks exposed above his scuffed loafers. Chuck was holding his chattering, screeching monkey up to an enormous, ancient mirror so the monkey could admire his tuxedo and hot pink bow tie identical to Chuck's. Wow. And Nate thought *he* had problems.

Nate turned away and searched his father's face for some kind of recognition or understanding, but Captain Archibald seemed oblivious to what Nate was trying to say.

His father smiled and clinked glasses with Nate again. "I'm glad it helped, son. You certainly are one lucky kid," he repeated, looking at Blair appreciatively. Blair giggled and squeezed Nate's hand. Nate just buried his nose in his champagne.

Glug, glug, glug.

"Nathaniel!" He heard someone call from behind him and turned around to see his mother approach from the neighboring Egyptian exhibit. She wore bright red lipstick, a red poppy in her dark hair, and a sweeping red gown that looked like it had come straight from the set of *Carmen*. "Darling," she cooed in her French accent, kissing her son on either cheek. "Your father's told me the good news. I'm so glad. But I'm afraid we can't stay to celebrate—we're off to the opera."

Throughout Nate's life, his mom had spent more time shopping and attending the opera or a gala to benefit the opera than she had with her only son, leaving precious little to talk about. Once a year, at Christmas time, she met him for a drink at the bar in the Carlyle Hotel, where she'd attempt to pry into his love life. It was totally embarrassing.

"I'm so . . . glad you're glad, Mom," he responded lamely.

"Congratulations, *mon cherie*." His mother gave him another kiss, squeezing his hand before she dragged the Captain away to their waiting town car.

Nate turned to Blair, ready to confess to her how confused and freaked out he felt, but she was chatting with the bartender while he tried pathetically to get her number. Maybe Blair had bigger balls than he did, but she couldn't figure this out for him. No one could.

Except maybe that joint in his pocket.

this is your life, b. . . .

Eleanor Waldorf Rose stood on the landing of the Met's great staircase, a tiny silver microphone in one hand. The gold sequins of her gown glittered in the spotlight, casting a disco-ball effect across the Met's Great Hall. Blair thought she looked like a seventies-era Statue of Liberty.

"Hello everyone," she chirped, beaming at the collection of partygoers who had been shuffled from the Ancient Greek room into the Met's impressive entryway. "I hope you're having a good time!"

"We are!" Cyrus cheered from his perch on the steps below. He raised his nearly empty glass, his eyes bulging idiotically. Blair sank a little lower in the thronelike seat Davita had provided for her next to a table adorned with special gold-flecked Magnolia cupcakes. She could tell things were about to get extremely embarrassing.

"I can't believe all of you wonderful children are leaving for college tomorrow," Eleanor gushed into the microphone. "It seems like just yesterday that we were dropping you off at preschool! And now you're all grown up."

The crowd cheered wildly. The anticipation of being at college in only a day or two was getting to them. Eleanor nodded at Davita, who was in the far corner of the room, murmuring instructions into her headset. "But before you go forward into your new lives," Eleanor continued, "I thought it might be fun to take a look back and see just how far you've all come!" she crowed. She stepped back and the lights dimmed. A huge screen was lowered from above, as if it had come from the heavens.

Nope, just from Bang & Olufsen.

Blair picked at an uneaten cupcake, steeling herself for "Lean on Me" or whatever cheesy-ass song her mom had chosen to set the slide show to.

What you gon' do with all that junk?

All that junk inside your trunk?

Suddenly the first notes to the Black Eyed Peas' "My Humps" filled the air. Had her mom seriously picked this song for the slide show of Blair's *life*? Wasn't it a song about *boobs*? Or *butts*? Or *vaginas*? What in hell was she smoking?

And where can we get some?

Photographs began flashing over the screen. First came Blair's kindergarten class picture, Blair and Serena holding hands and kneeling in the front row wearing matching dorky white turtlenecks. She remembered that they'd had to take the class picture five times, because every time the photographer got to "cheese," Blair and Serena had promptly stuck their tongues out, not caring that all the other girls were getting fidgety and annoyed—that had made it all the more fun.

Next came a photo of the two girls at tennis camp, the one summer Serena's parents had forced her to go. Both girls wore their hair in ponytails, their skin tan against their tennis whites. Serena was playing her racket like a guitar, her eyes closed as she strummed the strings in a rock-star pose, while Blair was doubled over laughing right next to her, tears in her eyes.

Blair looked up at the enormous photograph, and much to her surprise, her own eyes began to fill with tears. She wiped them away hastily, trying not to ruin her makeup. Looking up at their smiling, happy faces, she couldn't help really missing Serena—and how simple things used to be. She couldn't believe that as of tomorrow they'd be in two totally different places, living totally different lives. Blair looked over at Serena, who was sitting at a table next to Chuck and his disgusting primate. On the other side of the table were Kati and Isabel, Isabel perched on a chalky white fake-statue model's lap.

At least someone's enjoying the party!

Serena turned and caught Blair's eye. She grabbed a plate from the table in front of her and pretended to strum it like she'd played the tennis racket in the picture, putting it back down again and giggling. Then she blew Blair a kiss.

Blair laughed, then sniffled. For the first time in their lives, she and Serena wouldn't be able to walk over to each other's houses whenever they felt like it, or sit on the steps of the Met gossiping for hours. Soon she and Nate would be at Yale, living together like real grown-ups, and Serena would be here in the city, busily becoming the next big thing. Blair shook her head, bewildered by how much things had changed in what really was so little time.

Serena watched Blair's foxlike profile as the slide changed

in time to Eleanor's completely ridiculous music selection. On-screen, Serena, Nate, and Blair were ten years old, eating Fudgsicles in Central Park on Blair's favorite navy blue Yale blanket. Nate sat cross-legged while the girls perched precariously on each of his knees. Serena's eyes filled with tears at the realization that even back then, they were sharing him.

Sharing is caring, right?

As much as things had changed, some things had always been the same. She looked around for Nate and spied him standing near the Met's front doors, his gaze locked on the screen. She raised her hand and waved, trying to get his attention, but he didn't see her. She grabbed the snowy white tablecloth in her fist and squeezed the material between her fingers as Chuck's white monkey climbed onto her arm and began picking at her blond hair.

"Sorry," Chuck whispered, removing the monkey from her shoulder and placing it in his lap. "If you don't behave"—he wagged his index finger in the monkey's face—"I'm sending you to the zoo. And I think we both know they don't have cupcakes and champagne there."

Vanessa watched the screen, surprised to see her own enormous face smiling down at her as an image of her Williamsburg apartment appeared. Her shaved head was tilted toward Blair's shining brunette mane, their tongues stuck out at the camera, near-white polish gleaming on Blair's nails as she held one hand up in the peace sign. Vanessa smiled, still clinging to Dan's hand as she waited for the next slide.

"It's so weird that you guys were roommates," Dan muttered.

"Totally," Vanessa whispered. But even though they still had nothing in common, Vanessa was glad she and Blair were friends. As different as they were, they'd accepted their differences and painted each other's toenails. And wasn't that what true friendship was about? Vanessa nearly gagged at her own sentimentality, but it was all true, so fuck it.

Dan stared up at a large photograph of Serena at the Raves show, suddenly noticing himself up on stage in the background, sweat dripping from his black T-shirt, his hair flying as he jumped into the air, mike cord wrapped around one skinny arm. He laughed at his own idiotic antics and squeezed Vanessa's fingers for reassurance. Vanessa had been with him through every bizarre moment over the last year—from back when he was just a nerdy guy scribbling in a shabby notebook all the time, to a published poet in the *New Yorker*, to an almost rock star.

Almost. Except for the whole puking-on-stage part.

And now, on the verge of a road trip out West that would lead him God knew where, she was still here—and still holding his hand.

You love my lady lumps. Check it out!

The screen flicked to an ad for Serena's Tears. Serena stood in Central Park in a skimpy yellow dress, one lone tear glistening on her smooth, perfect cheek. Next came a shot of Blair, starring in her fourth-grade production of *Annie*, an enormous grin on her face. She'd refused to wear a wig and had chosen brown pigtails instead, calling it artistic license.

Next Nate recognized a photo he'd taken of Blair sunbathing on his roof, one eye closed in an adorable wink. Then there was a picture of Serena on the set of *Breakfast at*

Fred's, wearing an enormous wide-brimmed black Bailey Winter hat, a triple strand of creamy white pearls around her throat, blowing the camera a kiss. And finally came a photo of Blair's and Serena's faces pressed together, beaming at the camera, the frame so tight that there was nothing else in the picture but their two gorgeous faces.

Nate ran his fingers through his hair. The only thing missing from the photo of Blair and Serena's smiling faces was his own face wedged between them. He'd always been there, in between them—coming between them.

Nate watched as Serena got up from her seat and hurried across the room to Blair's table. The two girls stood in front of one another for a moment and then Serena opened her arms, pulling Blair in for a hug and resting her shining blond head on Blair's shoulder. Blair turned her head to the side, and Nate could see the tears streaking her face, even in the dim light of the darkened room.

As he watched the two girls he loved holding each other and crying, a smile crept across his face. It slowly grew and grew and the rest of his face brightened. He pushed through the glass doors of the Met just as the lights went up and slipped out into the warm August night, running down the stone steps. They were the same steps he'd sat on with Blair and Serena a million times, their perfect legs extending from their short, itchy Constance uniforms, cigarettes and coffees in their hands. At the bottom of the steps he stopped and looked back at the imposing stone building with its brightly colored banners. He was going to think with his balls once and for all.

Uh-oh. Is he going to steal more Viagra?

Disclaimer: All the real names of places, people, and events have been altered or abbreviated to protect the innocent. Namely, me.

hey people!

This late night post-party wrap-up is coming at you from the luxurious confines of my boudoir, cats and kittens, where I'm lying in bed wrapped in one-thousand-thread-count Egyptian cotton sheets. I'm also scarfing the only surefire hangover buster—chocolate croissants from Balthazar. But none of this is nearly as deliciously or delectably yummy as **B'**s goodbye party. All I have to say is, if you weren't there, too bad. You missed out on the party of the year—if not the century. But I won't rub it in your faces—*too much.* After all, there's always next year. Or not.

Anyhoozle, I've just taken my La Mer ice mask out of the freezer and am ready to lie back in bed and depuff my tired lids, so this will have to be a quickie. And everyone knows that sometimes, quickies are just what the doctor ordered. Not *that* kind of quickie! Get your mind out of the gutter.

sightings

C and his new friend **G** are inseparable—and the party was no exception. Those of you who stuck it out until the bitter end will remember **C** and **G** dancing around a fast-melting ice sculpture—while **C**'s fuzzy white snow monkey stuffed his furry muzzle with gold-flecked cupcakes. . . . **K** and **I** in the Met's bathroom stalls, their arms and legs streaked with white paint, taking turns holding one another's hair out of their faces. That flight down to Rollins together is going to be brutal. **B** having her picture taken arm in arm with **S** on the front steps of the Met—guess those two kissed and made up—again. . . . Speaking of performances on the steps of the Met, how about those crazy Czech weirdos, doing their encore performance of "Ode to Love" at about 4 a.m.? Were they even *invited?* . . . **N** walking down Fifth Avenue talking in hushed, excited tones on his cell. Was he calling his dealer?

Dawn will be here soon enough, and you know I'll be the first to report on what the new day brings when I wake up. 'Night, all.

You know you love me.

gossip girl

all aboard—or not

Tick-tock, tick-tock . . .

Blair stood beneath the giant clock atop the information booth in the middle of Grand Central Station, searching the crowd impatiently for Nate. The main hall of Grand Central was mass pandemonium. Travelers rushed to their trains, suitcases dragging behind them, seemingly oblivious to the train station's elegant beauty. Grand Central was so much nicer than any other station in the world, with its marble floors, gold leaf molding, and beautiful sea green mural of the constellations on the ceiling. When Blair was little she'd loved searching for the scorpion, her zodiac sign.

Not that she was really in any mood to appreciate the beauty of the old train station today. As the impatient commuters streamed past her, Blair felt like the only person standing still in the whole place. She checked her watch again—not that she needed to, considering she was standing under the biggest fucking clock in the world. Their train was leaving in less than ten minutes, and Nate wasn't there. She hadn't seen him since she'd toasted the good news about Yale last night with his dad. He'd disappeared at the end of the party, presumably to go home and pack. Of course, he was bound to bring all the wrong things and forget his lacrosse stick. He was so totally helpless when it came to packing. Blair grabbed her cell from her black-and-white Balenciaga bag and held down the number three again, sighing as it rang and rang and then went to Nate's voice mail. Again. What was the holdup? She couldn't wait to just get on that train and watch the landscape change as they sped away from the city—and everything that she knew.

She straightened the hem of her fitted black Chanel dress, which she wore with black ballet flats and gold hoop earrings, a chic white hat in her purse. The outfit reminded her of Audrey Hepburn in *Sabrina*, on her triumphant return home from a year in Paris. Sabrina had left her home in the suburbs of New York a brokenhearted and shy girl and had returned a stylish, sophisticated, and mature woman. Blair had always been stylish and mature, but at Yale she would become even more so. She threw her cell back into her bag, tapping one of her ballet flats against the floor as she waited, and waited, for her Humphrey Bogart.

Serena hurried through Grand Central, her yellow flip-flops slapping the marble as she ran. She'd planned on getting to the train station at a quarter to ten to say one last goodbye to Blair, but of course she'd overslept—the result of one too many flutes of Dom Perignon last night. She'd thrown on her white eyelet Anthropologie sundress and her largest pair of vintage white Chanel sunglasses. Getting stopped for autographs would only slow her down and make her even later than she already was.

Tough life.

Finally she spied Blair standing in the middle of the main hall, tapping her foot impatiently and checking her watch. Seeing her all alone, looking so small amidst the bustling throngs of people, Serena felt horrible for not getting there earlier. Blair looked so worried, craning her head to look over the crowd.

But where was Nate? Serena had assumed he'd be there already to say goodbye to Blair. She smiled brightly as she approached. "Hey! I'm so glad I caught you!"

"Hey." Blair's forehead wrinkled in surprise when she saw her. "What are you doing here?"

"I just wanted to say one last goodbye," Serena threw her arms around her friend and hugged her tightly.

Blair's tense shoulders relaxed in Serena's arms. "Thanks. That's really sweet of you." She frowned and glanced at her watch again. "I shouldn't even still *be* here right now—Nate's fucking late as usual."

Poor Blair. It was just like Nate to keep her waiting one last time. Serena pushed her sunglasses farther up on her head. "You must be excited to finally be leaving though, right?"

Blair craned her head and looked over Serena's shoulder, searching the crowd nervously. "Yeah, but I just want it to get on the train and *go* already!"

Even though Blair was being impatient and crabby, Serena smiled. No matter how much things changed, Blair would always be the same. "So, did you ever end up getting in touch with your roommate?"

"Yeah, she wrote me an e-mail. She seems okay." Blair pulled a black Nars compact from her bag and checked her makeup. "She's from L.A. Her dad's a dentist."

"That's convenient." Serena smiled. Maybe Blair would be okay at Yale on her own after all. "You can hang out with her on breaks and stuff."

"I seriously doubt I'll be going to L.A. for break." Blair slid her compact back inside her bag. "Nate and I will probably spend vacations together." Serena felt a little sick. Blair really thought she and Nate would still be together come Thanksgiving.

Blair pulled her cell out of her bag and looked at it, checking her call log before tossing it back in her bag again. "Knowing Nate, he's probably still packing."

"Huh?" Serena demanded, totally bewildered. "What for?"

"For college?" Blair looked through her bag distractedly, pulling out her train ticket. "I mean, I know he wears about the same five shirts over and over again, but I seriously hope he's bringing *something*."

"But . . . you told me he wasn't going to Yale with you." What was Blair *talking* about? What was going on? "He told me he didn't even get his diploma."

"Oh . . . right. No, my dad got him back in. I didn't tell you last night? I guess I forgot once I told him." Blair put her ticket back in her bag. She couldn't stop scanning the crowd of commuters for Nate's face, or checking the time on the giant clock directly above them. She was starting to get insanely nervous. Not to mention pissed off. If Nate didn't get there soon, he'd miss the train. Not that that would be the end of the world—he could always catch the next one. But she really wanted them to have the experience of starting their new life *together*. And if he didn't get there *now*, it wasn't going to happen.

"What? No. When did this all happen?" Serena's normally smooth brow wrinkled in confusion. "He didn't say anything—"

"Last night. He must not have had the chance to tell you either." Blair pulled her cell from her bag with an exasperated sigh and dialed Nate's number again. It rang and rang and then went to voice mail.

Again.

hello, goodbye

"God, Dan." Jenny's voice rang out in the early-morning sunlight as she dumped a big box into the trunk of Dan's robin's egg blue 1977 Buick Skylark. Even though it was only 10 a.m., the pavement on Ninety-ninth Street and West End Avenue was already blazing hot, and the garbage bins were starting to smell like rotting dog poo. Jenny straightened up, wiping her hands off on her jeans. "Do you think you packed enough crap?"

Dan scowled, taking a scuffed-up Samsonite suitcase from his sister's tiny hands. "They're *books*," he muttered, gently placing the luggage in the trunk, "not crap."

"Well, whatever's in there is heavy." Jenny was panting in the oppressive August heat, her white FCUK wifebeater streaked with grime. Dan threw a duffel bag into the backseat—along with a blanket and pillow, his notebook, and a few bags of stale H&H bagels. He couldn't wait to park by the side of the road at night and sleep looking out at the stars. It was going to be so *On the Road*. He'd even brought the audio book to play on the car's outdated tape player. He was going to spend the next week out on the open road, looking for truth and the meaning of life.

This from the guy who couldn't figure out his own sexual bent.

Vanessa appeared from the Humphreys' ramshackle apartment building, holding a plastic container of Folgers crystals. She looked cool and comfortable with her shorn scalp, wearing one of Dan's old black Raves T-shirts and a pair of his black boxers.

"Hot enough for you?" Dan called lightly, even though the sight of her was breaking his heart.

Vanessa grabbed a bag from the sidewalk and stuffed it in the trunk. She stopped to wipe her face on the hem of her T-shirt. "I hate you," she mumbled grumpily. "Don't forget this," she added, handing him a half-empty Folgers container.

"I can't believe I'm actually leaving," Dan said nervously, to no one in particular, mechanically grabbing the coffee from Vanessa as his mom and dad stepped out of the apartment building and onto the curb. Jeanette wore a bright purple satin kimono with a large dragon on the back embroidered in gold thread, and her mousy brown hair was a mass of snarls. Despite the heat, she was also wearing her favorite pair of purple fuzzy slippers. Rufus was wearing an obscenely tight pair of electric blue spandex bicycle shorts, and a canary-yellow T-shirt with a colorful picture of a sunset on the front, that said YOU BETTER BELIZE IT. Dan was certainly going to miss his parents, though he wasn't sure whether he'd miss their bizarre fashion statements.

"You two could help, you know," Jenny commented,

throwing an army green duffel bag in the trunk and wiping the droplets of sweat from her eyes with the back of her hand.

Rufus crossed his arms over his chest. "Why do you think we had you two? Free labor!" He and Jeanette burst into peals of laughter.

"Oh, Rufus," Jeanette moaned, composing herself, a note of sadness creeping into her voice. "Our baby's all grown up!" She flew at Dan, the sleeves of her kimono flapping in the breeze like wings, and Dan opened his arms, resting his head against his mother's shoulder.

Looking around, Dan realized that this would be the last time that his family would be all together—for God knew how long. He was off to college today, and tonight his mom was flying back to Prague and her boyfriend, Count Dracula. Tears welled up in his eyes and he blinked them back. His mom patted him on the back like she was trying to burp him. "Sweetie," she whispered in his ear, "I know you and Vanessa are back together, and I just wanted to let you know that it's okay—I still love you, even though you're straight," she sniffed. "You're my baby boy, and I just want you to be happy."

Dan just shook his head. Why his mother wanted a gay son so badly was beyond him. But if his brief venture into homosexuality had finally brought her back to visit, he couldn't really complain.

"It's okay, Mom," he said between thumps on his back. "Just remember next time you send a gift that I'm a men's medium, not a kids' size four, and I'm sort of not into pink spandex anymore."

"Well, Dan." Rufus appeared at Dan's side smelling like curry and enveloped his son in a huge, hulking bear hug. "It's time to begin the next great adventure of your life." Dan held onto his dad for a long moment. He knew that when he woke up tomorrow morning, that wherever he was—no matter how beautiful and picturesque the scenery —it would feel totally bizarre not to see his dad padding through the kitchen making brussels-sprout pancakes, wearing his long white nightshirt and purple flip-flops. "And don't forget to write it all down," Rufus added, slapping his shoulders affectionately.

Vanessa helped Jenny fit the last suitcase into the oversize trunk and stepped back. Was Dan imagining things, or did he see actual tears in Vanessa's eyes? She swiped at them furiously, refusing to look at him. He walked over and took her in his arms, running his fingers over the stubbly scalp he adored. He could hear the rapid sound of her breathing, and he hugged her even closer.

"I'll call you every day," he said, his voice trembling. "I promise."

"Me too." She sniffled.

Jenny slammed the trunk of the robin's-egg-blue car shut. "Let's get this boat on the road!"

"It's not a *boat*," Dan snorted, letting go of Vanessa. "It's a 1977 Buick Skylark convertible, and it deserves some *respect*."

"Okay, Mr. Only Got His License like, *Yesterday*." Jenny gave him a sweaty hug. "I was only kidding." She buried her head against his chest, her curls bobbing up and down. "I'm going to miss you so much," she said quietly as the tears rolled down her round cheeks.

Dan closed his eyes, squeezing his little sister tight. "You too," he muttered, trying not to cry any harder.

"But I know you guys probably have some stuff to um . . . do." Jenny looked up at Vanessa meaningfully and then shuffled away, fanning her face with one hand as she joined Rufus and Jeanette on the curb.

Vanessa grabbed Dan's hand forcefully, pulling him behind the car so that they could have some privacy. She kissed him hard—a little reminder of their long night last night—and then pulled back, grinning. She was sad to see Dan go, but they were together again—and she had some ideas for how to stay in touch.

"Not only will I call you every day," she said, swooping in for another kiss, then lowering her voice to a throaty whisper, "but I'll be sending you some *movies,* too." She winked, her face wicked.

Dan blushed bright red. "Rated R, I hope," he whispered in her ear.

Finally she pried herself out of his arms, and he got behind the wheel of his huge automobile. He slammed the door and Vanessa backed slowly away, joining his family on the curb. There they were: his crazily dressed father, his long-absent mother, his sweet little sister, and Vanessa, the bald, beautiful, love of his life. He jammed the key into the ignition, fighting tears.

The car coughed once, twice, and then . . . died abruptly. Dan closed his eyes. He couldn't face another round of goodbyes. He turned the key once more. This time, the engine caught, coughing and sputtering, before coming to life with a giant roar.

He jerked the car forward, trying to remember everything his dad had told him about defensive driving, and watched his family get smaller and smaller in the rearview mirror, all four of them waving wildly and wiping their eyes as he sped up West End Avenue. His blood felt electric, and he could hardly wait to get out on the open road, to feel the sun on his face as it streamed through the windshield. Hopefully, by the time he found an Internet café, he'd already have a Vanessa Abrams original in his inbox. One meant for his eyes only.

And sure to make its way into the public realm—nudge, nudge.

n picks up another girl

Nate glanced at his beat-up platinum Rolex as he hopped out of the cab and into the blinding morning light. He shaded his eyes from the sun as he looked up at the street signs, trying to get his bearings. "Thanks, man." He turned to the cabbie and handed him forty bucks.

"Sir, you overpay—" The driver handed back one of the twenties, but Nate had already turned away.

"It's all yours," he called as he hurried down the street. He checked his watch again. Nine fifty-five. Only five more minutes.

He started to run now, his loafers slapping against the pavement as his feet made contact with the hot asphalt. A few paces and he was panting. The sweat trickled down the back of his gray T-shirt. The balls of his feet hurt and he wished he'd worn sneakers—and maybe eaten some breakfast.

Of course he'd be thinking of food at a time like this.

His phone rang and buzzed in his pocket. He pulled it out and looked at the screen. Blair. Again. He silenced the phone and put it back into his shorts.

Finally he rounded a corner and there she was, the sweet girl he'd be spending the next year with.

Who?

Nate raced down the Battery Park City wharf—the same dock he and Blair had sailed into ten days ago, although it felt like much longer. It was as if the moment he'd set foot on dry land, his days had turned into a confusing tangle of getting stoned and hurting the people he loved.

Story of his life.

Nate leapt onto the deck and strode into the stern of the *Belinda*, crashing into a pile of life preservers. He looked at his watch again.

"Nine fifty-nine!" he called out. "I'm early!"

Chips appeared from the cabin with a grin. "Glad you made it." He was wearing his "traveling clothes," a pristine pair of white duck cloth sailor's pants and a navy blue windbreaker. His white hair was combed back from his deeply lined face, and his blue eyes sparkled as he moved around the boat, his bad leg dragging behind him but an excited spring in his step. He bent at the waist, untied a mass of rope at his feet, and began to raise the anchor with the hand crank. That's what Nate was going to love about sailing with Chips. No computerized anything. Everything was done the old-fashioned way, with maps and muscle. "*Belinda* and I thought we might have to leave without you."

Nate grinned, extracting himself from the pile of life preservers, and started to help Chips with the rope. "I just wanted to make you sweat a little."

His phone rang again in his pocket and he pulled it out—even though he knew who was calling. He silenced the ringer.

Chips arched an eyebrow. "Which one is it? Does she know where you've gone?"

"She doesn't. Neither of them knows, actually. They both think I'm meeting them at Grand Central right now." Nate thought about Blair and Serena standing in the train station, wondering where he was, and felt bad—but only for a minute. He closed his eyes as he pictured Blair's excited, happy face and Serena's wide, gorgeous smile. It really was better this way—for everyone—whether they realized it or not. Serena and Blair would be friends again—without him getting in the way all the time.

"You didn't even tell them?" Chips coiled a length of rope around one arm, his brow furrowed. "Did nothing of my using-your-balls speech make its way through that thick hair of yours and into your head?"

Nate looked out to sea. The sky above him was flooded with bright morning light that bounced off the calm surface of the water. "No . . ." he began. "I got it. It's just . . . better this way. If I'd told them, they would have tried to stop me from leaving." His phone started beeping wildly, breaking the perfect silence of the calm morning. Nate pulled it out of his pocket and silenced it again. "And I might have let them."

He glanced at the phone in his hand and its screen flashing 18 MISSED CALLS. He flipped it open and punched at the keypad, knowing exactly what he needed to say in his text. He pressed SEND and then SEND again. And then he brought his throwing arm back and tossed the phone out to sea. It made a tiny splash as it hit the calm surface of the water.

Chips nodded approvingly and Nate grabbed a rope to

hoist the sail, giving it a fierce pull. The sail rose above him, fluttered in the breeze, and then grew taut.

"We're off!" Chips cried as the boat motored out into the harbor.

Nate watched the dock grow smaller and smaller. Maybe college was the right choice for most people, but it wasn't for him—at least not now. Yale could wait. He needed time to figure out who he was and what he really wanted, and he was never going to do that if every spare minute was taken up with classes, papers, and . . . Blair. Or Serena.

The tall buildings of Manhattan began to recede into the distance, and the spires of the Chrysler building and the Empire State building became tiny toy versions of themselves. The island Nate had called home his whole life suddenly looked . . . small. He planted his feet on the teak planks of the deck and turned his head into the wind as they sailed off into the sparkling, endless blue.

Like we're never going to hear from him again? Not a chance. The world is big, but not *that* big.

the long goodbye

Blair crossed her arms and tapped her toe impatiently on the platform as the train began to fill up with hundreds of luggage-toting passengers. She was so fucking on edge that she felt like she might throw up. The bright silver train cars were momentarily engulfed in a white cloud of exhaust, and Serena coughed, one hand covering her mouth.

Blair dialed Nate's number for the bazillionth time and sighed as it rang and rang and then went to voice mail. "Nate, it's me," she snapped into the phone. "I'm here on the platform at Grand Central . . . waiting. *Where are you?*" She glanced around and exhaled heavily, blowing her dark hair off her now-sweaty forehead. "You better get your ass here in *two seconds* or you'll miss the train!" She closed her cell with a snap. Where could he be?

Serena's voice broke through her thoughts. "Blair, I—I don't think Nate's coming."

Blair whipped around to face her. "What do you mean, *not coming*? Why not?"

Serena looked down, playing with the ends of her hair.

Her voice was small and slightly muffled. "Just because you got him into Yale again doesn't mean he wants to go." She lifted her head, her eyes shining. "The truth is, Blair . . . the truth is, I love Nate too. And he knows. Because I told him."

Uh-oh.

Blair opened her mouth in shock, but before she could utter one venomous word, both girls' phones began to chirp maniacally.

Serena pulled her phone out—anything to avoid Blair's angry eyes. The screen read, ONE NEW TEXT MESSAGE. She opened it.

"It's from Nate." Blair whispered, holding up her phone. *"To both of us."*

Serena looked down at her screen and read:

B AND S—SAILING AROUND THE WORLD. I LOVE YOU BOTH. ALWAYS HAVE. ALWAYS WILL. TAKE CARE OF EACH OTHER. -N

The train hissed on the tracks. Serena bit her bottom lip and looked up at Blair's shocked face. Nate had left—left them both. He loved them, but he didn't want to be with either of them. Serena hugged herself, feeling unsteady on her feet. Blair looked like she was about to pass out.

And then, to Serena's utter surprise, Blair began to giggle, small, hiccupping, hysterical giggles. Serena threw her arms open and hugged her friend, laughing and crying at the same time.

"Oh, Serena," Blair gasped, "Don't you see? It's *so* classic. He just sailed off into the sunset without even saying goodbye." As much as she wanted her own life to be like an old black-and-white movie, Nate's departure was far more cinematic than anything she could have come up with.

The two girls clutched each other, their faces wet with tears as passersby on the platform turned to stare and whisper. The loudspeaker above their heads crackled with static, and then a booming voice filled the underground space.

This is the 10 o'clock to New Haven stopping at Stamford, Noroton Heights, Darien, South Norwalk, Norwalk, Bridgeport, Stratford, Milford, and New Haven. Ten o'clock to New Haven. All aboard!

Blair wiped the tears from her cheeks and straightened the bottom of her dress. Nate wasn't there, but she still couldn't wait to get on that train. Serena was going to be a big movie star, Nate was off sailing around the world, and she was going to Yale—her dream since she was a little girl. And who knew what might happen there? Maybe she'd meet some gorgeous lacrosse player with golden blond hair and glittering green eyes who wasn't a total flake.

"'Bye." Serena whispered in her ear, her voice giddy with emotion. "Call me?"

"Definitely." Blair boarded the train on her own, adjusting her white pillbox hat and black Chanel sunglasses. She didn't know what Yale—or the future—would hold, but she couldn't find wait to find out.

Serena stepped back on the train platform as the doors began to close. But before they shut entirely, she and Blair blew each other kisses one last time, and yelled in unison: *"You know you love me!"*

gossipgirl.net

hey people!

It's time to say goodbye, my darlings, because at this point, everyone who's anyone is on their way to college. Except for those of us who have the good sense to stay right here in old NYC. But if you find yourself feeling left behind, don't be sad. There's *always* a silver lining. Like . . .

(5) Now that your older (probably prettier and more perfect) best friend is gone, it's your turn to really shine. By the time the first day of school rolls around, you'll be ruling the hallways and wearing that imaginary diamond-encrusted tiara.

(4) No one's here to scoff at your new back-to-school look—so go for it. After all, this coming school year will probably be the most important of your social existence, so go for those new, sex-kittenesque bangs. The boys will come barking—trust me.

(3) You're finally free to make out with everyone you've ever had a crush on. Senior year is basically a get-out-of-jail-free card—like Las Vegas, whatever happens during senior year stays here, so its okay to take some chances and flirt your tushy off—you never know what might happen if you do!

(2) The city is now yours—take advantage. Remember, next year you might be stuck on the green, leafy campuses of Yale or

Princeton with nary a Barneys or Bergdorf's in sight. Time to explore the limits of your charge card—as if you need the reminder.

(1) And the number-one reason not to feel sad about being left behind is . . . things are not going to get boring around here—not if I have anything to do with it. Which, of course, I will.

sightings

D's mom **J** at the Upper West Side branch of the New York Public Library, wearing a silk kimono and purple fuzzy slippers, attempting to donate the book *HomoSensuality* while insisting it's essential to any great library. **B** on the train looking very Audrey, being helped with her bags by a hottie in a Yale T-shirt. **S** walking past La Goulue on Madison, a big smile on her face, getting stopped by *everyone*. **D** at a rest stop in Pennsylvania, cooing sweet nothings into his cell phone while drinking entirely too much black coffee. **V** strolling through the NYU campus near Washington Square Park in the early afternoon, manically filming everything. Something tells me that **V** will attempt to document every moment of her college existence. Those tapes will probably be worth a fortune someday. **N** . . . nowhere in sight. And finally, three new sightings:

After **B** left her apartment this morning, headed for Yale, three gorgeous new faces arrived for a quickie tour: I have it on good authority they're the **C** triplets, set to move into **B**'s pad any day now. There's blond **A**, looking every inch the Upper East Side bombshell she *isn't*. Her adorable brother, **O,** whose chiseled features and white-blond hair are like a who's who of hotness. And then there's the über bohemian chic **B,** which I've heard stands for "Baby." Her real name—or just what guys call out to her on the street? Because yes, she's really that beautiful.

Well, my darlings, that kind of wraps it up . . . for now. If you're wondering why I'm so chipper when **B, S, N, D,** and **V,** and all their wild friends have left, it's because it looks like next year might be even more fun than this year, and I'm not going anywhere. That's right, you heard me, I'm here to stay. Why leave when there's going to be *so* much more to talk about?

Whatever I do, you know you'll *always* love me.

Once upon a time on the Upper East Side of New York City, two beautiful girls fell in love with one perfect boy. . . .

Turn the page for a sneak peek of

it had to be you
the gossip girl prequel

and find out how it all began.

by the #1 *New York Times* bestselling author
Cecily von Ziegesar

Disclaimer: All the real names of places, people, and events have been altered or abbreviated to protect the innocent. Namely, me.

hey people!

Ever have that totally freakish feeling that someone is listening in on your conversations, spying on you and your friends, following you to parties, and generally stalking you? Well, they are. Or actually, *I* am. The truth is, I've been here all along, because I'm one of you.

Feeling totally lost? Don't get out much? Don't know who "we" are? Allow me to explain. We're an exclusive group of indescribably beautiful people who happen to live in those majestic, green-awninged, white-glove-doorman buildings near Central Park. We attend Manhattan's most elite single-sex private schools. Our families own yachts and estates in various exotic locations throughout the world. We frequent all the best beaches and the most exclusive ski resorts. We're seated immediately at the nicest restaurants in the chicest neighborhoods without a reservation. We turn heads. But don't confuse us with Hollywood actors or models or rock stars—those people you feel like you know because you hear so much about them, but who are actually completely boring compared to the parts they play or the songs they sing. There's nothing boring about me or my friends, and the more I tell you about us, the more you're going to want to know. I've kept quiet until now, but something has happened and I just can't stay quiet about it. . . .

the greatest story ever told

We learned in our first eleventh-grade creative writing class this week that most great stories begin in one of the following fashions: someone mysteriously disappears or a stranger comes to town. The story I'm about to tell is of the "someone mysteriously disappears" variety.

To be specific, **S** is *gone.*

In order to unravel the mystery of why she's left and where she's gone, I'm going to have to backtrack to last winter—the winter of our sophomore year—when the La Mer skin cream hit the fan and our pretty pink rose-scented bubble burst. It all started with three inseparable, perfectly innocent, über-gorgeous fifteen-year-olds. Well, they're sixteen now, and let's just say that two of them are *not* that innocent.

If anyone is going to tell this tale it has to be me, because I was at the scene of every crime. So sit back while I unravel the past and reveal everyone's secrets, because I know everything, and what I don't know I'll invent, elaborately.

Admit it: you're already falling for me.

Love you too . . .

gossip girl

the best stories begin with one boy and two girls

"Truce!" Serena van der Woodsen screamed as Nate Archibald body-checked her into a three-foot-high drift of powdery white snow. Cold and wet, it tunneled into her ears and down her pants. Nate dove on top of her, all five-foot eleven inches of his perfect, golden-brown-haired, glittering-green-eyed, fifteen-year-old boyness. Nate smelled like Downy and the Kiehl's sandalwood soap the maid stocked his bathroom with. Serena just lay there, trying to breathe with him on top of her. "My scalp is cold," she pleaded, getting a mouthful of Nate's snow-dampened, godlike curls as she spoke.

Nate sighed reluctantly, as if he could have spent all day outside in the frigid February meat locker that was the back garden of his family's Eighty-second-Street-just-off-Park-Avenue Manhattan town house. He rolled onto his back and wriggled like Serena's long-dead golden retriever, Guppy, when she used to let him loose on the green grass of the Great Lawn in Central Park. Then he stood up, awkwardly dusting off the seat of his neatly pressed Brooks Brothers khakis. It was Saturday, but he still wore the same clothes he wore every weekday as a sophomore at the St. Jude's School for Boys over on East End Avenue. It was the unofficial Prince of the Upper East Side uniform, the same uniform he and his classmates had been wearing since they'd started nursery school together at Park Avenue Presbyterian.

Nate held out his hand to help Serena to her feet. She frowned cautiously up at him, worried that he was only faking her out and was about to tackle her again. "I really am cold."

He flapped his hand at her impatiently. "I know. Come on."

She snorted, pretended to pick her nose and wipe it on the seat of her snow-soaked dark denim Earl jeans, then grabbed his hand with her faux-snotty one. "Thanks, pal." She staggered to her feet. "You're a real chum."

Nate led the way inside. The backs of his pant legs were damp and she could see the outline of his tighty-whiteys. Really, how gay of him! He held the glass-paned French doors open and stood aside to let her pass. Serena kicked off her baby blue Uggs and scuffed her bare, Urban Decay Piggy Bank-pink-toenailed feet down the long hall to the stately town house's enormous, barely used all-white Italian Modern kitchen. Nate's father was a former sea captain-turned-banker, and his mother was a French society hostess. They were basically never home, and when they *were* home, they were at the opera.

"Are you hungry?" Nate asked, following her. "I'm so sick of takeout. My parents have been in Venezuela or Santa Domingo or wherever they go in February for like two weeks, and I've been eating burritos, pizza, or sushi every freaking night. I asked Regina to buy ham, Swiss, Pepperidge Farm white bread, Grammy Smith apples, and peanut butter. All I want is the food I ate in kindergarten." He tugged anxiously on his wavy, golden brown hair. "Maybe I'm going through some sort of midlife crisis or something."

Like his life is so stressful?

"It's Gra*nny* Smith, silly," Serena informed him fondly. She opened a glossy white cupboard and found an unopened box of cinnamon-and-brown-sugar Pop-Tarts. Ripping open the box, she removed one of the packets from inside, tore it open with her neat, white teeth, and pulled out a thickly frosted pastry. She sucked on the Pop-Tart's sweet, crumbly corner and hopped up on the counter, kicking the cupboards below with her size-eight-and-a-half feet. Pop-Tarts at Nate's. She'd been having them there since she was five years old. And now . . . and now . . .

Serena sighed heavily. "Mom and Dad want me to go to boarding school next year," she announced, her enormous, almost navy blue eyes growing huge and glassy as they welled up with unexpected tears. Go away to boarding school and leave Nate? It hurt too much to even think about.

Nate flinched as if he'd been slapped in the face by an invisible hand. He grabbed the other Pop-Tart from out of the packet and hopped up on the counter next to Serena. "No way," he responded decisively. She couldn't leave. He wouldn't allow it.

"They want to travel more," Serena explained. The pink, perfect curve of her lower lip trembled dangerously. "If I'm home, they feel like they need to be home more. Like I want them around? Anyway, they've arranged for me to meet some of the deans of admissions and stuff. It's like I have no choice."

Nate scooted over a few inches and put his arm around her. "The city is going to suck if you're not here," he told her earnestly. "You can't go."

Serena took a deep shuddering breath and rested her pale blond head on his shoulder. "I love you," she murmured, closing her delicate eyelids. Their bodies were so close the entire Nate-side of her hummed. If she turned her head and tilted her chin just so, she could have easily kissed his warm, lovely neck. And she wanted to. She was actually dying to, because she really did love him, with all her heart.

She did? Hello? Since when?!

Maybe since ballroom-dancing school way back in fourth grade. She was tall for her age, and Nate was always such a gentleman about her lack of rhythm and the way she stepped on his insteps and jutted her bony elbows into his sides. He'd finesse it by grabbing her hand and spinning her around so that the skirt of her puffy, oyster-colored satin tea-length Bonpoint dress twirled out magnificently. Their teacher, Mrs. Jaffe, who had long blue hair that she kept in place with a pearl-adorned black hairnet, worshipped Nate. So did Serena's best friend, Blair Waldorf. And so did Serena—she just hadn't realized it until now. Serena shuddered and her perfect skin broke out in a rash of goose bumps. Her whole body seemed to be having an adverse reaction to the idea of revealing something she'd kept so well hidden for so long, even from herself.

Nate wrapped his lacrosse-toned arms around her long, narrow waist and pulled her close, tucking her pale gold head into the crook of his neck and massaging the ruts between the ribs on her back with his fingertips. The best thing about Serena was her total lack of embarrassing flab. Her entire body was as long and lean and taut as the strings on his Prince titanium tennis racket.

It was painful having such a ridiculously hot best friend. Why couldn't his best friend be some lard-assed dude with zits and dandruff? Instead he had Serena and Blair Waldorf, hands down the two hottest girls on the Upper East Side, and maybe all of Manhattan, or even the whole world.

Serena was an absolute goddess—every guy Nate knew talked about her—but she was mysterious. She'd laugh for hours if she spotted a cloud shaped like a toilet seat or something equally ridiculous, and the next moment she'd be wistful and sad. It was impossible to tell what she was thinking most of the time. Sometimes Nate wondered if she would've been more comfortable in a body that was slightly less perfect, because it would've given her more *incentive*, to use an SAT vocabulary word. Like she wasn't sure what she had to aspire to, since she basically had everything a girl could possibly want.

Blair was petite, with a pretty, foxlike face, blue eyes, and wavy chestnut-colored hair. She let everyone know what she was thinking, and she was fiercely competitive. For instance, she always found opportunities to point out that her chest was almost a whole cup size larger than Serena's and that she'd scored almost 100 points higher than Serena on the practice SAT.

Way back in fifth grade, Serena had told Nate she was pretty sure Blair had a crush on him. He started to notice that Blair did stick her chest out when he was looking, and she was always either bossing him around or fixing his hair. Of course Blair never admitted that she liked him, which made him like her even more.

Nate sighed deeply. No one understood how difficult it was being best friends with two such beautiful, impossible girls.

Like he would have been friends with them if they were awkward and butt-ugly?

He closed his eyes and breathed in the sweet scent of Serena's Frédéric Fekkai Apple Cider clarifying shampoo. He'd kissed lots of girls and had even gone to third base last June with L'Wren Knowes, a very experienced older Seaton Arms School senior who really did seem to know everything. But kissing Serena would be . . . different. He loved her. It was as simple as that. She was his best friend, and he loved her.

And if you can't kiss your best friend, who *can* you kiss?

upper east side schoolgirl uncovers shocking sex scandal!

"Ew," Blair Waldorf muttered at her reflection in the full-length mirror on the back of her closet door. She liked to keep her closet organized, but not too organized. Whites with whites, off-whites with off-whites, navy with navy, black with black. But that was it. Jeans were tossed in a heap on the closet floor. And there were dozens of them. It was almost a game to close her eyes and feel around and come up with a pair that used to be too tight in the ass but fit a little loosely now that she'd cut out her daily after-dinner milk-and-Chips-Ahoy routine.

Blair looked at the mirror, assessing her outfit. Her Marc by Marc Jacobs shell pink sheer cotton blouse was fine. It was the fuchsia La Perla bra that was the problem. It showed right through the blouse so that she looked like a stripper. But she was only going to Nate's house to hang out with him and Serena. And Nate liked to talk about bras. He was genuinely curious about, for instance, what the purpose of an underwire was, or why some bras fastened in front and some fastened in back. It was a big turn-on for him, obviously, but it was also sort of sweet. He was a lonely only child, craving sisterhood.

Right.

She decided to leave the bra on for Nate's sake, hiding the whole ensemble under her favorite belted black cashmere Lora Piano cardigan, which would come off the minute she stepped into his well-heated town house. Maybe, just maybe, the sight of her hot pink bra would be the thing to make Nate realize that he'd been in love with her just as long as she'd been in love with him.

Maybe.

She opened her bedroom door and yelled down the long hall and across the East Seventy-second Street penthouse's vast expanse of period furniture, parquet floors, crown moldings, and French Impressionist paintings. "Mom! Dad? I'm going over to Nate's house! Serena and I are spending the night!"

When there was no reply, she clomped her way to her parents' huge master suite in her noisy Kors wooden-heeled sheepskin clogs, opened their bedroom door, and made a beeline for her mom's dressing room. Eleanor Waldorf kept a tall stack of crisp emergency twenties in her lingerie drawer for Blair and her ten-year-old brother, Tyler, to parse from—for taxis, cappuccinos, and, in Blair's case, the occasional much-needed pair of Manolo Blahnik heels. Twenty, forty, sixty, eighty, one hundred. Twenty, forty, sixty, eighty, two hundred. Blair counted out the bills, folding them neatly before stuffing them into the back pocket of her peg-legged Seven jeans.

"If I were a cabernet," Blair's father's dramatically playful lawyer's voice echoed out of the adjoining dressing roo.., "how would you describe my bouquet?"

Excusez-moi?

Blair clomped out of her mom's dressing room and reached for the chocolate brown velvet curtain hanging in the doorway of her dad's. "If you guys are in there together, like, doing it while I'm home, then that's really gross," she declared flatly. "Anyway, I'm going over to Nate's, so—"

Her father, Harold J. Waldorf, Esquire, pulled aside the velvet curtain, dressed in his cashmere tweed Paul Smith bathrobe and nothing else, his nicely tanned, handsome face looking slightly flushed. "Mom's out looking at dishes for the Guggenheim benefit. I thought you were out. Where are you going exactly?"

Blair stared at him. He wasn't holding a phone, and if her mom was out, then who the fuck had he just been talking to? She stood blinking at him with her hands on her hips, tempted to peek inside his dressing room to see who he was hiding in there.

Does she really want to know?

Instead, she stumbled out of the master suite, clomped her way across the penthouse, grabbed her blood orange–colored Jimmy Choo treasure chest hobo, and ran for the elevator.

Outside it was breathtakingly cold, and fat flakes fell at random. Usually she walked the twelve blocks to Nate's house, but today Blair had no patience for walking—she had just discovered that her father was a lying, cheating scumbag, after all, and a cab was waiting for her downstairs. Or rather, a cab was waiting for Mrs. Solomon in 4A, but when

.iform–clad doorman saw the terrifying
.rmally pretty face, he let her take it.
.ailing cabs in the snow was probably the high-
.is day.

.he stone walls bordering Central Park were blanketed in
snow. A tall, elderly woman and her Yorkshire terrier, dressed
in matching red Chanel quilted coats with matching black
velvet bows in their white hair, crossed Seventy-second
Street and entered the Ralph Lauren flagship store. Blair's
cab hurtled recklessly up Madison Avenue, past Agnès B.
and Williams-Sonoma and the Three Guys coffee shop
where all the Constance Billard girls gathered after school,
and finally pulled up to Nate's town house.

"Let me in!" she yelled into the intercom outside the
Archibalds' elegant wrought-iron-and-glass front door as she
swatted the buzzer over and over with her hand.

Inside, Nate and Serena were still cuddling in the
kitchen. Serena raised her head from his shoulder and
opened her eyes, as if from a dream. The kiss they'd both
been fantasizing about had never actually happened, which
was probably for the best.

"I think I'm warm now," she announced and hopped off
the counter, composing her face so that she looked totally
calm and cool, like they hadn't just had a moment. And
maybe they hadn't—she couldn't be sure. She grinned at the
monitor's distorted image of Blair giving her the finger.
"Come on in, sweetness!" she shouted back, buzzing her
friend in.

Nate tried to erase the disturbing thought that Blair had

caught him and Serena together. They weren't together. They were just friends, hanging out, which is what friends do when they're together. There was nothing to catch. It was all in his mind.

Or was it?

"Hey, hornyheads." Blair greeted them with snow in her shoulder-length chestnut brown hair. Her cheeks were pink with cold, her blue eyes were slightly bloodshot, and her carefully plucked dark brown eyebrows were askew, as if she'd been crying or rubbing her eyes like crazy. "I have a fucked-up story to tell you guys." She flung her orange bag down on the floor and took a deep breath, her eyes rolling around dramatically, milking the moment for all it was worth. "As it turns out, my totally boring, Mr. Lawyer father, Harold Waldorf, Esquire, is like totally having an affair. Only moments ago, I caught him asking some random babe, 'If I was a wine, how would you describe my bouquet?' and they were, like, totally hiding in his closet." She clapped her hand over her mouth, as if to keep the words in.

Or her breakfast.

"Whoa," Serena and Nate responded in unison.

"He just sounded so . . . slimy," Blair wailed through her fingers.

Serena knew this might be even grosser, but she just had to get it out there. "Well, maybe he was just having phone sex with your mom."

"Sure," Nate agreed. "My parents do that all the time," he added, feeling a little sick as he said it. His navy admiral dad was so uptight he probably wouldn't have phone sex for fear of being court-marshaled.

Blair grimaced. The idea of her tennis-toned-but-still-plump, St. Barts–tanned, gold-jewelry-loving mom having any kind of sex, let alone cabernet phone sex, with her skinny, preppy, argyle-socks-wearing dad, was so unlikely and so completely icky she refused to even think about it.

"No," she insisted, wolfing down the uneaten half of Serena's Pop-Tart. "It was definitely another woman. I mean, face it," she said, still chewing, "Dad is totally hot and dresses really well, and he's an important lawyer and everything. And my mom is totally insane and doesn't really do anything and she has varicose veins and a flabby ass. Of course he's having an affair."

Serena and Nate nodded their glossy golden heads like that made complete sense. Then Serena grabbed Blair and hugged her hard. Blair was the sister she'd never had. In fourth grade they'd pretended they were fraternal twins for an entire month. Their Constance Billard gym teacher, Ms. Etro, who'd gotten fired midyear for inappropriate touching—which she called "spotting"—during tumbling classes, had even believed them. They'd worn matching pink Izod shirts and cut their hair exactly the same length. They even wore matching gold Cartier hoop earrings, until they decided they were tacky and switched to Tiffany diamond studs.

Blair pressed her face into Serena's perfectly defined collarbone and heaved an exhausted, trembling sigh. "It's just so fucked up it makes me feel sick."

Serena patted Blair's back and met Nate's gaze over Blair's Elizabeth Arden Red Door Salon–glossed brown head. No way was she going to bring up the whole being-sent-away-to-boarding-school problem—not when her best friend was so upset. And she didn't want Nate to mention it either. "Come on, let's go mix martinis and watch a stupid movie or something."

Nate jumped off the counter, feeling completely confused. Suddenly all he really wanted to do was hug Blair and kiss away her tears. Was he hot for her now, too?

It's hard to keep a clear head when you're surrounded by beautiful girls who are in love with you.

"All we have is vodka and champagne. My parents keep all the good wine and whiskey locked up in the cabinet for when they have company," he apologized.

Serena slid open the bread pantry, where most families would actually keep bread, but where Nate's mom stored the cartons of Gitanes cigarettes her sister sent from France via FedEx twice a month because the ones sold in the States simply did not taste fresh.

"I'm sure we can make do," she said, ripping open a carton with her thumbnail. "Come." She stuck two cigarettes in her mouth like tusks and beckoned Nate and Blair to follow her out of the kitchen and upstairs to the master suite. If anyone was an expert at changing the mood, it was Serena. That was one of the things they loved about her. "I'll show you a good time," she added goofily.

She always did.

The Archibalds' vast bedroom had been decorated by Nate's mother in the style of Louis XVI, with a giant gilt mirror over the head of the enormous red-and-gold toile canopy bed, and heavy gold curtains in the windows. The walls were adorned with red-and-gold fleur-de-lis wallpaper and renderings of Mrs. Archibald's family's summer château near Nice. On the floor was a red, blue, and gold Persian rug rescued from the *Titanic* and bought at auction by Mrs. Archibald for her husband at Sotheby's.

"*Bus Stop*? *Some Like It Hot*? Or the digitally remastered version of *Some Like It Hot*?" Serena asked, flipping through Nate's parents' limited DVD collection. Obviously Captain Archibald liked Marilyn Monroe movies—*a lot*. Of course, Nate had his own collection of DVDs in his room, including a play-by-play of the last twenty years of America's Cup sailing races. Thanks, but no thanks. His parents' taste was far more girl-friendly. "Or we could just watch Nate play Nintendo, which is always hot," she joked, although she kind of meant it.

"Only if he does it naked," Blair quipped hopefully. She sat down and bounced up and down on the end of the huge bed.

Nate blushed. Blair loved to make him blush and he knew it. "Okay," he responded boldly, sitting down next to her on the bed.

Blair snatched a Kleenex out of the silver tissue box on Nate's mom's bedside table and blew her nose noisily. Not that she really needed to blow her nose. She just needed a distraction from the overwhelming urge to throw Nate down on his parents' bed and tackle him. He was so goddamned adorable it made her feel like she was going to explode. God, she loved him.

There had never been a time when she didn't love him. She'd loved the stupid lobster shorts he wore to the club in Newport when their dads played tennis together in the summer, back when they were, what—five? She'd loved the way he always had a Spider-Man Band-Aid on some part of his body until he was at least twelve, not because he'd hurt himself but because he thought it looked cool. She loved the way his whole head reflected the sunlight, glowing gold. She loved his glittering green eyes—eyes that were almost too pretty for a boy. She loved the way he so obviously knew he was hot but didn't quite know what to do about it. She loved him. Oh, how she loved him.

Oh, oh, *oh*!

She blew her nose with one last trumpeting snort and then grabbed a pink, tacky-looking DVD case from off the floor. She turned the case over, studying it. "*Breakfast at Tiffany's*. I've never seen it, but she's so beautiful." She held the DVD up so Serena could see Audrey Hepburn in her long black dress and pearl choker. "Isn't she?"

"She is pretty," Serena agreed, still sorting through the movies.

"She looks like you," Nate observed, cocking his head in such an adorable way that Blair had to close her eyes to keep from falling off the bed.

"You think?" Blair tossed her dirty tissue in the general direction of the Archibalds' dainty white porcelain waste paper basket and studied the picture on the DVD case again. In the movie that began to play in her head, she *was* Audrey Hepburn—a fabulously dressed, thin, perfectly coiffed, beautiful, mysterious megastar. "Maybe a little," she agreed, removing her black cashmere cardigan so that her hot pink bra was clearly visible beneath her blouse.

Blair picked up the DVD case again. Audrey Hepburn

looked so fabulous in the pictures on the back, but also sort of prim and proper, like she wore sexy underwear but wouldn't let a guy see it unless he was going to marry her. Blair pulled her cardigan back on and buttoned the top button. From now on, her life's work would be to emulate Audrey Hepburn in every possible way. Nate could see her underwear, but only once she was sure that one day they'd be married.

That makes sense—to her.

"I watched that movie with my mom," Nate confessed, causing both girls' hearts to drip into sticky puddles on the floor. "It's kind of bizarre, actually. I think it's supposed to be romantic, but I'm not sure I even understood it."

That was all the girls needed. Blair stuck the DVD into the player while Serena mixed martinis at the wet bar in the adjoining library. This involved pouring Bombay Sapphire into chilled martini glasses and stirring it with a silver letter opener. It was only 11 A.M.—not exactly cocktail hour—but Blair was in crisis, and Nate tended to take off his shirt when he got drunk. Besides, it was Saturday.

"There," Serena announced, as if she'd just put the finishing touches on a very complicated recipe. She handed out the glasses. "To us. Because we're worth it."

"To us," Blair and Nate chorused, glasses raised.

Bottoms up!

Before **V** filmed her first movie,
D wrote his first poem,
and **J** bought her first bra.

Before **B** watched her first Audrey Hepburn movie,
S left for boarding school,
and before **N** came between them. . . .

it had to be you
the gossip girl prequel

Coming October 2007

Blair Waldorf and Serena van der Woodsen
were the reigning princesses of the Upper East Side.

Until now.

Something wild and wicked is in the air.
The Carlyle triplets are about to
take Manhattan by storm.

Lucky for you, Gossip Girl will be there
to whisper all their juicy secrets. . . .

**A New Era Begins
May 2008**